THE GOLDEN STATE

THE

GOLDEN STATE

LYDIA KIESLING

MCD  FARRAR, STRAUS AND GIROUX   NEW YORK

MCD

Farrar, Straus and Giroux

175 Varick Street, New York 10014

Printed in the United States of America

First edition, 2018

Library of Congress Cataloging-in-Publication Data

Names: Kiesling, Lydia, 1984– author.

Title: The Golden State / Lydia Kiesling.

Description: First edition. | New York : Farrar, Straus and Giroux, [2018]

Identifiers: LCCN 2017057600 | ISBN 9780374164836 (hardcover)

Subjects: LCSH: Mothers and daughters—California—San Francisco Bay
    Area—Fiction. | Desertion and non-support—Fiction. | Moving, household—
    California, Northern—Fiction. | California, Northern—Rural conditions—
    Fiction. | Domestic fiction.

Classification: LCC PS3618.I39265 G46 2018 | DDC 813/.6—dc23

LC record available at https://lccn.loc.gov/2017057600

Designed by Abby Kagan

Our books may be purchased in bulk for promotional, educational, or
business use. Please contact your local bookseller or the Macmillan Corporate
and Premium Sales Department at 1-800-221-7945, extension 5442,
or by e-mail at MacmillanSpecialMarkets@macmillan.com.

www.mcdbooks.com • www.fsgbooks.com

Follow us on Twitter, Facebook, and Instagram at @mcdbooks

10 9 8 7 6 5 4 3 2 1

Home is so sad.

—PHILIP LARKIN

THE GOLDEN STATE

DAY 1   I am staring out the window of my office and thinking about death when I remember the way Paiute smells in the early morning in the summer before the sun burns the dew off the fescue. Through the wall I hear the muffled voice of Meredith shouting on the phone in laborious Arabic with one of her friend-colleagues, and in my mind's eye I see the house sitting empty up there, a homely beige rectangle with a brown latticed deck and a tidy green wraparound lawn to its left, a free-standing garage to its right, and beyond that an empty lot with juniper shrubs and patches of tall grass where the deer like to pick. Technically it is a double-wide mobile home, although it does not look mobile—it's not on wheels or blocks; it has a proper covered foundation, or at least the appearance of one, and could not be mistaken for a trailer. Technically I own this house, because my grandparents left it to my mother and when she died she left it to me.

The house is waiting for an occupant; my uncle Rodney, who didn't need it and thus didn't inherit it, has been paying someone to come every month to tend the geraniums and cut the grass for the last five years. He pays for a low, persistent hum of electricity and gas through the winter so as to avoid the effects of a hard freeze. The idea is that someone will one day want to buy this house, and my uncle Rodney is keeping it nice until then, I suppose as a favor to me.

I hear Meredith send valedictory kisses through the phone and amid the sparkling glass and chrome splendor of the Institute I see the faux-wood paneling of the house and the nubbled brown upholstery of my grandmother's two soft couches, still in situ with the rest of her furnishings. And then I feel something tugging—first from across the Bay, the dingy living room where Honey and six other babies spend ten hours a day toddling, then from the long stretch of road, nearly four hundred miles of road, leading up to the high desert. And then I stand up from my office chair and open the right-hand desk drawer and put a Post-it on the petty cash box noting my outstanding debt of $64.72 to the petty cash fund, and after a moment's hesitation I put the Dell laptop and charger paid for with endowment income from the Al-Ihsan Foundation into my bag. And then I turn off my monitor, slip on my ill-fitting flats, call goodbye to Meredith ("Have a good night," she calls back, at 10:00 a.m.), and walk out of the building and down the main walkway through campus, the Bay before me and the clock tower at my back.

On BART I stare out the window and consider why it is that I am homebound at 10:15 in the morning with my eye to the northeast. The morning was not worse than most mornings. The alarm went off at six and I hit snooze six times at 6:10 6:19 6:28 6:37 6:46. Honey called from her crib like a marooned sailor and I guiltily left her there to take a shower after calculating the number of days without, four, too many. Then half-dressed and still dripping I pulled her wailing from the crib and wiped her tears changed her diaper replaced her jammies gave her kisses carried her to the kitchen. I put her in the high chair and gave her a fistful of raisins and realized there were no eggs or yogurt or fruit, which meant oatmeal, which takes an additional eight minutes by the most optimistic estimate, and so because of my own late start and the absence of the eggs I had to rush her through breakfast, and lately she hates to be rushed, hates to have things cleared away before she is ready, so when I took the oatmeal away she started wailing and when I carried her into our room she screamed and stiffened and threw her body back against my arms, a great dramatic backward swan dive with no regard for whatever might lie behind. And when I hustled her onto the floor to get dressed and held up the onesie and tried to invest her in the process like they say you should she started shrieking and thrashing anew and it felt very distressing, very critical, very personal, and I gripped her arms tightly, too tightly, arriving at a threshold of tightness that felt dangerous but obscurely good in a way I wouldn't care to investigate further. And then I tugged the onesie over her head looked at the time put my own head in my hands and sobbed for thirty seconds.

Engin's primary criticism of me is that whenever he tries to initiate a serious conversation I start crying, which activates his innate gallantry and sympathy, and which effectively halts whatever potentially challenging conversation we are having. He calls it a *taktik*; I call it a *refleks*. "What do you do when they criticize you at work?" he asked me once, and I told him, truthfully, that at work I am perfect. Whatever the thing is, my taktik or refleks, it worked on Honey, because she paused and I seized the moment to stuff all her limbs into the onesie the pants the socks. Then I put her down and got dressed while she rampaged cutely around the bedroom and messed with the doodads on my bedside table, evil eyes and icons and various other apotropaics I keep meaning to hang up on the wall. And then I dutifully put the little rice-size grain of tooth-paste on the little toothbrush festooned with Elmo and friends and sang the song from the Elmo video, but she clamped her mouth shut tight and pearly tears squeezed from her eyes and I gave up which I do four times out of ten.

But all this was par for the course. In fact it was a small miracle that we were out the door at 7:55 for a nearly on-time daycare arrival of 8:05. Then to the streetcar, then to the train, there to zone out with the Turkish work of midcentury social realist fiction I've been trying to read for three years, then switch trains, then to the planter boxes of a Wells Fargo to smoke a cigarette, then up the hill to arrive at work at 9:35 which is a little over one hour later than I am supposed to be there according to the terms of my offer letter. But I'm still the first in the office, and if I bring Honey to daycare at 8:00, the earliest they accept kids, I can't get to work any earlier than 9:30, even if I don't smoke a cigarette—it is physically impossible.

In the office things had proceeded more or less as usual. I visited the Visa Status Check page of the National Visa Center website to see the status of Engin's green card, which was, is, in perpetuity, "At NVC," which means nothing except that not a single thing that needs to happen has happened. I checked the bank balance, $341 checking; $1,847 emergency. This had five months ago been a plump and hopeful $4,147 until the forced abandonment of Engin's green card and immediate forced return of Engin to Turkey at our expense, and the subsequent retention of an attorney to reapply, and the new application fee, and the recent additional lawyer's fee to understand why it has been At NVC for five months with no perceptible forward movement—which is, we have lately been told, a probable "click-of-the-mouse error." I paused to silently pray that whatever future emergencies might arise can be resolved for under $1,847. I checked the credit card balance, $835 less $483 in pending reimbursements for Miscellaneous Catering Expenses. I checked the University Purchasing Portal to see the status of my pending reimbursements, and verily they were still pending. I checked my retirement balance, $9,321, which was theoretically comforting although I cannot of course access it without penalty for twenty-seven years. I checked an immigration thread on BabyCenter, very short, and a Subreddit, very sad. I looked at a WeChat picture from daycare showing Honey's diaper and a troublingly small turd. I checked WhatsApp for Engin's last greeting and sent him the picture of the turd. And finally I listened to a voice mail from the Office of Risk Management relaying that I would have to make a statement regarding the death of student Ellery Simpson and injuries sustained by student Maryam Khoury in a taxi outside the Fidanlik Park refugee camp on a research trip supported with funds from the Al-Ihsan Foundation and partially arranged for by me. And then I looked out the window and thought of death and remembered the smell of the Paiute air and the dew on the fescue grass.

I reach my stop and take the streetcar to my block and stop to smoke a cigarette in front of the door of our building, staring at a free newspaper in a waterlogged bag on the pavement and picturing the long road up to the house. It's been a year since I made the drive, the miles of sprawl, then the huge swath of territory punctuated by alkali lakes and picturesque homesteads and tree stands, then the stretch of increasingly far-apart tiny townships and ruined general stores and abandoned trailers, the place where you think you've absorbed the beauty and caution of the territory and it must be time to get where you're going but you've still got eighty miles of rattlesnake plain left to go. I imagine the swift elevation up from the plain through sugar pine and juniper and more pine and the sudden descent onto another great basin, this one checkmarked with fields and cattle and pieces of wetland, its silvery grass and wet places shimmering pink in the twilight, a cattleman's paradise five thousand feet high. And then my own abandoned homestead in Deakins Park, to sink into those soft nubbled couches and take in the cool morning air of Altavista, the seat of Paiute County.

I put out the cigarette in a flowerpot and go inside and pull out a tote bag and a suitcase, and all of the focus that has lately abandoned me at work materializes and I run through the checklist: clothes diapers Pack 'n Play baby bedding sound machine high chair Ergo stroller toys books bib sippy cup snacks and, in a flash of motherly inspiration, socket protectors. There are thirty-some Costco string cheeses in the fridge and several bags of shriveled horrible natural apricots in the cupboard. I put on jeans and I stuff my jammies a housedress a few of Engin's T-shirts and my sweatshirt that says "I Climbed the Great Wall" into the suitcase. There is no Business Casual in the high desert and none of my nice things fit in any case. I put everything in the trunk of the car in two trips and then I pause before locking the door and run back in to get our passports because you never know. Then I stand on our dingy wall-to-wall carpet thinking now is a moment to reverse course and drive south to the airport and find the soonest flight to Istanbul and get us one ticket since Honey is still free and then I recall I have this thought every single day like a goldfish and every time it ends back at the $1,847 in emergency.

My mother-in-law is not rich but she is not poor and I suspect she would happily buy the plane ticket to get her hands on her granddaughter so I suppose it's not only the $1,847 that keeps me from this course. The other thing is that I have this objectively marvelous job, a world-historically good job, a job at one of the best universities in the country or the world, a job wherein I got to make up my own nonsense title which is Director of Engagement and for which I make $69,500 a year all by myself, an extremely arbitrary figure which is somehow not enough to live on here but well above the national median household income and with which I pay our rent our daycare and our food and appreciate but do not rely upon the sporadic lump sums from Engin's video gigs. "Always have a job," my mother told me when I was eleven, and again when I was seventeen, and then again, when I was twenty-three, right before she died, when we sat together at her dining room table going over the papers that would give me the mobile home and all of her own furniture and household effects. "Don't ever live on someone else," she said to me over her glasses, her dainty head wrapped in a silk scarf I remember for no reason that my dad bought her at the Alhambra gift shop in the dead of a cold Spanish winter.

So I suppose it is the $1,847 that keeps me here, but it is also my glass-walled office, my gold-plated health care, our below-market rent in a top-five American city. And there's

Honey, born here. If we leave I am pretty sure we are never coming back, and she's a California baby now and if we leave she won't be ever again. So I abandon Istanbul with a pang as I do every time I think to take flight, and I smoke another cigarette against the hours in the car to come. Then I walk the two blocks to daycare to collect Honey, who gives me a radiant smile when she is brought to the door, which I accept as confirmation of the rightness of my actions thus far.

There are two ways you can drive up to Paiute County from San Francisco. You can take I-5 which runs up through the central agricultural flatlands, or you can head way east up the mountains that encircle Lake Tahoe, all the way to Reno and then north from there up the endless state roads. Mom always went up the mountain and down the valley so I decide that's what we'll do too.

Honey is happy enough when I put her in the car seat even though I do so with hideous pangs because she should be facing backward but faces forward. I switched it when her unusually long baby legs started to seem cramped and then read she should stay facing backward for many more months but couldn't get it tight enough by myself when I tried to turn it back around. The idea of calling the fire department or one of the daycare parents to do it for me is so humiliating that for now I've abandoned her to her fate in a front-facing car seat which I secretly prefer anyway because now I can see her and at red lights I can reach back and squeeze her feet. I give her a string cheese but I panic at the first stoplight remembering that it's a choking hazard in a moving car and first I scrabble my hand back ineffectually and then I pull over before the entrance to the highway so that she can eat the string cheese under supervision, but I have ruined it, and she throws the cheese and cries, and she cries all the way over the bridge and into the customary grid-lock by the IKEA, the clogged highway branching off into miles of parking. I smell the foul bay-mud around the base of the bridge, and look across the water to Angel Island and the container ships making their placid hulking way through the Golden Gate and I say "look look look Honey, big boats, BIG BOATS" but she is still crying forty minutes after we've left the house and she is still crying forty minutes after that.

The Buick is a beautiful heavy boat built for long voyages, with soft taupe upholstery and a bench seat in the front with seat belts for three across. It is a 1997 LeSabre that I inherited from my grandparents before I inherited their house, and it is now pointing toward its place of origin like a giant beige hom-ing pigeon. I wish I could put Honey up here next to me but that would obviously be a thousand times worse safety-wise than having her facing forward in the back. When Engin and I made this drive the first time, he drove the complicated part to get over the bridge and onto the open road and I sat in the middle seat nestled against him, pointing things out as we passed Berkeley passed El Cerrito passed Richmond until we were well into the golden hills scarred with cheap motels and roadside churches and housing developments. I showed him my favorite lone farmstead past Hercules, an 1800s beauty hun-kering down amid a stand of poplars, beyond it rolling hills dotted with cows. It must have been one of the loveliest pieces of land on God's earth and now it looks out at a highway lined with trash.

If Engin and I can be said to have anything in common, anything that forms the basis of a solid lifelong marital foundation that is, it's a shared aesthetic, so that the landscape of California moves and offends us in equal parts. Thus he admired my farmhouse and the hills of the coast range, yellow as they were, and lamented with me the cheap hideous housing tracts around Vallejo Fairfield Vacaville, and then the god-awful Nut Tree, a township comprised entirely of big-box commercial establishments, mattress stores and Starbucks and fast casual dining a stone's throw from endless choking traffic, the smell of exhaust faintly perceptible even in the padded coffin of the Buick.

But now it is Honey and I and I am driving straight-backed right up against the wheel with my shoulders up by my ears, sweating and worrying over my precious squawking cargo and feeling so increasingly perturbed by her crying that soon I have to pull the car over again in a highway-adjacent dialysis center and cry into the steering wheel for three minutes along with her. Honey knows we have stopped the car and her crying becomes more urgent and her body begins straining against the straps of the car seat and she makes a glubbing sound and I look back at her and before I can do anything her mouth opens wide and her eyes open wide with the unmistakable panic of imminent barfing and I say "no no no" and a small torrent of milk water cheese pieces and noodle bites from daycare sprays forth onto her and the car seat and her eyes are terrified. I lunge back and am trying to unbuckle her as another torrent comes forth and then she recovers her breath and screams so I know she is not dying. I get out of the car and sprint around to her door and undo the restraints from which she is frantically trying to free herself and pick her up and first hold her at a shameful arm's length before motherlove grinds into gear and I press her against me and cradle her hot head against my shoulder and smooth down her damp curls while she sobs. I grip her with one arm open the trunk dig in the tote bag find a T-shirt and a pack of wipes and a new onesie and I get her more or less wiped off and changed and sit her in the passenger seat and tackle the car seat with one eye on her and I am obscurely proud to see her return quickly to higher spirits and make a renewed effort with her cheese; she has a nice sense of equilibrium. I take my shirt off and put on one of Engin's and we do a little walk around the parking lot and finally she gives me a smile and squawks merrily when I kiss her on the mouth and do a zerbert into her neck.

We have some water and she finishes the cheese and I put her back in the car seat and roll down the windows for the smell and as I move down the exit and wait for some window between the terrifying rush of enormous trucks pickups SUVs she has started up crying again. But once we get on the road and make our way through the perpetual snarl of traffic that surrounds Nut Tree and finally get through Davis and Sacramento and head into the Sierra, she is asleep, and as we say goodbye to the dusty median oleanders of the flatlands and begin to feel the incline signaling our ascent to the high country I have the slightest bit of that road-trip feeling, that opening up, the road rising up to meet us, the marginal loosening of cares.

The road is beautiful now, pine forests and limestone slabs and glimpses of Donner Lake in the distance. Once you get over the top of Donner Pass and some kind of geological divide, suddenly the forests are gone and the land is brown and stretching out for miles and miles and that's Nevada. Then through Reno, its outer ring of subdivisions and lawns trying to be green, its downtown its modest multistory casinos and the suggestion of tree-lined neighborhoods just hidden from view of the highway. In Altavista this is the small-c city, four hours away, where Mom and Uncle Rodney bought their prom clothes and their dress-up shoes and had white-tablecloth meals at the regal art deco hotel they demolished fifteen years ago. Every time I see the trees and think of the home prices I think maybe Engin and I should try it out here, but Engin having grown up in the heart of the world's greatest metropolis is ruined for two-bit cities, for him San Francisco is just a town, and I can't quite picture him on this patch of desert.

Before Honey and I traverse the vast territory between Reno and Altavista we have to eat, so we stop on the Nevada side at a little tiny casino called State Lines which is where Mom and I always used to stop to get a cheeseburger for reasons that now escape me since it's a low-lying unprepossessing building with tinted windows on a plateau overlooking the warehoused suburbs of Reno and a vast dry lakebed. When you open the door, on your left is the gambling section with indoor smoking and on the right is a diner. The people are friendly and the food is bad and the seats are vinyl and the art is mustardy paintings of waterwheels and gold-rush diggings. Honey sits on my lap and plays with the spoon and the fork and I order the jumbo hotdog and share with her, cutting her half into tiny pieces, but she whines and mostly wants to take bites off mine like a big girl.

Engin and I stopped here on our solo trip and I said as I

had said for the days weeks leading up to it, "Prepare yourself for a lot of downtrodden white people." And there were the customary white people saddled up to slots with oxygen machines and cigarettes smoldering in the ashtrays beside them, bearded men in shirts reading e.g. "Donkey Kong Is My Spirit Animal," every one with his hat on, women with big legs and bad hair and rambunctious children. Now I am here, a white person not particularly downtrodden but with big legs bad hair and rambunctious child although she isn't really that rambunctious, not really, and at this moment she is peaceful in my lap, happy to be out of the car happy to be smiling at the hostess who is not white but brown and who chucks Honey's cheek and touches her curly fuzz and Honey points at a bronco in a painting and says "daggy daggy daggy," the only real word she can say. She sucks ketchup off the French fries and I analyze her food intake today and it is unbalanced and I wonder how I will go about balancing it. I exchange smiles with two very old people sharing an enormous sandwich, he with a trucker hat and suspenders, the picture of my beloved Burdock grandfather, but this man looks menacing to me as everyone looks menacing to me lately. We finish our meal, my fingers already swelling from salt, and I stand and pluck my pants from my butt and haul Honey through the smoky side to the bathroom and I pee and there's no changing table so I change Honey's diaper outside in the back seat of the baking car. Zerberts zerberts and more zerberts and baby laughs and so docile getting into the car seat I think I can do this and trot around to the driver's side with just the slightest bit of pep in my step.

We leave State Lines and Honey looks happy. I have the windows down and the hot wind is whooshing around the car and the fuzz on her head is standing up and I crane to make eye contact with her in the rearview mirror and I smile and she smiles back. I like this stretch here the most because this is the real way there, all the obstacles of Davis Sac Reno behind you and the sparse hills rolling away from the road like a moonscape and you understand you're really going somewhere special. But it doesn't last long before the road becomes long and monotonous and the distance starts to feel threatening and somehow irrevocable, the only movement the occasional flocks of sheep impossibly far from shelter. When Engin saw this part for the first time he said "My god, it's like the steppe." When I was a child we did this pilgrimage every year, hours and hours and hours in the plane and then stepping bewildered into the fog of SFO, only to get in the car and drive into this otherworld where my grandparents waited on the deck with drinks for my parents and ice cream for me. But now for me it's only the memory that beckons, the strength of all the associations that still cling to the land and the road leading to it.

Honey is quiet and the Buick is devouring miles, the ride so smooth you don't feel the road beneath. We are swiftly out of radio opportunities and I have to pee again but Honey is fast asleep so I press the pedal and we are flying on the empty road at ninety miles an hour until I can't stand it anymore and find a dirt place to pull over, a forest service fire road or a rancher's road with a cattle gate stretched across. I leave the car on and spring around to the side and pee right next to the car so I can peer in the window and keep an eye on the sleeping Honey. And then it's back on the road, now passing the tiny depleted burgs before the Paiute border. In the distance I see a little shack with a big black flag reading "Kafir" in Arabic, which was here when Engin and I came up last time. "Bu ne yaa," he said when he saw it. *What is this?* And I said, "It says kafir," infidel, the same word in Turkish. "It's for anti-Islam dickheads to show that they are anti-Islam dickheads." He looked aghast and then laughed, I thought because it sounded so odd to hear the obscenity in my accent but then was informed that sik kafalı is way more obscene apparently than dickhead is in English—the type of thing where you might have to fight someone. I'm always miscalibrating profanity since you can't learn it in a book.

The sky is just starting to mellow into the warm pre-twilight light, bruising faintly at the horizon, when we get out of the last stretch of plain and up over the forested hills to the basin where Altavista sits. Honey wakes up now, crying. "We're so close, sweet one," I tell her. "Hang in there," but she's justifiably grumpy and she cries and I listen to the crying and roll down the window to imbibe the juniper and try to bolster myself for the sight of the wildlife preserve and the fields and the town that will greet us over the crest of these little mountains, but as with everything up here it's the scale and the sparseness that are striking, and the thrill of recognition at first sight is replaced almost immediately with a feeling of deflation, the knowledge that there's no one waiting on the deck to greet us. The highway turns into the main street and we pass the area they called Indian Town which is a rocky slope just outside of where the grid begins and presumably where the people were made to live who weren't shipped off to Oklahoma after the Indian Wars or into one of the tiny rancherias out yonder.

And then we are in town proper, Honey crying past the abandoned false-front emporia past a few shops past the High Desert Hotel past the tiny movie theater with by god a newish release spelled out on the marquee. My heart sinks as I take in the empty sidewalks and empty storefronts, the gas station, the railroad tracks now defunct, everything looking like it was the last time I was here, that is, not exactly thriving.

The drive is supposed to take six and a half hours but somehow we have been on the road for eight when we come to the wooden sign sunk into grass that signifies the entrance to Deakins Park. Although Honey is still caterwauling, passing the sign feels like entering protected land, something apart from the ravages of the town. It sounds like hair-splitting to parse the varieties of mobile home, like something only a person obsessed with imperceptible class minutia would do, but there are mobile homes and mobile homes and despite how mortified I used to be by the fact that my grandparents lived in one now I happen to think Deakins Park is just as nice if not nicer than many a suburban cul-de-sac of for example the Nut Tree–adjacent variety. It's a circle of nicely appointed and discreetly mobile mobile homes of different styles and patterns built on either side of a large circular street, each kept up nice and with a good-size yard. The outer ring of houses is bounded by a split-rail fence, and beyond this the town gives over to the high desert, with low, prickly sagebrush and rafts of tumbleweed through which jackrabbits bound and antelope poke delicately in the cool mornings. Everyone has plenty of space and a view of the low-lying mountains ringing the basin. It's a little neighborhood on the frontier. Home on the range, if you will.

I drive past what was the original eponymous Deakinses' place, left empty by their deaths like my grandparents' and also kept up by their children, and down the road ahead of us I see my grandma's birch tree with its white paper skin I picked strips off of as a child and its luxuriant fall of green and the low chain-link fence and the tidy squares of yellowing grass bordering the concrete walkway up to the porch.

I pull up to my grandparents' house, or my house, I should say, and the empty lot next door which is technically also mine. There's a Realtor's sign stuck into the front yard, curling at the corners and cutting off the final vowel on the Basque name of a local gal who handles all the dealings for a hundred miles. Every few months someone makes as though they want to buy it, ranch hands or frail retirees hoping to be closer to grandchildren, but they tend to melt away after their first inquiries to the bank, or some issue with the required paperwork. Uncle Rodney informs me that last winter the only title company in Paiute County closed, precipitously leaving all real estate deals such as they are in even greater disarray.

Honey is quieter now but still mewling hungry and tired of being squished up in her car seat, long past her bedtime already. I park in the driveway in front of the garage and step out to release her and once she has tottered around on the front grass a bit to stretch her legs I get her to hold my hand and together we climb the back steps and I fumble for the key I keep on my keychain even though I've only been up here twice in five years. I hoist Honey up on my hip and open the door holding my breath. It's been more than a year since the last time I walked in this door and I think what if it's been colonized by local youths meth-users or pillheads or whatnot and I prepare myself to see something I don't want to see. But it's as pristine as it was when my grandmother presided, with its all-over faux-wood paneling which somehow comes together with her couches her dining room table her Indian baskets her hutch her milk glass her torchère lamp, everything left as it was, cozy and immaculate, my grandfather's encyclopedia and his World War II books on the low shelf by his recliner. The house is an aesthetically closed circuit, not a detail out of place, its mobileness less apparent within than it is without. I breathe in the smell, the smell as it's always been, the smell of old paper in a dry cedar cabinet. I eye the woodstove on its brick platform and think how cozy it will be in here and remember that it's summer and I won't need to use it. Or not yet, I think, and then unthink it, because we are not prepared to travel that line of inquiry.

I feel the enormous squishy heft of Honey's diaper and set her down and consider leaving her while I go back to the car to get the diaper stuff but see too many incipient hazards about the place. So I heave her back up and trot back out to the car and pull out the tote bag with the essentials and trot back into the house and change her diaper on the living room floor, and she looks at me with a surprising amount of good cheer given the strange day she's had, and I feel that we are two gals out on an adventure. I button the onesie and pull up the pants and consider the living room and the hazards and, patting myself on the back for being so conscientious and prepared considering my general frame of mind, take a bunch of clean rags from the pantry and tape them over the razor-like corners and edges of the brick platform under the woodstove, and since I'm at it I take my thirty-pack of socket protectors and stick them around, and I put the heavy brass lamp down on the floor where she can't pull it down onto her head, and I feel the mirrors and still lifes the cowboy ephemera and weavings to make sure they're secure on the flimsy walls, and then I lie down on the couch and watch as Honey makes her first lap around the living room, poking and stumbling on little legs that have only just learned how to walk. It's very, very quiet and I wonder what we are going to do next. Then I consider what Honey has eaten today and I get up and make for the pantry and there are cans of baked beans and peas and I bustle around the kitchen and get them into a little saucepan and I survey the house. My house. My house. "This is my house," I say aloud, and everything in the house contradicts me, down to its dubious foundation. "You're a visitor," the house seems to say. But it still welcomes me, even if we have mutually rejected the existence of an owner-owned relationship between us. We are safe in the house, I feel.

Despite the caretaking efforts of my uncle the house is beginning to show the signs of disuse. I can see that rain comes through the master bathroom window; there's a small soft place in the wood at the sill. The shadows of deceased bugs are visible in the white bowls of light fixtures. Carrying Honey I slide open the screen door which complains a little in its tracks and step onto the porch and see that something has got at the feathers that once hung from the dreamcatcher wind chime, and its remaining wood and metal are in a little broken pile below. A cow skull propped against the house is minus a horn.

I peer around at the neighboring houses and note the absence of any lights blinking cozily across the park. I note the mountains with the slightest bit of snow still on their peaks in the distance, neither the Sierra nor the Cascades, but some weird in-betweener range. I feel enervated rather than invigorated by the landscape. But the air feels warm and good and smells like juniper like I promised myself it would, and the light is otherworldly purple, indisputably beautiful.

Honey is starting to do high-wattage squawks that indicate she is way past tired and I know I have to hustle to try and get the sleeping situation configured in the most soothing routine-looking way possible. I decide we won't sleep in my accustomed twin bed in the little side room overlooking the birch tree with the framed telegraph from my great-great-grandmother on the wall and my mother's bronzed baby shoes on the dresser which I pause and consider weeping over but don't. No, the "master suite," my grandparent's room.

I clip Honey's high chair to the tiny laminate table in the kitchen and spoon her some of the baked beans and peas and she pats at them with her spoon and for a moment I worry about botulism and then stop worrying because I'm suddenly so desperate for her to eat something so I can get her into bed and smoke a cigarette and have a minute to figure things out. While she eats I set up the Pack 'n Play in the closet off the room with the king-size bed which eerily has clean sheets with military corners and the polyester floral cover spread over them smooth as cream and Grandma's chest of worn Pendleton blankies at its foot.

Finally we sit in the big bed and have milk which is warm in the sippy cup from this morning because I haven't brought a carton and we have two stories *Goodnight Moon* and *Goodnight Gorilla*, trying to emphasize the goodnight aspect and the sleeping aspect, and I decide to forgo brushing teeth and then think no no no it's too easy to fail to establish good habits and I haul her into the bathroom and poke at her with the toothbrush and she clamps her mouth shut and cries and then I lay her in the Pack 'n Play turn on the sound machine say "I love you I love you I love you" and close the door and listen to her scream.

I find my phone which I know will not have service here for love or money and there is a mystery Michelob in the fridge and I take it onto the porch with my cigarettes and stretch out as much as I can in the plastic chair. I unbutton my pants which are creasing the fat of my stomach, my embonpoint I sometimes try to cheer myself up by calling it. I open the beer and light the cigarette and feel repose fill my soft anxious body.

When I unlock the phone it wheezes to life, tottering along on one bar and I see that I won't be able to Skype Engin, something we will have to deal with tomorrow. I manage to load a few e-mails and I make a reflexive mental note to submit a reimbursement to the Institute for the overage this will undoubtedly accrue, datawise, and then make another mental note that I will not be reimbursed for anything going forward. I peck out a WhatsApp message to Engin that I'm in Altavista and will call him tomorrow and I watch the app labor to send the message for two minutes, my nerves chirping until it finally whooshes off and I have completed my major obligations for this day.

I haven't had a cigarette since we left the City and I feel a little high sucking this one down in the frictionless air. I have secretly had a pack of cigarettes with me at all times for eight months now. I'd like to say that I've had them since after I weaned Honey but if someone is surveilling the search history on my Institute computer which I suppose they could be apart from visa questions they would find many variations of "nicotine" "breastmilk" "nursing" "damage" "bad" etc. The problem with reproduction is that it is stressful, I mean becoming pregnant having the baby raising the baby, and all the measures I employ to deal with stress involve some measure of self-harm, and once you have a baby in or around your body that body is no longer just your own to harm. Engin has some investment in it, of course, not wanting me to die an early death, and shortly after we got married he took what I consider to be a rankly hypocritical position about my smoking, since he has smoked since infancy practically and I'm sure he's sucking them down on his mom's balcony right this moment, that is, morning his time. Unfortunately for him, given the various demands on my physical person over the last two-plus years smoking is now what I consider to be a feminist issue and I take a big drag and watch the smoke go out in the cooling air and think how every time I quit smoking I invest that last cigarette with a lot of ceremony—big, weighty drags, clasped hands, heart lifted up in supplication to God. But I can't remember the last time that I nursed Honey, and that really was the last time, the last time in the history of man that I had my baby at my breast.

This reminds me that my breast pump is still sitting in the basement of Oberrecht Hall. I remember this approximately once a week but while I was on campus I couldn't bring myself to go down the three flights to get it. It's in Ted's server closet, which is tiny and full of whirring machines and one office chair and kept at sixty-three degrees. Ted and I had a system, which was that I would go in there and turn off the AC and lock the door and disrobe and attach myself to the pump and if he needed to come in and check on the servers he would knock which thank god never happened. Sometimes I would go in there and find an orange or a little stack of paper napkins on the table, and know that Ted had shortly beforehand been sitting in the seat and eating his lunch and futzing with his servers. Ted has very long fingernails, which I imagined digging deep into the skin of the orange. I thought about this when I was half naked in his chair with plastic hoses attached to my breasts, and the little bottles of milk placed around his desk and on his papers and next to his servers.

Honey has stopped screaming and it is now very, very quiet and dark. A light pops on in the house behind us, neighbors I don't know.

The issue with the breast pump was that the things it came with, flanges they are called, were too big for my nipples. A whole great chunk of my breast was pulled in along with the nipple, and the skin blistered against the plastic as it was chafed by the motion of the pump. I found online a smaller insert, 22.5 millimeters, but the insert wasn't compatible with the tube thing that the flange stuck in, so that I had to stick it into the original too-large flange, and then stick that into the tube, and some of the milk sort of stuck between the insert and the flange and dripped all over the table when I took them apart. Invariably during the assembly or de-assembly one of the flanges would fall on the linoleum and I'd pick it up covered with hair and fuzz, and I would wipe it off with my clothes and the hand sanitizer that sat on Ted's desk, or one of his napkins. I asked Engin if I had in his estimation smaller than usual nipples, and he asked why and I got waylaid looking up the Turkish word for flange and I never found out about his estimation of the relative size of my nipples.

When I was in the hospital after I had Honey I told the nurse I wasn't sure the breastfeeding was working and she held my hand and looked into my eyes meaningfully and said, "You have all the tools you need." She was in her late forties and had very white, likely false teeth and tattooed eyeliner and lustrous black hair. I asked if she was from Paiute County because she pronounced the word "Sunday" just like my grandmother, "Sundy," but it turned out she was from Southern California with a mom from Okinawa, not like my grandmother at all. Her parents must have had a cross-cultural marriage, I think now. I should have asked her about that, not the breastfeeding which is in the scheme of things a very small part of life. I light another cigarette in honor of this woman, who reassured me that I could do it, feed Honey that is.

But once I went back to work, less and less started to come out of the tubes, and when I looked online about how to sustain the milk it seemed like an insane project—feed the baby, pump after feeding the baby, wake up and pump every two hours, etc., even if the baby is sleeping. So then I gave her formula, and the more formula I gave the less milk I made, and all the things that I read on BabyCenter came to pass vis-à-vis my "supply." I used to lie on the couch after work and look at pictures of nursing mothers on my phone and cry.

Engin's mother begged me to take more time off work for

the good of the baby, but the standard leave policy of the University is six weeks off at 50 percent of your salary, and after many bewildering and misleading conversations with the morons in HR I elected to pay twenty-eight dollars out of every paycheck from the time I started work so that I could instead receive 70 percent of my salary, and then I took the additional six unpaid weeks that were my right by federal law, except Honey was born two weeks late and so that ate up two of those precious weeks and no one in HR ever told me I was legally entitled to tack them on later. I seem to always meet University staff who are just coming back from their second or third six-month absence but those are unpaid and in any case at the discretion of your supervisor. Hugo earnestly counsels his female graduate student against procreating and I felt that he felt that spending any additional time away from work would be frowned upon but to be honest I never even asked so I don't know and thus I went back when she was a mere ten weeks old. I felt so certain that the Institute truly could not function without me because there were grant reports to file and federal compliance to ensure and events to orchestrate and nobody knows how to do any of this but me and it all felt so important it would make me laugh now if I weren't so furious.

If I had just weaned her when I went back to work I never would have had to pump milk half naked and freezing in a closet with Ted's servers and napkins and oranges. Then again if I hadn't gone back to work at all I wouldn't have missed days weeks months with my child that I will never have again in this life.

My thoughts are finding their familiar melancholy groove of love for my child and sadness about our fleeting life together and then I think of Ellery whom I have assiduously avoided thinking about for most of the day, whose life on earth and with her own loving parents is now at an end, and I feel the mustard sting behind my eyes as her face and Maryam's face are summoned up before me from the night air. I never actually met Ellery despite being circumstantially wrapped up in her doom. Two months ago Maryam sent me a cheery progress report, two days before the accident, two days after having dinner with my sister-in-law Pelin and her husband Savaş and their daughter Elifnaz, which I arranged so the girls—young women—could have some kind of cultural experience beyond carousing with hot guys from New Zealand in their Tünel-adjacent hostel. Attached to the e-mail was a photo, the two of them in the Rüstem Paşa Camii, Ellery a lively looking girl with great eyebrows white teeth huge smile, her face lit up with the secret joy game white girls feel upon donning a headscarf in a culturally appropriate context, and Maryam who is a Palestinian Christian from Bakersfield by way of Amman duckfacing with a worn mosque-provided paisley sheet wrapped around her short shorts and her arms wrapped around her friend. The memory of this photo, the thought of them setting out on their adventure with their backpacks and their water bottles and their bag of warm bread from Pelin's favorite bakery, and then of these smiling girls being thrown into the windshield of their speeding taxi with no seat belts is several orders of magnitude too large and awful to contemplate and I shake my head hard in the dark, a dimly remembered gesture of my father's whenever he wanted to stop thinking about something he didn't want to think about.

I have one more cigarette brush my teeth look in at Honey

splayed out in her Pack 'n Play in the dark closet and stroke her head and cover her with the blanket and climb into bed. Then I think of all this big expanse of bed and Honey cooped up in the closet alone and get back out and gently lift her out and carry her over and put her next to me which I've always wanted to do but have not done because of all the things you read about sleep habits and people who sleep with their children until they are five. I've never had her in bed with me through the night, just mornings during the early weeks months when she hardly moved at all. Now I put my arm under her rear and sort of encircle her with my mouth against her fuzz. But she senses the change and squirms and wakes up and looks at me and smiles and starts fidgeting and says "da da daaaaaah" with curiosity and I feel her little hands on my face and I say "shhhhh sleeping" but when I open my eyes I can see the whites of her eyes in the darkness gazing at me like an inquisitive turtle and she kicks her feet and squirms toward the edge of the bed and I can't get her to lie down and I know I've made a mistake and carry her back to the Pack 'n Play and she cries.

My grandmother who slept in this bed with my grandfather lost her father before she was even born. He was twenty-one years old and was carried off by flu when my great-grandmother was six months pregnant. I thought about this all the time when I was pregnant and Engin was home with us and when he was late coming home from the store or the studio he sometimes rented time in I would hold my stomach and know he was dead and he would find me crying over the kitchen sink. Now sometimes I have to remind myself that Engin is not actually dead, just in Turkey. I want to think good thoughts about Engin so I think about those magic weeks after Honey was born when Engin and I hung around the house with tiny her lying on her blanket. In the mornings we would tuck her between us like a hot dog, and we would loll around until 11:00 and Engin would fix breakfast. Then we would have a pro forma argument about the in my view mistaken Turkish belief in a forty-day sequestering period for babies and new mothers that I pointed out he only knew and pretended to care about because his mother told him he should, and finally we would bundle her up and take her for a long, slow walk around the City, and we would stop for ice cream or beers and hold hands and gaze at each other and at the perfect creature that we made.

The last thought I have is that Engin is not in fact in Turkey at this moment, he is in Belgrade helping his friend Tolga shoot a commercial, and he'll be back at his mother's tomorrow night. I lie there feeling guilty that I have forgotten this, and also relieved that he likely hasn't been sitting around his mom's house waiting for Honey's face to light up his screen, until I finally fall asleep.

DAY 2   This morning while fixing Honey what I tell her and myself is a cowboy breakfast of warmed-up beans string cheese and cut-up apricots I look out the window and see Cindy Cooper, who lives in the lot kitty-corner from Grandma's pansy bed. She has a green State of Jefferson sign on her front lawn, which means I believe that she takes a dim view of government activities and thinks the North State and southern Oregon should throw in their lot together and form a new state where there are no rules of any kind. They have something about it in the *Chronicle* from time to time. I never heard my grandparents say word one about it and I've never seen one of these signs in the wild before, but now that I see hers I realize they were dotted across homesteads the whole drive up, three or four counties' worth.

Cindy Cooper is I am pretty sure a Johnny-come-lately who came from I don't know where and bought her lot in Deakins Park a couple of years before Mom died. As I watch her pick up her copy of the *Paiute Recorder* and peer skeptically at a mean-looking dog tied to a mailbox across the street I feel the thinness of the skeins that tie me to the town. My relation to Altavista is so glancing, so filtered through the perceptions of my mom, who spent her life establishing a safe distance between herself and here, that I really have no idea who is new and who is old.

In their twilight years my grandparents' friends broke up the weekly bridge and martini nights to spend winters in more temperate climates, Stockton or Sac. But my grandparents stayed right where they were, the Deakins Park house they bought when they retired. The house was a source of perpetual sorrow to my mother, who believed that only what you might call white trash lives in mobile homes.

It does feel like the concentric circles that described social life in Altavista have expanded wider and wider until their essential structure has stretched and broken apart. My grandparents worked for the school, the Forest Service, the Bureau of Land Management, sundry local enterprises, but their friends were landholders, ranchers, outdoorswomen in pressed jeans, friendliness undergirded by the dignity of long years spent on a single piece of soil, and none of them seems to live here now. Uncle Rodney never criticizes the town but when Engin and I spent the one mournful Christmas here with him, he peered at every face we saw in the store and along the main street, looking for some sign of lineage, the innate quality of rootedness. It may be that just our family died out and moved on, and that everyone else is thriving in unknown houses. But even when my mom was alive she would point out the empty storefronts, the junk in the yards, and say it's not the place it once was.

Honey is chewing up her apricots and spitting them out and splatting her spoon on the surface of the beans to demonstrate that she is unimpressed by the offerings and I realize we will need to deal with the food situation. I sponge her off change her diaper get her dressed pull on the clothes I wore yesterday and hustle her out toward the back door. The morning is spectacular; it's 7:15, and the sun is at a friendly low angle, and the sky is blue, and it's cool cool cool and birds are cheeping in the birch tree.

We drive over to the Holiday which is an honest-to-god grocery store on the edge of town. Everything is on the edge of town; the town is comprised of edges, the streets are so wide and haphazard beyond the tiny core grid of four blocks by four blocks. I'm pleased nay amazed to see the store has gotten a makeover since the days I helped my grandmother do her shopping—there is organic produce and a classier kind of frozen food. During my inventory of the kitchen this morning I spotted an almost-full bottle of Popov in the freezer where it must have been sitting since my grandmother died and I think what the hell and get a carton of orange juice. I get two feel-good frozen pizzas, I get noodles, yogurt, more beans, eggs, milk, apples, Cheerios, bananas, strawberries, blueberries, avocado, sweet potatoes, and a bunch of broccoli since it's the only green thing I can get Honey to eat. I am wondering if this is all going to be enough or too much and then I realize I have no idea how long we are going to be here and the indecision this awakens in the aisle causes my heart to beat very fast. I have been eerily calm for twenty-four hours but I remember suddenly all the e-mails I need to write all the explaining I'm going to have to do and I almost wheel the cart out with Honey and our unpurchased produce in it. But then I think Meatloaf like a message from someone and I get ground beef and bread-crumbs and onion soup packets you can't get at Whole Foods or the Chinese grocery at home. And then I go ahead and get a cardboard box of the cheap yellow vanilla ice cream we always ate after dinner with my grandparents, and a can of Hershey's chocolate syrup to put on it, and then I think what else did Mom and Grandma make and I say "Pancakes" and I get flour vanilla extract baking soda buttermilk. The women at the check-out aisles are ancient and I wonder if they know anyone I know but I decide not to ask and they coo over Honey and she waves her little paw at them beaming and says "Hi! Hi! Hi!"

We drive back home. It's 8:15 a.m. Honey roams around the living room and I turn on the TV which has ABC, CBS, fuzz, fuzz, fuzz. I put it on some morning show. We don't have TV at home and just watch shows on the laptop and the bright lights loud voices taut arms brassy makeup are just too much and I start to feel the very specific kind of deeply down-in-the-mouth existential despair brought on by network television and I turn it off and then I say to Honey, "I guess we could make pancakes." This is the only thing I can make without consulting the recipe and I made them every Sunday when Engin was here. He is crazy for these pancakes. Most pancakes are garbage; the secret, which I learned from Mom, is you have to separate the yolks and whites and mix the yolks with the milk and beat the whites and then mix them into the finished batter. I do all this and Honey is more or less transfixed on the linoleum floor by some pots and pans I pull out for her and when it is all over we eat the pancakes and I am stuffed and she is stuffed and there is a huge mess and it's 9:20. I lie on the couch and Honey rollicks around on my stomach and tumbles off the couch and lunges for my grandmother's raw-hide coasters and throws them all across the living room and zigzags around the house and I think we need to find some-where with Wi-Fi and call Engin and then I remember he is flying back from Belgrade and I can't yet muster the energy for a walk in any case and so instead I lie there and just will the hours to pass until lunch, which kills four minutes, with Honey standing by the couch pinching the fat around my elbow and laughing. I think how can I enrich her so I collect the books I brought, eight books, and I scoop her up and I read every single one and then I put a sweet potato in the oven to roast so she will have something nutritious ready to eat later on and then it is 9:57.

During Honey's nap I discover that if I bring the Institute computer out onto the very end of the deck toward the back of the house, I can latch on to the ass-end of someone's unsecured wireless network, maybe Cindy Cooper's. This is excellent news because it allows me to smoke while I check e-mails. I try Skype and the connection is too weak to sustain video, although this gives me more time to figure out what I am going to say to Engin when I finally reach him. His response to my WhatsApp is short, or terse, I can't tell which. "Call me." I check the Check Visa Status portal and it's At NVC, the same the same the same the same it's been for five goddamn months. I see how far down I can draw my cigarette with one drag.

I e-mail Hugo and Meredith to say I am sick. Mercifully my work e-mail does not yet reflect my absence from the Institute, although my body does; I blow my nose and big green slabs streaked with blood shoot out onto the Kleenex. You can't feel the altitude here right away, it comes on days two and three with the dramatic boogers and the cracked skin of your hands and the blistering sunburn you'll get if you aren't careful. I open the least threatening-seeming e-mail, which is from the head of the Social Sciences and Humanities Diversity Committee and informs me that the meeting to discuss our Diversity Action Plan is postponed indefinitely due to the Vice Provost's recent resignation for sexual misconduct. My task for the Action Plan was to survey existing Action Plans on campus and summarize them for the group.

Ted sent me an e-mail too. I assume this would be some characteristically poky and roundabout Ted message about my stealing the Institute laptop, but it is only a reminder to do the overdue software patch on my office machine by clicking the "Agree" button instead of the "Snooze" button when the window pops up. This means he doesn't yet know that I'm gone. Moreover, I'm fairly certain no one knows how many laptops the Institute has. The last person the University sent around to do an inventory was a hapless work-study asking about mystery machines no one had seen in years. "On whose authority are you conducting this survey?" Hugo had asked in his imperious way, and the boy stammered and went away with his clipboard hanging low. In addition to Ted's e-mail there is a letter of recommendation portal login e-mail of the type that Hugo reflexively forwards to me, which means, importantly, that Hugo doesn't know I'm gone either. I've gotten good at these letters over the last couple of years; I like to think that several highly desirable teaching positions and postdocs were secured for his students through my efforts. Ironically Hugo himself doesn't have a Ph.D., although you would never ever know from the way he is lavished with lecture invitations and NPR appearances. But he was the last noncredentialed person into the academy and he barred the door on his way in. Meredith of course has one from Princeton but as Hugo never tires of reminding her she has no publications.

We at the Institute are nesting dolls: Karen the admin assistant who has no M.A., then me who has an M.A. but dropped out of the Ph.D., then Meredith with her Ph.D., with Hugo encircling us all. Meredith is sensitive to slights from Hugo; I am sensitive to slights from Meredith and Hugo; Karen is sensitive to slights from everyone. The hierarchy is all we have. We are all publicly rather flirtatious with Hugo, privately disdainful, and occasionally afraid. I have spent so much time with these people that I can't tell whether I hate them or whether I can't live without them.

Meredith endlessly counsels me to go back and finish. "You're so smart," she says. "You *need* to get a Ph.D.," oblivious to the universe of condescension that lurks behind this formula. In my secret heart I am susceptible to the formula too, but since working at the Institute has amply illustrated the precarious shitshow that is a life of the mind in 2015 I can always talk myself out of it. The only time I think it's not a bad idea is when something comes along like THE CONFERENCE as Hugo calls it when he e-mails me about it, and people I've never met are e-mailing me lists of demands regarding how to arrange the program, who will give the opening remarks and who will give the lunchtime keynote and who will introduce the person giving the evening keynote and who will be the panel chairs. Apart from the recent death and maiming THE CONFERENCE is the thing that is most intolerable about the Institute. It's a big anniversary spectacular deal which has been looming for two years now and which I had been assured I wouldn't need to take too great a hand in the execution of, but like so many things in the University it acquired so many cosponsors demonstrating so many exemplary strains of interdisciplinary collaboration that no one was actually tasked with planning it. Every few months in a desultory way someone would ask whether I had found a venue, or created a budget, or made the arrangements for the speakers and sooner or later it was clear I better make it my business to do these things.

The more education you have the more removed you are from the ineluctable yawning core of work at the University, which is not in fact teaching but is the filling out and submission and resubmission of forms, the creation of scheduling Doodles, the collection of receipts and the phoning of caterers, the issuing of letters and the ordering of supplies and the tallying of points in poorly formatted spreadsheets. The secret work of us administrators—of everyone at the University—is to put as much distance between ourselves and this yawning core as possible, to be the thing rather than proximal to the thing. Your relative position in the hierarchy will dictate how much Doodling will be your responsibility, how many humiliating interactions with incensed French experts whose taxi got lost on the way to the lecture hall.

I guess I could have kept up with the Ph.D. and *also* married Engin, but I wasn't an optimal Ph.D. student to begin with. Doctorates require specialization, specificity, and all I ever wanted was to speak Turkish perfectly, to speak Arabic perfectly, to speak Persian perfectly, to understand everything, to go everywhere. Turkic verbs and Persian poetry; religion and migration; art and civilization and change. But choosing religion means learning classical Arabic and hours of reading hadith and hadith interpretation and counterinterpretation and choosing migration means counting surnames in dusty archives and making GIS maps and choosing change means picking one very specific thing like Mongol legal practice and establishing how it evolved after they invented postage stamps or whatnot, and choosing language means linguistics and all those god-awful equations and formulas on the white board. I wanted to study the world-altering beauty of Muslim civilizations, but that's not a topic, it's an enthusiasm, it's a fetish for rug-collecting Berkeley-dwellers. But I made a show of choosing and thus have approximately one-third of a Ph.D. in Turkish Republican literature, clearly a mistake since it has taken me three years to not even finish for example a seminal work by Sait Faik Abasıyanık on the BART train.

In a sense working at the Institute is perfect for me, since now I can just listen to all the people who did choose and presumably weave them into some tattered tapestry of erudition. But then I have to reimburse them for their taxis to and from the airport and write effusive introductions about them for Hugo to deliver.

Reflexively I navigate to the Purchasing Portal to see whether my $483 in miscellaneous catering expenses has been reimbursed. Half of them have gone through, although this only means they have successfully navigated the labyrinth of approvals associated with the original submittal. This means that our financial analyst looked at the fund number and confirmed that the Al-Ihsan Foundation would theoretically countenance the expenditure of endowment income on twenty-four donuts two meze platters and two coffee cambros to enliven a workshop on Islam: Theme and Variation, but that no one has actually released the money to pay me. I remember that I had to pay for extra daycare for that workshop for which I will not of course be reimbursed. I also remember that a man named Todd spent most of the allotted time talking about Yarsanism, which as far as I can tell has to do with Islam in only the most arcane and theoretical sense, and that Faisal from Religious Studies spent the rest of the time talking about Islamophobia, which is more of a unifying Islamic experience than a variety of it, and that Hugo then chided me mercilessly for letting things get off track. Hugo is of course notoriously and militantly irreligious, if not actually Islamophobic himself, but he has an Arab surname and family origin which was presumably what impelled the Vice Provost to appoint him director of the Institute, a post highly sought by many faculty members due to endowments that provide over 300K in no-strings-attached funds annually, most of it from Saudi entities with no mailing address. In fact currently none of the staff of the Institute for the Study of Islamic Societies and Civilizations is a Muslim. Not me, not Meredith, not Karen, not injured Maryam, and not the other work-study, a poli-sci-majoring redhead from San Diego whom we think Hugo personally interfered in the hiring process to select over Meredith's and my preferred and head-scarfed applicant from Senegal because he found her sexually compelling. He can do this because we live in a lawless shadowland, one of the hundreds of Institutes and Centers and Programs and Initiatives that have blindly replicated themselves over the body of the University so that it is like a once-vigorous person covered with tumors that behave exactly as they please.

I look at my remaining e-mails which are various things dealing with THE CONFERENCE. I already know that the end result of all these e-mails will be great personal frustration and the expenditure of $20,000 of endowment funds in direct costs and untold taxpayer dollars in person-hours. We will be left with a series of badly lit recordings wherein people either (a) deliberately ignore the exhortation not to read prepared papers and drone on at length from a journal article they are polishing up (b) talk in extreme generalities about things that any fool could read about online or (c) deliver a cogent and accessible statement on the topic at hand based upon a vast body of knowledge they have amassed in the course of their research. The latter people are typically about to be denied tenure or are in the middle of negotiations with another university and will be somewhere else within the year. The taxpayers are rarely in evidence at these events, although they are all ostensibly free and open to the public.

There is no e-mail about Ellery, but I know the voice mail from the Office of Risk Management is still sitting inside my office phone like an evil charm. I smoke one more cigarette and then I feel sick and then I go back inside and lie down on the couch. With the eight books for Honey I brought no book for myself, the TV has five channels, I don't have my Turkish notebook or poor Sait Faik, I have literally nothing to do except mother my child who, thank god, is still in her Pack 'n Play giving me a respite from this obligation. I am thinking about how stupid I am and wondering when Honey is going to wake up and suddenly I am myself waking with a start, my hand over my face and the skin baking a little in the sun.

I dreamt people were queued up at the reception desk to see me and Maryam wouldn't let them in. Prior to the accident Maryam sat at the front desk of the Institute between five and nine hours a week, answering phones and cheerfully dealing with Hugo's bullshit and on slow afternoons going on Facebook to post memes about Palestinian liberation and watch tutorials for face contouring. I think about her broken fibula her broken occipital bone her concussion and then I am powerless not to remember the day she came into my office asking advice about summer research for her and her project partner, the offscreen Ellery, and I talked to her about Turkey and sent her to Meredith to talk about Syria and from what I understand Meredith told her "Of course to really dive into any substantive research you have to go abroad" and got Hugo to give the two of them an unofficial grant with Al-Ihsan money and had me write the ex post facto award letter and then I thought I might as well set them up with Pelin before they went east to Diyarbakır, and it was all so careless, so ad hoc, although I know that life is careless and ad hoc; as Hugo rather callously observed to Maryam's parents on the phone, the truth is that she would be just as likely to get in a car accident in America. "In fact," he told them, "the sad fact is that students are safer abroad than they are on U.S. campuses," after which he was contacted by the Office of Risk Management and told not to have any further contact with the family without a representative present. I wrote the Institute's formal statement of condolence to Ellery's parents for him to sign.

Hugo excels at unwelcome true remarks. When he found

me crying in my office after Engin's green card was taken and Engin returned ignominiously to Istanbul he patted my back tenderly and said "I know this must be very hard," before his innate didacticism was activated. "In some respects, Daphne, you are experiencing a sort of very mild form of Casualties of Capital!" (This is Hugo's catchphrase; he has a very well-known book on South Asians in the Gulf.) "Just last week I read a dissertation chapter about Filipinas who leave their children to become nannies in the U.S. My student is doing her fieldwork in Westchester County. Imagine it!" This made me feel ashamed to feel so very sorry for myself, although Hugo has no kids and no fucking clue what that would really be like. "But I *have* capital, sort of," I sniffled. "This is a casualty of militarized bureaucracy and nativism." He laughed and patted me again. "Do you think those things aren't related?" and then gave me the titles of two books I probably won't read but will try to find summaries of at some later date. Hugo can be obscurely comforting on his better days.

I bury my head back in the couch cushion and count to twenty. I forgot how utterly quiet it is here.

Honey is still asleep, going on three hours, a miracle. Poor monkey. She must be very tired and mixed-up. I go back out on the porch to smoke. Cindy Cooper steps out onto her porch at the same time and we exchange a formal wave. "Hello," I say. "Hello," she says. "Haven't seen anyone up at the house in a while," and I say "I'm Jeannie's daughter," and she says "Yep I remember, I met Rodney a few times." She lights what looks like a Capri 120. "What brings you up here?" "Well, I have the baby" and she nods and says "How old" just as I am starting to say "Well I just wanted to show her—" and I decide to forge ahead "—the place now that she's a little bit older, check on the house. Ah, she's almost sixteen months about." Cindy nods. She looks to be in her late forties and has long thin brown hair and mild rosacea on her cheeks and some weight around her middle and slouches down into her lower back, one arm resting across her paunch, the other bringing her slim cigarette back and forth to her mouth. I am having a little pity party on her behalf until I catch a glimpse of myself in the sliding glass door, a pudgy apparition like a Cindy of yesteryear. In those first eight weeks or so after Honey was born I can't believe how good I looked, I mean I never looked better in my life. The weight just incinerated right off, for one. They tell you that breastfeeding will ruin your boobs, but they don't tell you that if you're small-breasted they'll first flare out into archetypal perfection and give you just long enough to become accustomed to filling out a dress properly. It's not just your original body that you can't get back—you can't get your pregnant body back either. Since weaning I'm heavy across the shoulders and hips and thighs, and the pouch that Honey vacated has achieved greater prominence. And my boobs— now they are little coin purses, the overall effect being that my body is much smaller on the top and much bigger on the bottom.

Cindy's placid reaction to my arrival is a good reminder that the exigencies of my situation may not be immediately clear to anyone else. It is anyway a true statement on its face. I am visiting the house, which is my house and Honey is my child. I have not stolen, except for the laptop, which I will at some point return. We are fine here. I know with my lizard brain that it is not my fault that a twenty-year-old girl is dead,

even though other parts of my brain, say, the part that manu-
factures dreams, are still not sure. When my mom was mad at
me in adolescence she told me I was a "hard creature" and
sometimes I think that's true and sometimes I don't think I'm
any harder than anybody else. But Cindy doesn't need to know
all this. I put out my cigarette and say "See you later" and step
inside and Honey has started to coo and I feel a legitimate
surge of happiness at the prospect of seeing her face searching
for mine from within the closet dark.

I get her out of the Pack 'n Play and change her diaper
and she kicks her legs and grins at me and I put my mouth on
her stomach and blow and she grabs my hair and pulls hard.
If she is confused about our situation she doesn't show it. I
like to think actually that she is having a nice time scooting
across the wall-to-wall carpet. Moreover due to my smart forward thinking of the morning I have a nicely roasted sweet
potato to feed her. I mush this up and fry her an egg and cut it
into small pieces and wash some blueberries and arrange them
around the side of the plate and set her in her high chair with
her sippy cup of milk and the feast before her. She has very
good motor control and uses her little spoon to scoop up the
sweet potato and before long the plate is empty and I feel the
atavistic pleasure of having provided a reasonably balanced
meal for my child with things that I made or had, requiring no
angst no digging no last-minute run to the store no cooking
plain noodles with butter because there was nothing else in
the house. Whenever I have this feeling which is maybe full
force in one-third of meals and a faint glow in one-fourth, I
think I could live on the feeling, like this could sustain me as
a life pursuit, but it only lasts a few minutes and then there's

the next meal to think of by which time I've usually decided to go to the Chinese place around the corner where we go at least once a week.

I smear some sunscreen on Honey and take her outside in her T-shirt, her little diapered butt shuttling back and forth while she runs unsteadily around on the grass periodically sitting down hard on her butt. I make to chase her and she shrieks and I think good good this is fine and I run and scoop her up and fall onto my back squeezing her and cover her face with kisses and she screams with joy.

The proprietress of Honey's home daycare speaks to the babies in Cantonese. Engin is very distressed that he is not here to speak to her in Turkish, and asks me every time we talk whether his linguistic interests are being represented. I have told him that based on my limited understanding of human speech development, it's no good for a nonnative speaker to talk to a baby, because the essential somethingness of it won't be transferred. Engin feels however that hearing something is better than hearing nothing. What's interesting to me is that on the rare occasions when I do force myself to speak Turkish to Honey beyond the terms of endearment that I use to give our conversation at least a sort of Turkish affect, she looks at me with perceptible puzzlement. She knows enough to know that I'm doing something different from what I normally do, which makes me feel both proud of her for being so discerning and bad that I'm being an American imperialist parent and boxing her dad out of her cultural formation. It has always been my policy to speak English to her because I pride myself on my English and Engin's English is good not great and frankly a bit of a mystery since he so seldom uses it. But I want Honey's

English to be native perfect because English is her mother tongue and mine and I'm helpless not to love it, full of senseless grammar and airless flat vowels though it is. I have to remind myself, Engin is her father and we are married and his interests must be represented and I want her to be fully bilingual, trilingual even. It's a gift a gift a gift to speak another language, my deepest wish is that I could do it effortlessly, that I was born to it.

I look at my watch and once again we have missed the window to speak to Engin who is by now back in Istanbul but in bed probably after trying fruitlessly to Skype us again and again and I go limp and lay back on the grass staring up at the unsmiling blue sky and wonder when they are going to get some fucking cell service up here. I have at this point developed a shadow sense of time like two clocks on a banker's wall, San Francisco and Istanbul, but so far having this shadow sense does not translate into actually timing my actions appropriately to contact him at the right time, and usually this just means that I am perpetually feeling harassed to make contact in our circumscribed window. During the week I am rushing too much to get to work to have a meaningful morning conversation. Engin is a night owl but Honey comes home at 6:00 and goes to bed at 7:00 which is 5:00 a.m. Engin time so typically we have a brief viewing on weekday mornings so he can at least look at her and exchange kisses, and then I call him before I go to bed and we can actually talk, which actually I hate, it's boring to talk to someone on the phone every day. In the beginning there was a siege mentality—the Emergency had happened and there was the painful but necessary recounting and commiseration re: hours spent on hold with fucking USCIS and the NVC, there were action items and fact-finding and document checks and sharing of information. But now we are stalled waiting for something to happen and we talk about the future as though it's a fantasy island we both know we'll never see. I know that calls in these long-distance situations are not really about the sharing of news but about the maintenance of connection, the assurance that each party still exists and is living breathing in the world sending love across the sea, not to mention reassuring our child that her father still exists and giving him some glimpse of the true love of his life, but it's come to feel like another fucking obligation. I know women who live apart from their men who keep Skype on in the background to chat while they cook or clean up the living room or paint their nails, but I do enough inane pointless narration at Honey. It's easier to have TV shows on; the show doesn't need anything from you. So I go about life thinking of Engin as something like my partner in a challenging and as-of-yet mostly unprofitable business venture, waiting for our ship to come in, until those moments when I really remember what he is like and would give anything to be sitting next to him on the couch, laughing with our shoulders together and Honey across our laps.

Honey is trying to tear the head off a geranium and I say "That's not what we do to flowers, gentle, gentle" and I suddenly feel so tired and I think how nice it is to be with her and how simultaneously not-nice. I did not have a thought in my head except go go go when I bundled her into the car yesterday and started the drive northeast but now I wonder if I just wanted to be not in the office and whether I might have achieved this by taking a day off work and going to the playground for god's sake. Honey for ten hours during the day is a blank space to me, that's how my brain treats her, as though she functionally ceases to exist when she is at daycare, until all at once I get desperately lonesome for her and look at the videos the day-care proprietor sends on WeChat and strain to hear her voice among the cacophony of little babies cooing together on the rug. But I have no knowledge of the texture of her days there. I have always found Honey to be a very sunny caring conscientious baby—a generous temperament—I wonder how much of this is the daycare and how much is me. I know the blank spot where those fifty hours a week should be is a blessing, surely it is the absence of worry that allows me to blot her out like someone who has been etherized, kind of like I do to Engin. Maybe it's because I don't care enough. I don't think that's it, though.

When I went back to work Engin stayed home with Honey, which is undoubtedly what prompted him to decide to go back to Turkey to improve his prospects of employment. I remember I felt jaunty and efficient setting out for the office that first day, leaving him with a supply of frozen breastmilk I had been dutifully collecting since she was born. I answered e-mails while I pumped in Ted's closet and put pictures of Honey up on my bulletin board and I ignored the fact that pumping took up roughly two hours of the workday and generally felt that things were going to be okay. But when I got home that evening I ran up the street to the house only to discover from Engin's apologetic face when I opened the door that he had put Honey to bed.

It's pathetic but I don't feel like I have spiritually recovered from that week somehow even though I went back to a beautiful glass office and not to a sweatshop or a goddamn Subway sandwich shop or to be a nanny in Westchester County. When I came back Meredith was trying to be supportive and talked constantly of how awful it is and told me how she used to pace like a wild animal when she was away from her children and I both felt guilty because I had not yet paced, and how odd it was that we should both be sitting there saying "yes, it is very bad" when we could instead be staging a revolt. But her kids are teenagers and she is over it and in fact grateful to come to a quiet beautiful office now so her moment for revolution has passed.

And now I am here with Honey trying to eat a geranium and I'm, yes, extremely bored and I would love for her to tire herself out and go back into her Pack 'n Play and go to sleep for two more hours. It's been one day. I hate myself.

The only insight I have developed about parenting so far even though I always forget it is that when you feel like dying you should try to leave your physical location and go to another one. Blow the stink off, as my grandpa Burdock used to say. I think to myself what if we go to the Golden Spike and have a steak, and I immediately feel so buoyed by this idea my awareness of our bank balance notwithstanding that I grab Honey with renewed joy and say "Come on sweet pea we are gonna go out on the town," which, ha. I say "Do you wanna take a bath with Mama" and she says "Yahh" and we go inside to the master bathroom with its cheap Jacuzzi tub and rotting sill and I pee and smell must rising up from between my legs and the bath is none too soon for either of us. I look in the mirror and I have flakes in my eyebrows and in my unfortunate little sideburns and around my hairline. I spray the mummified mosquito hawks down the drain and put Honey outside of the bathtub with the handheld shower and I get into it and spray myself down and do my shampoo and conditioner and then I step out dripping everywhere strip off her grassy pants and onesie and get her into the tub and do a mild hose-down while she vacillates between protest and glee. We sit down on our butts, she between my legs and facing me poking at my stomach. I look down at myself in the fluorescent light and see very white dough and moles and a giant thatch of hair, which has been more or less par for the course since I got pregnant. My understanding is that most Turkish women take it all off and when I was there I went with the flow and allowed myself to be thus denuded but I hate it and anyway now I don't have the time or the money or a man on the premises. Engin and I have had only the most brief and strangely awkward conversation about hair and preference and he claimed not to care but this is probably a lie which makes me feel bad again until I think of the Golden Spike and how good it is going to be, not maybe in the food sense but spiritually.

The Golden Spike is just a short walk out of Deakins Park over the train tracks and along Route 235, or rather it's a very very short distance in your Buick or your enormous pickup your Ford F-150 your Dodge Ram in which it's a matter of moments to get there but like everything in town takes what seems like an unwarranted amount of time on foot, which I forget until we are at the tracks. Apart from the excessive space in this town, the pavement is so hard, the land is so flat, the air so thin, and the sun so strong even on the downhill slope to evening that your destination, visible though it may be, comes to feel like a mirage. The ground is hard on your knees and there's no sidewalk out here by the tracks. I put Honey on my shoulders and grip her ankles tight and she claps her hands above my head. We see the big old sign of the Golden Spike in the near field and behind it the cinder-block box with an illuminated bar sign in its sole visible window.

The Golden Spike is one of the family-style Basque joints you can find across the west, the California west, the Nevada west, where a hundred years ago the shepherds who left Spain settled. The model is "family style plus a meat," so you get a lamb chop, or rib eye, or fish, and then there's a large salad of iceberg highly dressed, and sometimes a chickpea and lamb stew—presumably a taste of the Basque past—and tomato soup with barley or noodles. It's ruinously expensive and not really very good but it excites me in some kind of primal way. I like the carafes of chilled red vinegar wine and the huge slabs of beef.

We reach the door of the cinder-block box and even though it's 5:00 p.m. and the breeze has started up I'm sweating. We enter the vestibule that separates the dining room from the dusty parking lot, a strange, carpeted anteroom with an unused little piano pushed up against one wall, and then the main room and it's almost empty and I feel immediately deflated at the discrepancy between the cozy hum I had pictured and this dark depopulated cave. The hostess says hello and leads us to a table and asks whether I'm just passing through and I tell her the name of my grandparents and she doesn't recognize them.

Then we are getting settled and Honey is in a high chair playing with a spoon rapping it on the plate and I'm pouring her the smallest little glass of water from the brown melamine pitcher and myself a glass of wine from the cold carafe that is already on the table and a cheery server arrives and clucks at Honey and says "What an absolutely gorgeous baby" and I say thank you because I think so too even though I try not to say so, try not to say beautiful try not to say pretty girl or any variation thereof. I order the rib eye with garlic which means they put six to eight cloves of garlic on top of a rib eye steak the size of a plate. There is going to be a baked potato too. Honey takes her cup of water in her hands and brings it to her mouth for a surprisingly tidy sip and maybe it's the wine but I'm bursting with pride to see it. I spoon soup for myself and Honey who has in addition to her looks great talent with a spoon and she tucks in and I butter a thick slab of the pale crumbly house bread. While she's eating her soup I listen to the hostess and the server both white women of a certain age shooting the shit and the server is saying "I tell you I got all frazzled yesterday—we had a fight, which I never seen here before. It frazzled me right up!" and the hostess makes moos of concern and asks what happened and the server says "You know that old guy who comes in sometimes and gives himself a shot for his diabetes and he always leaves the needle on the table on a napkin? Normally I don't say anything I just put it in a milk carton and throw it away. But yesterday Donna Dellomo is here and she hollers at him that us girls are gonna get stuck with that thing and he better throw it away himself, and he's a mean old guy and tells her to mind her business and then her husband says 'Don't talk to my wife like that' and then the old guy stands up and they just start trying to slug at each other. I was worried someone was gonna run out to his truck and get his gun." They move to the far side of the host stand and carry on a stream of conversation I don't quite hear but I hear the server say "I don't even know which hole to put it in" and laugh and then as if she didn't get the reaction she had hoped for or conversely wants to relive the nice reaction she did get says "I'm like 'I don't even know which hole to put it in'" but the hostess doesn't really laugh and I am close enough I wonder whether I am part of the audience and whether I should laugh but I feel this would intrude and I hope the needle wasn't at the table we are at now. Good for Donna Dellomo, whoever she is. Fucking men leaving their biohazardous garbage around for women to clean up.

My steak comes and I cut up little pieces for Honey that she mostly doesn't eat preferring the soup and the bread and soon I have demolished my portion and am feeling like a stuffed tick and Honey is tired of sitting and being a good girl and is now agitated, troubled by some unknown thing that makes her scramble to vacate the high chair so I pick her up and she stands on my knees, pulling up on my shirt with stew hands and starting to bleat, our window of relatively civilized fine dining dying without ceremony in the air-conditioned chill of the cinder-block.

At this moment I see John Urberoaga stroll through the front door, the cousin or maybe brother of our Realtor, Rosemary. John looms large in my mythology of the town but I doubt we've had a conversation longer than two sentences. He was at Grandpa's funeral and like almost all the men in the room I saw him wipe away a tear when Davis Birgeneau sang "That Old Rugged Cross" and played the guitar. I feel the tiny flair of feeling that comes from recognizing someone, but it fades as quick as it came.

He walks past our table and stops to cluck at Honey with big-man friendliness and I smile at him and say hello and he stares at me for a beat until I prompt him with my mother's name. "Jeannie's daughter. Frank and Cora Burdock's granddaughter." "That's right!" he beams at me and his large presence his belt buckle are enough to subdue the bleating Honey. "You know Rosemary's sure been workin' on gettin' that place sold." "Well, no rush," I tell him. "Rod up with you?" he asks. I feel suddenly threatened by being narced on but I don't know why my taciturn uncle Rodney, patron of the mobile home, shouldn't know I'm here, in fact I don't know why I didn't just call him to tell him myself. "Not this time," I tell him, "but I thought it might be nice to get the, um, cobwebs out," and he nods. The proper maintenance of immovable property or cars or livestock is a central concern to citizens of the high country. The great sorrow of my aging grandparents was seeing the disorder that crept into the town, shaggy lawns strewn with toy limbs and decaying copies of the *Paiute Recorder*. Rusted lawn mowers, sweatpants in the market, cars with rusted tailpipes— their lawn stayed pristine, their Buick polished, their small finances in impeccable order. I am looking a little down-at-the-heels myself, I realize. I am wearing a maternity shirt and Honey has smeared a substantial portion of the stew all over. But I am keeping cobwebs out of the house and the water moving in the pipes.

I shouldn't be snide. The reason Honey and I are sitting pretty all things considered up in Deakins Park is that good old Uncle Rodney cares enough to keep the place maintained, to keep the water in the pipes, while my helpless disdain at the bourgeois mysteries of property maintenance would probably leave the town with another rusted-out mobile home. Uncle Rodney, never married, lives in a nice cabin outside Quincy, many basins south and west of here. He has worked for the Forest Service his entire life and has a very long-term off-and-on relationship with a surprisingly bubbly woman named Helen who works at a quilt shop of the sort that Quincy is cute enough to sustain. He and my mom had not a lot in common except their happy memories of summers at the lake and winters in the snow, girl scouts and boy scouts and high school hijinks and bridge nights with drunk parents letting the kids run free. In the end what she wanted was to get out, to get Elsewhere, and Rodney won't even come to San Francisco except for when Honey was born. ("Not a city person," he told Engin when we met him.) But he never made a peep when my mom got the house, and now he keeps the water in the pipes for me.

John Urberoaga doesn't ask me where Honey's dad is which seems curious and I wonder whether it is some sense of social nicety and not asking what don't concern you or whether it just had not occurred to him to have any curiosity about my life which I suppose would justly match the general lack of curiosity I have about his and he ambles off to a table with his wife and Honey is now struggling so much to get down onto the floor that I know we've got to go and I crane around for the jokey server to bring us the check and she laughs at Honey and says "She's feisty" and it soothes me. I hate being an archetype—woman struggling alone with fractious baby—but it really does feel horrible and a little humor delivered with a deft hand can go a long way. Too much sympathy and help is bad though, it's very obligating.

In the parking lot Honey is frankly obstreperous. The absence of sidewalk on the highway back to the railroad tracks makes me anxious about the prospect of navigating it with Honey on her uncertain legs but when I pick her up she loses her mind, struggling and crying and pushing against me with her small fists. I put her back on the ground and she sits down abruptly and then flings her head straight back onto the pavement and then screams furiously in pain and rage. I scramble to pick her up and put my hand on the back of her head saying "No no oh no." I hold her tight while she struggles against me, her sobs eventually giving over to little yells issued at an interval of three or four seconds. I turn to face the fields to the east of the Golden Spike should anyone come out and see me having not the least amount of success controlling or comforting my hysterical baby who is still trying to hit me. "Be a calming presence for your distressed toddler," some baby blog whispers to me, and even though I reject categorically the idea that she is yet a toddler I hold her body to me and rub my hands on her hot back and say as soothingly as I can, "Hey. Hey, Honey. I know, sweet baby," and it actually seems to be working, first she stops struggling and then she finds the place to put her wet face in the crook of my neck while I whisper to her and dust the gravel off the back of her head and I feel she is tired, that's what it is, she is very very tired. Then she leans away from my body and smiles into my face, plucking at the front of my shirt where the stew is with both hands. "Daaaaah," she says to me, her eyes wide and wondering. "Daaaaaah," I say to her. I carry her home, heavy heavy, too heavy for me to carry with my flabby muscles atrophied by administrative tasks, but we make it over the train tracks into Deakins Park and she keeps one arm slung around my neck and her eyes on the horizon like a princess alert on her palanquin.

She is sticky with stew and dust and so she goes back into the bathtub and then she goes into her almost-too-small pajamas and before she goes into the Pack 'n Play in the dark of the closet we scramble up onto the big bed with her milk and *Goodnight Moon* and I lean against the pillows with my knees up and she leans against my knees with her legs on either side of my waist and she begins to chat happily and conspiratorially to me in non-words, just babbling cheerfully like a brook. She puts her hands on my breasts and pulls at my shirt and pats my face and tells me all sorts of things I don't understand and I think this is the happiest moment of my life not only because of the smile on her face the smallness of her body the love for me she communicates with her entire being but because of the almost erotic knowledge that soon she will be in bed, the whole evening ahead of me without her.

I put her in the Pack 'n Play and all the happy time on the bed vanishes without a trace and she is miserable again and I try to soothe her and then I say good night and leave while she wails with her hands on the netting of her cage. I remember that she is sixteen months old today.

Then I remember the bottle of Popov and the orange juice and I make myself a screwdriver and sit in the Wi-Fi zone of the porch smoking and listening to her faint cries through the screen door. I send Engin a generic greeting on WhatsApp and then I google "banging head against ground," the little wheel turning as the phone strains to hang on to Cindy's signal in the Paiute night. I feel my anxiety reach through the screen to comingle with the anxiety of the BabyCenter mothers, various in its particulars but always with the same root—let it not be serious, let it not be serious. Or perhaps some of them do want it to be serious. When I was younger I used to wait for something dramatic to happen—my period to come, my mother to die. Both things eventually happened and neither of them brought any glamour to life I can say with certainty. But if something happens to Honey I will die I will die I will die.

This line of thought leads me down the path of Ellery Simpson's mother and I picture Ellery's heavy eyebrows and brown eyes from the photo on an older woman lying in bed in a darkened room with her fist to her mouth. I know from one of the work-studies that Ellery has a younger sister and brother and I wonder if that makes any difference and of course not how could it, how could anything. There's the math of it, two being more than zero, but this is capitalist thinking—my mind somewhat hysterically conjures Hugo. And I still live in the universe of a single child where the idea of reproducing that love, the same dimension and volume of it, twice, three times, seven times, ten times, is incomprehensible although it is an irrefutable fact of life. I start crying. Eventually I stop and I hear that Honey has stopped too and now I feel lonesome for her and in a while I go back into the house back into the closet and get her out of the Pack 'n Play, her body heavy and limp. I hitch up onto the big bed and lean against the pillows with her head on my chest, feeling her back rise and fall with her curly head in the place on my neck. We stay like this for a while in the nearly pitch-black room with me just trying to transmit love to her until I put her back gently into the Pack 'n Play and return to the porch where I smoke three cigarettes in a row staring into the dark, ranging my fingers over my face and into my scalp and picking away at anything that feels remotely like a flake or a protuberance and feeling both not good and good at the same time.

DAY 3   We are finally going to call Engin. I put Honey in her stroller and we start the long walk down the highway that is also the main street leading out to the bird refuge at the far side of town. The sky is not so blue today as it was yesterday—it has a yellow tint and it is hot hot hot even at 9:45 when we hit the road after four stories and more pancakes. You think of heat having mass when it is humid but extremely dry heat has mass too unless you've got a good breeze or some shade, it is something you have to move against. Here and there I try to point out things to Honey—"there is the school where your grandma went" "there is the Elks" "that used to be a pharmacy" "that used to be the Tog-Shop" etc.—but once she is in the stroller her eyes basically glaze over and she lives in a strange place between sleep and awakeness but I'll take it because I can basically think my thoughts and just be with her without having to do anything *for* her.

There aren't very many open businesses on Main Street anymore, except the High Desert Hotel and the Frosty and the Rite Aid which is only a few years old and sure enough has annihilated the two mom-and-pop pharmacies that had coexisted peacefully for decades. The Frosty has a sign rising high up over the plains like a forlorn palm tree. Just past the sign my phone buzzes as we wander into a patch of service, and I see a voice mail icon, which fills me with dread. But I tap and there is only one and when I hold the phone to my ear I register that it is the voice of Uncle Rodney, who is the least threatening person who could be leaving me a voice mail at this moment. I stop to marvel at how quickly the frayed grapevine of my Altavista life has communicated to him that I'm in the house. John must have called Rosemary must have called Rodney. "Heard from Rosemary you were up at the house," he says on the voice mail sure enough. "Give me a call and let me know how it's looking, when you get the chance." I know this will be relatively painless but I decide I don't have the energy.

The sidewalks are completely empty except for a little group of youngish people in big T-shirts and short shorts for girls and big shorts for boys. Three kids are white and two are brown and I wonder if this is indicative of demographic change. There was one lone black family in town when Mom and Uncle Rodney were growing up but I don't know what became of them. The kids move slow and laugh among themselves and Honey and I pass them and I give a little wave which yields a murmur of "Hi"s. We walk all the way through town to the Desert Sunrise, which is the Indian casino which is three conjoined trailers with slot machines and a few poker tables inside. I took Engin there on his inaugural trip to Altavista because I wanted him to see something he'd never seen before and I'd never seen the Desert Sunrise myself but it's not like Las Vegas or even Reno where you can visit a casino if you aren't gambling—there are about six grim-looking men and women at the Desert Sunrise, and everyone stares. Engin fancies himself a man of the people and gets into involved conversations I suspect he secretly regrets with old men and aunties in Anatolian gas stations but the Desert Sunrise does not create an atmosphere of folksiness so much as one of incipient murder. So we moonwalked out of the trailer and I noted the "Silly faggot dicks are for chicks" bumper sticker in the parking lot.

I reflect on Engin's first visit to Altavista that Christmas with Rodney and Helen. Engin I think made certain assumptions about my class background which combined with certain assumptions that any foreigner has about what America is, which are no less bizarre and misguided than any American's assumptions about what another place is, led him to believe that a trip to my ancestral land would be something like the movie *Father of the Bride*, even though I tried to prepare him by using words like "village" and "cowboy" when I described the town. When he first came to California and we got married in Uncle Rodney's backyard in Quincy first we went up the Sonoma coast and then took 128 back inland through the golden country which if you squint looks Mediterranean and then we went inland to 49 up the Yuba and the Downie and the majestic forests and the stone peaks of Lassen and then into the green valley around Quincy and Quincy itself with its beautiful false fronts and historic theaters and the sound of water wherever you go and I could tell wherever we went that he got it. But then you get up in the north and east and things just get a little scrubbier, the buildings flatter and the people less likely to have started a playhouse with a free library out front. The beauty here is the great slate sky the sound of the birds in the morning the color of the hills and the fields at dusk. Engin said it reminded him of Ang Lee. But I told him that's not accurate, since Ang Lee trucks in the maximalist blue-sky beauty of Montana or Wyoming, blowsy hills like big green breasts, not the high, thin, stony West, full of volcanic stone washes and scrub oak. Then he pointed out that *Brokeback Mountain* was actually filmed in Canada and I said "How do you even know that" and he said "I googled it because I liked the scenery" and I laughed. Engin loves vistas.

When Honey and I hit the turnoff for the Desert Sunrise we turn back around in order to find Wi-Fi to Skype with our Ang Lee fan and thus we find ourselves at Sal's Café in the lobby of the High Desert Hotel on Main Street. It's open and populated by two tank-topped blond white teen girls at one table and a very, very old white woman with a gray bob who sits at another with a cup of coffee staring vacantly ahead. I buy a coffee from the proprietress maybe Sal herself and unpack Honey from her stroller and take a banana from the bag and squeeze it into pieces and she begins shoveling them into her mouth and I set up the laptop. I open Skype and put on the headphones but then realize Honey won't be able to hear so I will just have to be rude and let him talk to the room. I click Engin's face and it rings and he answers and there he is in the flesh or in the screen rather, his gray eyes pale skin brown hair and his newly clean-shaven face and I think how handsome he is and instead of feeling happy and proud I feel a pang because he has been unattended for eight months looking like that and I am here looking like this and then I remember that he is on the shorter side and his arms are also the tiniest bit too short for his body and maybe that will keep the women away and then I think God should just smite me we haven't even exchanged three words.

Behind him on the screen is his mother's tidy apartment, which is where he stays. He says "Finally, Defne"—in Turkish I'm Defne—and I laboriously flip a giant rusty lever in my brain to speak Turkish again and I say "Look Honey it's your baba look look" and she looks at me with some suspicion to hear the strange words and she looks at him and there is a pause and I am holding my breath and thinking please don't cry please don't squirm please don't hide but she smiles and stretches out her arms to him and he says "My cub, my darling, do you miss your daddy," and they coo back and forth at each other which puts off the moment when I have to apologize for running away and Honey touches the screen and says "Hi! Hi! Hi!" and I say "Say merhaba to your baba" and then my mother-in-law Ayşe is in the frame boxing Engin out entirely and there is a torrent of affectionate pitter-patter for Honey and it fills Sal's coffee shop and I look around at the proprietress and the teens and the old woman but nobody seems to care very much. Ayşe brushes away a tear and blows a kiss to me and says "Come to us my love, we miss you," and then she recedes and Engin lights a cigarette—it seems we're both smoking—and addresses himself to me and Honey stares rapt at the screen. "Don't smoke in front of the baby, yaa," I tell him, I mean come on, and he stubs it out with a rueful look and I feel guilty and smile and say "How was Belgrade," a sally whose fundamental insincerity he perceives and brushes off accordingly.

"Why are you in the steppe? Don't you have work?"

Although I have had plenty of time to ponder this I don't have an answer for myself let alone a soothing lie for Engin, which would be a reason of some kind, any kind, and not just a sudden urge for flight.

"Things were, ahh, not busy at work," I say, in Turkish, always in Turkish, I loved Turkish before I loved Engin. "And

I thought I haven't been up to the house for a while and I should go look at it." My grammar is distressingly lumpy. "Okay," says Engin in English, but I can tell he thinks it's weird, it is on its face weird, because had I been planning some recon mission I would have let him know in advance.

"Are you okay?" he asks. I begin to cry so suddenly and so copiously it's not a taktik or a refleks but more that my tears are a well-trained army and always mustered ready to unleash hell.

"My love, my soul, don't cry." Turkish has lots of endearments freely deployed. "Come on, why are you crying?"

I don't want to make him feel bad by saying I am crying because I am here and I am here because you went to complete a certificate course on postproduction in Istanbul and when you came back halfway through to see us surrendered your god-damn green card to DHS under pressure and under false pretenses that contravene established immigration practice and U.S. law and are undoubtedly rooted in xenophobia not to say Islamophobia, and because you were then sent back to Istanbul on the next flight at our expense rather than spending three desperately needed weeks with your wife and child, and because your second application submitted through the even more arcane National Visa Center for overseas consular processing is stuck in limbo due to what I learned after twenty-six nonconsecutive hours of waiting on the phone and the eventual expenditure of a thousand more dollars may in fact be a "click-of-the-mouse error"—theirs—and which we have already paid an attorney to ameliorate and resubmit through the correct channels and will presumably have to pay more to stay on top of until it is seen through and I am alone with our child whose first steps and first words you are missing and I sometimes fantasize about meeting you at the airport with her and kissing you passionately and then throttling you until you die, so I just say "I'm feeling sad," which is also true.

Honey twists around, bored, with her last bit of banana in one hand, and gives my descending bun a yank. Engin smiles at her while somehow simultaneously frowning at me. She finishes the banana and starts putting her fingers on the screen of the Institute's computer and I am still crying. The teens in the corner are openly staring. "How was Belgrade?" I manage to get out again. "Nice, actually," he says, joining the folie à deux of normalcy. "Really nice. We should live there." We are always opining about places we should live, which are always somewhere else than the place where either of us is living. "Tolga's thing is shit, though—really disorganized" but now I am crying again and unable to take in Tolga and his endless dubious multipronged film and web marketing schemes. Engin in his heart of hearts wants to be a video artist—make outlandish Björk videos and such—but to make money he signs on to shoot Tolga's promotional videos for private schools and Eastern European banking concerns instead.

"Tell her to bring my granddaughter and come here," his mother hollers from the kitchen. Engin smiles wanly and shrugs and says "You know you can come here" and I say "Do you want me to come there" and he says "Well you were staying there because you have a good job but if you are not going to work then I don't understand why you wouldn't come here" and I realize this probably cost him something to say because he thinks Hugo and Meredith are grifters but he knows also that work is important and that his work is feast or famine and not ideal for the maintenance of a family unit and then he says "As far as I know we hadn't planned for you to live . . . there," and he gestures at Sal's behind me and I nod. "I know," I say. "I thought maybe I'd go through some of my mom's stuff in the garage to see what I can sell." "By yourself?" and that leads us back to the fucking green card and I say "I'll leave the heavy stuff for when you come" and then I just feel so done and tired of talking I take two deep breaths and say "Honey has to have her nap" and "Really I'm fine, just feeling down" (Moralim bozuk, *my morale is spoilt*) and "I'll go back to work, I promise" and "Give your mother a kiss from me" and to Honey I say "Say bye-bye to your baba, give your baba a kiss," and she finally brings the palm of her hand to her mouth and lowers it toward the screen extravagantly open and proud of herself and I blow a kiss too and shut the laptop more abruptly than I intend.

I wipe my eyes and blow my nose on Honey's bib. I open the laptop again. I e-mail Meredith and Hugo to say that I am still sick. I message the daycare to say that Honey is sick. I need a treat of some kind and when a suitable interval has passed and I stop sniffling I hoist up Honey and leave our stuff at the table and buy a rice crispy thing from the basket next to the cash register. I wonder if the proprietor is going to ask whether she needs to call somebody but she just says "What language was that?" "Turkish," I say. "My husband's Turkish." I never have any idea what that will mean to anyone.

"Oh, my son used to live over there," she surprises the hell out of me by saying.

"Whaddayacallit, Injik, when he was in the air force." İncirlik, she means.

"Oh wow," I say. "Did he like it?"

"He loved it. Said it was just beautiful. Nicest people in the world." Everyone seems to agree on this point. "Turkish hospitality is famous," I say stupidly, aware of the clammy puff of my face and the crying hives and the runnels left by tears in my poorly moisturized undereyes. "Sorry," I gesture to my face and smile ruefully. "It's just hard to be apart sometimes. Gotta get him back here."

"What are you doing all the way up in Altavista?" She has an incredibly kindly look on her face, a narrow tanned white face with bifocals on an upturned nose and I just want to tell her everything.

"My mom's from here, Frank and Cora Burdock's daughter?" She looks blank. "They lived over in Deakins Park." "Oh," she says. "My brother's lady friend lives over there. Cindy Cooper." "Oh," I say. "My neighbor! She seems like a nice lady" and the proprietress laughs and says, "I don't know about that. But we love her anyway." Honey watches us talking and the proprietress says, "She's a good little thing isn't she," and I say, "Most of the time." "Pretty little thing," she says. "Look at those eyelashes," and Honey smiles at her out from under them.

I gather up our things and set Honey down and she toddles furiously toward the door and as we pass through it the crone who has been mostly motionless sitting at the table next to the door looks right at us. "Merhaba," I could swear she says, which is Hello in Turkish. Even Honey stills for a moment, pausing midflight in her headlong rush toward the sidewalk. "Hello?" I say to her politely in English, sure I've had an auditory hallucination. She looks down at her hands, her mouth closed and shy and Honey reanimates and flies out of the doorway and I fly after her, trailing a hand behind me in valediction at the crone. I catch the collar of Honey's shirt and stick my head back through the door to say something, but her head is still bowed. "Goodbye," I say. Honey chokes a bit with the neck of her garment up against her throat. We exit.

I decide that we will take the long way home by the cemetery and stop to visit Mom, since I have not seen her in more than a year. The cemetery is south of Deakins Park, but like Deakins Park it sits out on the edge of inhabited land. Honey is quiet in her stroller lulled by the wheeling as usual and I think about Engin's mother and what she said about us coming there to the small but airy matriarchal apartment in a nice neighborhood of Istanbul. This is the obvious thing to do, so obvious that we have danced endlessly around the idea, as though the idea were a slippery occult monolith upon which our minds can find no purchase. If you have two people and one of them is from what I believe is called an "emerging economy" and one is American you go to America, I guess is the usual thing, even though right now I am sitting in the middle of what you might call a demolished economy. (Casualties of Capital! Hugo says in my ear.) Plus I got the job at the Institute, and Engin did not have a stable income and was game to come to California, so this made sense. The whole trajectory of our marriage has been westward. It's true that in Turkey there is Erdoğan the tyrant sultan and also that there are safety concerns of various kinds but the last incident was the woman from Dagestan who bombed the police station and that was months ago and America is no picnic on that score what with roomfuls of murdered kindergarteners lying in their own blood. Oh God. We talk about buying a stone shack on the Aegean coast sometime in the distant future, when we've made it in some way, the way being as of yet unclear. But I guess we assumed that at least the first location of our making it would be in America. It occurs to me that I created a sort of budget version of my own family situation where my dad's work dictated that my mom live on foreign soil, and I'm now putting that on Engin, putting thousands of miles between him and his family and his friends not to mention momentous national events like Gezi, which he would have flown home for if we had the money and I wasn't pregnant with Honey.

And what do we have here? This house, such as it is. My uncle Rodney, such as he is. My mother, although she's in a buried urn in the grass in the high desert cemetery. We have her things—all her beautiful rugs and tablecloths and dishes packed away in the garage where the Buick ought to be. One of Engin's and my future projects has been the combing through and disposition or keeping of these when the mobile home sells, but it doesn't sell and doesn't sell. I have my job, sort of. I have the smell of juniper and the dew on the fescue, which seemed so urgent just two days ago. But I don't have the sound of seagulls by the Bosphorus, the clink of glasses, the sound of human enterprise and activity in the heart of the world. I don't have my husband, the father of my child. Honey doesn't have her dad and he doesn't have her.

Among things I generally choose not to think about is the absence of my own parents. When I envision my soul, such as *it* is, I picture a big pink lump of gnarled flesh, healed-over wounds that don't smart anymore so much as they tug painfully depending on which direction my thoughts travel. My dad was a weird dreamy man who worked for the government and died when I was eleven. He and my mom met overseas. She left Altavista to go to the same university that employs me now, and being an adventurous frontierswoman type, she graduated and saved her money and went with her girlfriend to Corfu, where my dad was enjoying R&R from his post in Romania, and they were both from California so they got married, and eight years later they had me and named me Daphne after the Greek myth, the nymph who turned into a tree. When I was born we lived on Cyprus where it was my dad's job to do things like assist with the forging of agreements between the hostile governments of Greece and Turkey while maintaining the sacred bewildering U.S. ratio which required that for every $7 million of military aid and muscle the U.S. government gave Greece it give $10 million of the same muscle to Turkey.

Then we spent four years in a humid house in Arlington, VA, before he was reassigned to Athens. And then one home leave, while Mom and I were visiting my grandparents in the mobile home Honey and I are occupying now, he took a little holiday after squiring around a delegation of some sort—Greek? American?—to Bulgaria, and got on a bus which somewhere between Sofia and Varna careened off the road with him inside. Mom and my grandpa flew to Sofia, where a hapless consular officer on his first tour, whose job was typically limited to issuing visas and consoling the pickpocketed, who had a tiny piece of toilet paper stuck to his razor-scraped face in my mother's vivid retelling, handed over a small canvas duffel with urn inside and held her hand and cried. We vacated our government-provided housing but stayed in Athens for two more years in a kind of paralysis until she sold the house in Arlington and moved back to the Golden State. His federal death benefit sustained her while she went back to school for her M.A.; the house money almost paid for me to go to an expensive high school and college in the muggy-in-summer-frigid-in-winter northeast; everything else covered her expenses when she was sick. I got a benefit too courtesy of Uncle Sam, and I spent it mostly unwisely, except it did buy my first plane ticket to Turkey.

Hence my remaining inheritance is the stuff in the garage, and the mobile home, which my grandparents quietly vacated by their deaths two years before my mother died, all of those deaths—their deaths and hers—taking place in my early-to-mid-twenties, which blurs together now as a time of both dealing with things and not dealing with things, a lot of logistics, the logistics of death mostly, and various bad jobs and blackouts and bad flings, until I started the stupid Ph.D.

I think, but don't know, that my father would have appreciated my marrying a Turk, although his personal feeling always lay with the Greek side; he and Mom were modern-day Philhellenes. It was Constantinople to them. My mother I suspect would not have appreciated it since when I first went to Turkey she explicitly instructed me not to marry a Turk, as though that were the likeliest outcome of any trip. She believed in "East" and "West," what we at the Institute know to be false categories, like "Clash of Civilizations," like "Middle East." She thought like ought to marry like, I think. But Engin and I *are* like, sort of, and she would have gotten over it, I know it. She would have liked him. She would have liked Ayşe and Pelin. And Honey! Well. The ideal child.

Honey isn't her real name, I sometimes do and sometimes do not explain to the people who ask about it. Her real name is

Meltem, which is a summer wind that blows in Greece and Turkey alike. When Engin and I decided to get married I was in my secret heart of hearts very excited to be able to have a baby with a beautiful Turkish name. I know this is Orientalist but I think anyone who learns Turkish is helpless against the names, because often they mean things, and not like English where you search Babynames.com and find out a name maybe possibly meant "Brave" in ancient Frisian or whatever, but tangible everyday meanings, like "Sea" or "Life" or "Horizon" or even phrases—Engin has a friend named "Take revenge." Anyway, we came up with Meltem, which is geographical and allegorical and alliterative. Meltem Mehmetoğlu. But when she was a baby I started calling her Melly in my singsong new-mom voice, and meli means "honey" in Greek, and then somehow I started calling her Honey, and Engin started doing it too sometimes, so now the baby I was so eager to name in Turkish has an American stripper name. But it's a secret tribute to my parents, who both spoke Greek. And it suits her. She is full of warm golden light. Although she is forceful too, I guess, like a wind. Honey Mehmetoğlu. You aren't going to forget her name, at any rate.

We arrive at the cemetery sweating—or I'm sweating, Honey pink in the cheeks but shrouded by her stroller. The road slopes gently upward so that the cemetery is perched on a sort of plateau, with a view of the flat plain and the bird refuge and the mountains in the distance, and a little church made of black volcanic stone at its back. There are a number of modest mausoleums built out of this black volcanic stone, all the way to the mid-1800s which passes for old here. The Burdocks, that is us, don't have a mausoleum, just flat stones, nothing flashy: my grandmother and grandfather and my grandmother's grandmother and grandfather and that grandmother's mother and father. We find my mom's stone, next to her parents. My dad, weirdly, upsettingly, does not have a stone here but lives in an urn in the garage of the mobile home because my mother could never figure out where she wanted him to go, and she knew he hated Altavista and wouldn't want to be up here, but also didn't want to put him down below in the South Bay where he was born; his family was as small as hers. I pause to feel guilty that I have not repatriated him at least to my apartment. "Beloved Mother," Mom's stone says, my idea. I take Honey out of the stroller and she sits down on the grass next to Mom. "Hi Mom," I say. Honey is pulling blades of grass out of the ground, delighted. "Do you see Honey?" I ask. "The last time she was here she was just a little squirt."

I think back to that visit, which is when my mother-in-law came to visit a month after Honey was born, bringing along Engin's niece, Pelin's daughter, the teenaged Elifnaz who was wild to see America. This being Ayşe's first visit not only to our home but to America I felt it could not simply be a meet-the-baby help-the-mother visit but had to be an elaborate exhibit of all the best America had to offer and I made it nightmarish by trying to cram in too many things. But first, when they arrived, I suddenly missed my mother so desperately I had to spend a day in bed, pleading illness, letting them take the baby and coo to her and whisper in hushed tones in the adjacent room. Then I recovered and it was showtime. Every time Ayşe and I have two glasses of wine together and I let loose the floodgates of my stilted Turkish we agree that there can be no ostentatious display of hospitality among family. But to me Ayşe's default mode of just finding a few snacks around the house to put out feels so elegant, so finely wrought, that I cannot believe her when she says it's no trouble at all. And she does this on top of running her own small but robust accounting business. My mother also reflexively put out snacks, prepared things, gave gifts, wrote notes, and I saw that those things were trouble to her, necessary trouble that gave her pleasure but took up her time, and the result was still less than what some Turkish women come up with when they are going all out. Whatever muscle I have in that department is weak and rubbery, but the urge is there—the worst combination. So that meant when they came there was the rental of an Airbnb in the City in a nicer neighborhood than ours, the price of which somewhat exceeded our ability to pay for it, and the arranging of a variety of outings, for wine tasting, for a boat to Alcatraz, for a hike at Point Reyes, and finally, although it boggles my mind and shames me to think of it now, a trip to Altavista so they could see "the real West."

Whatever misgivings my mother might have harbored about my irrevocably tying my fortunes up with a foreigner I knew she would have helped me finesse the visit, she would have pointed out the folly of taking them to Paiute, would have instead had them to her rented bungalow in Sacramento, would have suggested a weekend in Tahoe rather than two awkward nights in the mobile home and a chilly picnic lunch at Fort Bintner, where, I explained, by no means clear any longer on the details, how my great-great-great-grandparents cruised down the Emigrant Trail, got turned around between Shasta and Lassen, and for some reason decided to stay. In middle school I had to do a report about my hometown and

since I didn't really have one I picked Altavista, and my grandmother mailed me copies of all her historical society tracts and
some in retrospect extremely one-sided accounts of the Indian
Wars and I stood in front of the class with my poster board
and my diorama showing rodeo riders and told them my problematic inherited narrative of the west. Some details from the
report stay in my mind and I attempted to reinterpret them for
Engin's family. "No European saw this land until the 1820s," I
told them, which now seems remarkable, that we colonizers
are such a waterbug on the surface of this territory, temporally
speaking, yet so destructive. For the whites it was meant to
be a way-crossing, more people coming through the pitiless
basins on the way to something else than sticking around. The
ones who did stay wanted to be left alone except when they
needed the army to subdue the Paiutes the Modocs the Pit
River the Klamath the Hat Creek upon whose land they were
squatting. And once the Paiutes etc. were murdered or shipped
to Oklahoma or crammed into the nation's smallest reservations, the victors couldn't even agree what to call the land
or how to apportion it—Utah, Nevada, Mormon Deseret,
California, endless territory names, endless proposed states
and administrative divisions, endless skirmishes, with the
fractious settlers rejecting every tax levy until they wanted
something. The land was always being renamed and redrawn.
Finally they carved off this tiny, least-inhabited county, as-
signed it once and for all to California, and gave it the name of
their one-time enemy, out of scorn or fetish I don't know.

During the Mehmetoğlu visit I was gripped with anxiety
about making some hospitable tableau out of the limited tools

available, torn between warring inclinations: to try and re-create some approximation of the warm casual "drop in any time" of my grandparents, who had vodka and chips and peanuts on the deck every evening at five, or trying to do it nicer, with wine and cheese and an elegant home-cooked meal, and to arrange it all without making some careless cultural blunder. But Honey was also six weeks old, and nursed all the time, and really all anyone needed was to sit and hold her on a couch, could be any couch, and the realization that I had brought them all this way essentially for no reason paralyzed me with embarrassment for the entire time we were there. Fortunately Ayşe is an adventurous woman and an excellent sport, and Elifnaz, her whole life spent in the great navel of the universe, served as a kind of comic teen Greek chorus of one, constantly exclaiming "I can't believe anyone lives here," which finally allowed me to relax my strenuous efforts at historical interpretation and apologia and laugh along with Engin and his family, because it was, yes, absurd how long it took to get anywhere.

Engin indicated to me later that the visit was actually a stroke of deranged genius, because his mother and Elifnaz now have a sort of trump card of insights into America when the topic is brought up. I can see beautiful Ayşe, with her coiffure and her rakı and her occasional cigarette, sitting on the balcony in her apartment block in Kadıköy, trying first to describe the encampments of homeless people around San Francisco's City Hall, then trying to find the words to communicate the vastness of the high desert, the unsmiling plains, the pink sponge of tomato that graced her salad at the Golden Spike.

"The main thing you must understand about America is its barbarism," she probably says.

The now beet-red Honey has been tiring herself out running through the cemetery grass in the heat and I see her approach the outer reach of the plateau and spring after her, catching her near the edge of the property where she's looking as though transfixed by the expanse of sagebrush and patchy farmland of the basin. I pick her up and kiss her and plod back to the gravestones where our stroller is parked. I didn't bring any flowers with me so I fold up Honey's bib and put it on Mom's stone. "Love you Mom," I say. "I wish you were here," and a slow leak of tears starts up again. "That's your grandma," I tell Honey, who is stomping her little foot on someone else's stone. I pack her up in the stroller struggling and I'm suddenly exhausted and as I'm trying for the seventh time to buckle at least one of the buckles as she thrashes and strains resolutely forward to prevent me I say into the air "I'm going to *fucking* kill myself" which I sometimes do when I'm trying to cope with her equipage and I instantly feel bad since I'm sure we are standing on the final resting place of many untimely ends, shotgun blasts and death by drinking and getting rolled on by your horse. Finally I get her in and we roll down the hill to Deakins Park and I let myself think about Istanbul, about Engin and Pelin and Savaş and Elifnaz and seventeen million people or more humming along on either side of the Bosphorus in the June heat. She's asleep when we arrive and I scoop her into the Pack 'n Play so easily that I think my ancestors are rewarding me for visiting them.

I step outside to have a cigarette and Cindy Cooper is there on her deck and we each take a few steps in the other's direction and exchange greetings. "What do you do down there in the City," she asks me after a minute. "I work at the University." I could leave it there but I am curious so I say "At the Institute for the Study of Islamic Societies and Civilizations." As it happens Cindy has unreconstructed views about Islam and she begins airing them to me over the fence. "Gotta do something about them," she says and I say "What do you mean?" and naturally she means beheading people, murdering at *Charlie Hebdo*, etc. etc. I think about stubbing out my cigarette and going inside but this is honestly the easiest hill of tolerance to ascend and moreover my job as an employee of the Institute for the Study of Islamic Societies and Civilizations not to mention as a member of God's human family. "You know my husband is uh . . . Muslim," I say, wincing inside, since he would take grave offense at this, since as far as he is concerned he is not a Muslim, if he has a religion it is Morrissey, and he is in fact so much not a Muslim that he won't even say inshallah or mashallah or other things that warmly enfold the name of God into daily speech. I have heard Ayşe use what I am pretty sure but not positive is a pejorative term for heavily veiled women meaning "squished-head" but she is interested in spirituality and transcendental meditation and "Eastern" things although I do not know whether she actually does them. Engin's father, who is divorced from Ayşe and lives in Izmir, is a somewhat dissolute Marxist, anti-Islam, anti-Erdoğan, anti-American for that matter. But their parents were Muslims so they are loosely speaking culturally Muslims and since Cindy is starting from "Muslims are bad" and America more or less treats "Muslim" as an ethnicity rather than a religious choice it does not seem like a time for nuance, so for now I decide to deploy them as pleasant cultural Muslims in the jihad of tolerance. "Well," she says. "He's from Turkey," I say and she moves the corners of her mouth down as though to say Whaddaya know.

"Yeah, and he's stuck there now because the U.S. government has anti-Muslim policies."

I give her the rough outline of the unlawful relinquishment of his green card in the bowels of the San Francisco airport. So far the only thing worse than dealing with the green card situation has been explaining the green card situation to other people, even to know its full madness firsthand requires a graduate seminar in the Department of Homeland Security's U.S. Citizenship and Immigration Services unit and then the Department of State's National Visa Center and all associated forms and procedures and phone menus, menus where you press 3 to be hung up on after an hour of holding; numbers that due to the high volume of callers must be called back between the hours of 1:00 and 4:00; numbers that ring and ring and ring into the void, a human voice answering one in a hundred times; websites giving you instructions like "If you are granted an immigrant visa, the consular officer will give you a packet of information. Do not open this packet." I just tell her that he had one and they took it under false pretenses.

"There's this rule you have to spend six months of the year in the U.S., and Engin—that's my husband—went to do a course thing back in Turkey that was six months long, and when he came to visit us halfway through the course the border guys convinced him he was violating U.S. law by going back and forth, and that if he didn't voluntarily give them the green card he would be banned from the U.S. for five years, none of which was true. And since we had a baby, he got scared and gave it to them and signed the form they gave him. And it was illegal. And now he has to reapply a completely different way through a different agency since he's outside the U.S. And there's not a lot we can do now except wait for a new one which they are apparently too incompetent to get done." This seems almost to move Cindy, in some direction. She rolls her eyes.

"It's not very comforting," she says. "If they could do that with some normal person who's just trying to be with his family imagine all the terrorists they could just let in because no one was paying attention." Jesus Christ, I think. "Yeah," I say. "But I think the reason they did that to Engin is because some people think anyone with a possibly Muslim name is a terrorist, and now he can't be with me and our baby, so that's not a good policy either." Nonetheless I allow myself to agree without difficulty with her assessment that the Federal Government is a godawful bureaucratic clusterfuck and can be counted on to heartily fail at many things it undertakes. I suspect I don't want to hear whatever else she has to say about the Government, what she has to say about Barack *Hussein* Obama. I'm sure that's how she says his name, emphasis on Hussein like that is A Sign of Something and not one of the most common names in the entire goddamn world.

I gesture at the sign in her lawn. "What's sort of the main thing?" I ask. "About the State of Jefferson?"

"The 'main thing,'" says Cindy, subtly rearranging herself as though to start a recitation, "is that the people in Sacramento and Los Angeles don't know damn anything about the North State, not to mention the feds. They take our water for down south, and tax the hell out of us, and then they keep us from using our timber and land and tie us up in regulations. The feds just told Ed's cousin Chad Burns up in Oregon he owes eighty-six grand for grazing his damn cattle." I am curious about the "us" since if I have chosen correctly from my small and dwindling store of local knowledge Cindy does the books at the Flintlock, Paiute County's unexpected tiny municipal golf course where the clubhouse is a trailer and antelope run across the ninth hole. I can't imagine this is a full-time job but maybe it pays whatever bills you are likely to accrue here. Or maybe it doesn't, and that's why Cindy is so fired up about the return of extractive industries to the North State. My grandmother played at the Flintlock until she was eighty-four years old, in visor and immaculate white socks with little pom-poms.

But then Cindy says "Where'd you meet him, your husband I mean?" and I laugh and say "In a bar" and she laughs in her throat and says "I met my sweetie in a bar too."

She finishes her cigarette and grinds it out in a polished shell on her deck railing and says "Well, see you later" and I wave.

I sit down in a deck chair under the shaded part of the deck and light another cigarette and remember the fateful bar. Engin was the upstairs bartender and he had a lot of blurry tattoos and a proto-hipster mustache and he was rather tunelessly singing along with the Smiths who were blaring from the speakers into the summer night. We made desultory chitchat in my struggling Turkish and when I left I gave him a piece of paper with my phone number on it, the only time in my life that I have done this. I was thin and attractive at that time so I received an SMS from him the next day, and we began a relationship that mostly involved sitting in bars in the little tributaries that flow off İstiklal. I spent most of the time asking him what words meant and writing them down in my notebook. We had rather awkward sex and then sat in the living room with his friend Ali, a Kurdish guy who slept on Engin's couch and the rest of the time discoursed vigorously about politics, and I nodded along although in reality I had almost no idea what he was saying.

And then four weeks into our courtship which wasn't really setting the world on fire I found out Mom was sick, so I left Turkey to go back to California and that was it. I lived with her in Sacramento and did a bunch of random jobs and wrote in my Turkish notebook wistfully now and then and after three years she died. And then I decided I wanted to memorize more Turkish verbs and through some miracle I got into the Ph.D. program off a waitlist. And after the second year my advisor Murat had emergency gallbladder surgery and let me accompany a weeklong summer tour of Istanbul for rich university donors in his place. And on my night off I found that same bar in the backstreet of Nevizade and decided to go in, and Engin was sitting there like it had been a few weeks instead of five years. And my Turkish was much better, and what happened was so immediate so natural so inevitable that I decided to let Murat's flock return home by themselves at the end of the trip and I didn't go back to America and didn't take intensive summer Persian that the U.S. government paid for and didn't go back to school and thus ensured that I would max out at an M.A. rather than a Ph.D. but didn't care because the thought of being apart from Engin for so long was physically painful. So I passed the most beautiful summer of my life and at the end it was all clear to me that I had to marry Engin and not get a Ph.D. but find a job have a baby start my life and who knows one day speak perfect Turkish and be a true cosmopolitan. So I dropped out with a sympathy M.A. and a lot of thinly veiled hostility and concern by Murat who felt in loco parentis but was also a snob about Engin's academic pedigree although Engin is still what is fucked-up-edly known in Turkey as a "White Turk," that is urban, educated, irreligious. Engin means "vast" or "endless," incidentally. Maybe it was this sense of his being vast and endless in his capacity to surprise and delight, demonstrated by his sudden reappearance in my life after so long, that caused me to marry him so precipitously, with so little foresight.

There's an unspoken competition among American grad students in Middle East and related studies to be the least Orientalist and problematic and obviously by falling in love with a Turk during a hot Istanbul summer I lost this contest fair and square. But we are not mismatched as far as tastes, ways of being in the world go. The flings I had before I met Engin—ending up in someone's scandalized parents' apartment all the way out in Avcılar and then being driven around to fancy cafés and given expensive perfume I wouldn't wear and then trying to fade away and having to ignore dozens of increasingly tormented and then aggressive text messages—that was my main dalliance with the Other. But Engin rented his own tiny little apartment. We like the same minor-key indie rock, hold the same vague leftish politics, think succulents are the best plants. We are urban late-capitalist late millennials, as Hugo might put it; that shared vernacular counts for a lot. I think the moment I knew we would get married was when we visited his cousin, or his uncle's cousin, or someone's cousin, at a planned community outside a midsize town near Yalova. The cousin was a retired municipal employee who kept bees, and we were told it was baby bee season. We camped out next to the bee box and waited for the swarm of babies to appear because evidently if you don't catch them and hive them right away, they fly away and are lost in the universe. So we spent the day picnicking in the sun, waiting for baby bees to emerge, feeling just as rustic as we'd ever want to feel.

Sometimes I stop to consider that there is something wrong with both Engin and me, because of my many Turkish colleagues in graduate school none of them married Americans; two of my male Turkish friends told me they wouldn't consider it. Engin is different from those friends. I mean he is educated but not like they are—he went to Yıldız Technical University and took a longer-than-customary time to graduate, and they went to Robert College and then on to Bosphorus University or Harvard and wrote lengthy and beautiful treatises in English on materiality in Ottoman culture. I didn't speak Turkish with them because to do so would feel like an insult to their English. Engin's English is functional, let's say, I have heard him speak very shyly to my uncle Rodney, who is hardly a chatterbox. Maybe it's one of those things that keeps a marriage fresh. Back when I first met Engin, when I worked in the school, I had a different sort of Turkish colleagues, polished young women who spoke excellent English and were earning teaching credentials and dressed up beautifully every day. I could tell they found Engin vaguely troubling—some youthful caste and gender difference I never stopped trying and failing to translate to its American equivalent. He lived alone and slept with wayward Americans; they lived at home and married young, half of them divorcing right away as though the relief of being out of the house was enough. "He works in a *bar*?" One of them laughed when I told them about Engin the first time. Aman aman. *Oh my.* They always talked about setting me up with their brothers cousins friends, but never did.

Now I look at Cindy's sign across the fence and I think Engin, you poor bastard. I get up to go in and check on Honey who has now been sleeping a very long time and my first thought as always as I approach the door is that she has probably died in her sleep. I trip over the screen door on my way into the cool house and I think I went to Turkey and was careless careless careless about everything and now I have a pretty good life and my very own sweet baby, and Ellery went with a friend and a humanitarian research agenda and a 4.2 GPA and a suitcase full of modest clothing and small gifts to pass around and she is dead before her twenty-first birthday and I can't believe I told Maryam it was going to be the most meaningful experience of their lives.

Honey is not dead but alive and I hear her make the cry that indicates she has napped too long and deep and that returning to consciousness is like clawing the way back from death. I know this because this is how I nap too. Waking up hurts.

DAY 4   I wake up from a vivid sex dream before Honey starts making noise. If I do the math it probably means I can expect my period in a certain number of days. Since Honey turned four months old and my period came back my sex life—sex imaginary, I should say—has cleaved to a schedule. How else to explain three weeks of deadness in every nerve ending, and then about twenty minutes when I feel like a physical threat to every man I see, when the act of tracing my finger across the dirty BART window feels charged with sexual possibility, when I imagine sleeping with men with whom I've had only a cordial work-related e-mail exchange? Or even, gah, *Hugo* (but never Ted). And then when the mania passes you get a new e-mail or sit across from them in a meeting and they are just ordinary even repulsive people and you understand that sex is a trap.

I feel very cheerful and businesslike this morning—there are some mornings that just start out like that, where I transact matters of household or professional importance in an efficacious way. I remove the furze of orange juice and cigarettes from my teeth and I think Today things are going to be better. I am wearing the white shirt with the stew on it from dinner two nights ago. I strip naked and change Honey's diaper. She is cheerful too and she takes great amusement in my naked body, pulling at my boobs and poking at my nipple and giving me big smiles showing all her little tiny teeth. "Nipple," I say. I take her into the bathroom and put her down on the mat and shower with the curtain open so I can see her. She plops onto her butt and hauls herself back up and toddles over to the side of the bathtub and puts her hands into the water and cries. It is a very quick shower but it does the job. I tear through the house picking up all of our clothes and blankets and her stuffed animals and bedding from the Pack 'n Play and the dish towels and the bathmat for good measure and I stuff them all into the washing machine and wash them on hot. I feed her Cheerios and banana with a towel knotted around my body and I fill up the dishwasher with our modest dishes. I hazard a guess at the workings of the coffee machine. I read *The Runaway Bunny*. I put the things in the dryer. I take Honey out of her romper and put her into a clean pair of pants and a T-shirt. "It's important to get dressed and go out into the day," I tell her. We read three more books while she drinks milk. She prances around the living room and I watch as she learns how to step over the rags taped over the brick base of the wood stove. I'm so interested in her progress that she has gotten to the stove itself before I remember to tell her No. Not that the stove is on, of course, but it seems like stoves should always be avoided in case they are on. I have read on BabyCenter that you should not say "No" to everything that children want to do, but should instead make some other sound of guidance, like "Uh-uh," or "Mm-mm," and save the "No" for really bad situations. The stove does seem like one of those nonnegotiable things, so I look at her and say, gently, "No." She puts her hand onto the little handle of the stove and yanks at it. "NO," I bark at her, and she whips her hand back as though she's been struck. She starts to cry. I scoop her up and put her a safe distance from the stove. "We don't play with the stove," I tell her. She slams her head back into the ground and starts up the desperate wailing of two evenings ago. The golden hour of morning success comes to a close and I feel the endless day stretching out before me. I try to gather up her little flailing limbs into a hug and she bites me on the shoulder, very hard. "NO" I yell and I feel like biting her back and throwing her onto the carpeted floor but instead I lay her down a little too firmly and feel very marginal.

We go outside and I set still-crying Honey down on the grass so I can look at the laptop. I see many e-mails from Hugo about THE CONFERENCE but decide not to read them. It's Saturday, for one, I determine after a brief calculation. And enough brooding about the damn Institute, I think. I take Honey back inside. She is still oddly fussy and she wants to be put down and then she wants to be picked up and then she flails and then she's back down and then she's back up. Maybe she's getting new molars, teeth are always the explanation for everything it seems like. I don't have very many toys up here for her to play with so I get out a bunch of Grandma's wooden spoons, which are still in the ceramic pot by the sink where she kept them. Honey promptly hits herself in the forehead with one of them and cries again when I take it away so I pick her up and coo.

The clothes are dry. I pack up Honey in the stroller with her stuffed animals and we begin the walk to Sal's Café. I have also read that you are supposed to talk constantly to small children, this being the major thing that separates the smart and successful ones from their unfortunate peers. I always found this difficult when Honey was a very small infant but now I get the impression that she is actually interested in my voice. She is calm now and reasonably cheerful so I say "Look at that, that's Grandma's birch tree" and "Look at that, that's a pickup truck, and there's the split-rail fence, and there's the tumbleweed, and there's the sage, and OH LOOK HONEY IT'S A LITTLE COVEY OF QUAIL!!! Oh, look at the quail, Honey!!! Do you know what a quail is? It's a little bird, and in a group you call them a 'covey.'" "App, app, app!" Honey says, straining to get out of her stroller. I take her out and set her down on her feet in the empty street, and she runs toward the quail screaming with untrammeled joy and they immediately swarm through the fence and into the waste beyond Deakins Park. Honey stands looking after them bereft and I put her back into the stroller. It is 9:30 a.m. "There's a blue jay, and there's another blue jay, and there's the pile of garbage, and there's the Mormon Church, which is brand-new, and there's the railroad, and there's the Golden Spike where we went two nights ago, and down the road is Manny's Bar. Your daddy and I went there once and struck up a conversation with the guy who installed Grandma and Grandpa's deck and he bought us a beer." We don't see a single human being, although there are cars briskly passing through the intersection where state route meets state route.

When we arrive at Sal's the crone is there again in the same spot in the corner. "Good morning," I say to her. I start out to say Merhaba but the word dies in my throat a little and I turn it into a cough because I have to assume I imagined that she said it yesterday because I am I guess losing my mind. I've forgotten to fill the sippy cup with milk so I buy myself a coffee and a thing of milk from Sal and sit at a table adjacent to the crone so as to allow for easy intercourse. I pour the milk ineptly into Honey's cup, trying to fend off Honey's paws. "Heh heh eh eh" she says, which is what she says when she wants something, becoming increasingly distressed and needful until she begins crying for the milk. I give her the milk. I wipe the spilled milk from the table with the edge of my sleeve. I take out the computer. I open the computer and glance furtively at the crone, who is taking very slow, very small sips from a cup of black coffee.

I have been thinking yearningly of Elmo who is sometimes utilized at home and how Elmo would really help Honey and me pass the time here and while I know it is wrong for them to look at screens it would just be so nice to set her down and have her stay in one place slack-jawed and not running around rifling through things and I could do something, like answer e-mails on my phone I guess. Get a book from the library and read it. I bite the bullet and purchase two episodes of *Sesame Street* from Amazon and begin the download and think, just to have them, just in case of emergency.

I open Skype and click and soon Engin's face appears on the screen and he and Honey become effervescent with joy. There are still tears and red blotches on her face left from the milk conflagration. "My sweet one. Are you helping your mother?" he asks. "Come on, kiss your daddy," he says, and she kisses her hand and flaps it toward him, and smiles.

I feel like I need to convince him that I am still a functional person so I begin with serious matters. "I have e-mailed the lawyer"—not true but I will—"to ask what we need to do now about the click-of-the-mouse." I say "click-of-the-mouse" in English, it is now how we define the entire episode: "Engin is not here because of a click-of-the-mouse"; "we are working on my husband's click-of-the-mouse." He shrugs and I wonder if this is a bad sign—we've both just given up on it ever being resolved, which is probably what the Department of Homeland Security is hoping for, a general degradation of morale resulting in one fewer green card. I ask him what he is doing and he launches into a description of the project he is working on for the other friend who has the agency, not Tolga, and how the ad is in postproduction and while I don't care I find this somehow comforting, Engin is working, Engin is making money, I am staying home with my child, I am not doing anything wrong, my only responsibility is to my child, this is a globalized world and families don't always live under the same roof because they have to be where the opportunities are, it's all normal in the world-historical sense.

"You look beautiful," Engin tells me, also a lie. This feels like his tentative hand reaching across my back when I'm halfway asleep; thank you Jesus that he is five thousand miles away and I don't have to have sex, thank you Jesus.

"Seni seviyorum," *I love you*, I tell him, one of the first things I learned in Turkish, one of my least favorite things, alliteration only suitable for children, not for romance, to me it feels like you can't attach weight to a phrase like that. I like seviyorum seni which moves the verb to the front, but this is colloquial; knowing what parts of grammar can be kickily rearranged is part of good style I always think. Spur-of-the-moment I say "I want to come to you," and he says "Come, then" and then I have to think of all the reasons why it doesn't make sense to do that and in eight words we've moved back to square one.

Ayşe comes over to the screen and I valiantly endeavor to make pleasant chitchat with her and I wonder if she hates me. I wonder this all the time. I mean I assume that she finds me in some respects incorrigibly savage because I don't wear socks in the house or dry my hair before going outside, but I like to think we get along. Then again the current situation is one to try any mother's—any grandmother's—patience.

We click off, and then I hear it. "Seni seviyorum" the crone says. Ever since I started learning Turkish I'm always on high alert for people speaking Turkish, hear Turkish where it is not being spoken, and when it is being spoken put myself as close as I can to the speaker, and yet freeze when it's my opportunity to speak, instead doing a strange thing where I am silent until the very last minute and then freak everyone out by revealing I understood what they were saying the whole time. Much like this woman has just done to me.

"Merhaba!" I venture to her. "Siz Türk müsünüz?" She just looks at me. "Are you Turkish," I ask in English. "I went to Turkey with my husband a long time ago," she says curtly, as if she were not the one who just told a complete stranger I love you in a café.

"Well, that's quite a memory you've got," I say in the voice I use with all elderly people and the insane. I am deciding whether to stay and draw her out and hear about how friendly the people were etc. but she looks off in the distance and says

"I'm sure you want to be on your way" and there's really no response to that but to say "Well, I guess so. Hope to see you again soon!" and start to roll Honey out and head in the direction of home where we'll do god knows what for the rest of the day, but before I can put any distance between us she speaks again and says "It was the late 1950s, maybe 1960." Jesus, I think, because that's a long time ago, also a weird time, Turkey-wise—coup time, hanging time for what's-his-name Menderes. I halt the stroller and start scooting it back over to her table, raising my eyebrows to her in an inquiry as to whether our continued presence is welcome or a hindrance. "He used to—my husband—he used to set a little alarm and study Turkish for fifteen minutes at a time," she says. I lower myself into the empty seat at her table and roll Honey next to me. I'm worried she'll immediately start freaking out which she sometimes does at the cessation of motion but she is looking very seriously, very gravely, almost the slightest bit skeptically at this new person. It is probably the oldest person she's ever seen, I think, since Ayşe is under sixty and stunning and grandparents are an extinct species on my side of the family.

"I remember when we went there he was so frustrated that he couldn't talk to anyone." She stirs her coffee and sips it. "That's how I felt the first time I went there too," I say. I have a curious feeling of both wanting to stay and talk to someone and wanting to leave, because conversations are work and the elderly are work and I'm just not up for work of any kind but then I remember again the extreme quiet of the house and Honey is after all sitting here so rapt. "I remember we went to a mosque in Istanbul," she says it the American way, IS-tan-bool, instead of the Turkish way, "İ-STAHN-bul," which

I insist on saying now even though it sounds horribly affected when you are speaking English. "He was so excited because the mullah or whatever you call it spoke Arabic, and they could have a nice conversation."

"Oh," I say, intrigued. "Is your husband an Arabic speaker?"

"Was," she says. "He's gone now."

"I'm sorry," I say, and while I'm trying to formulate my next question she begins again. "I remember I was so sick I just wandered off into a corner and drank a yogurt drink a little boy brought me." She looks at Honey. "I was pregnant, is why." "Ah," I say. "Twins," she says. "Jesus," I say, my instinctive reaction to the possibility of twins. "That was before I knew it was twins, of course. It took me a long time to get pregnant. Almost ten years." Like my parents, I think.

"Was your husband American?" I ask. "Oh yes," she says. I offensively assume she means he was not also an Arab so I ask "Why did he speak Arabic?" I'm always hugely admiring of anyone who can learn Arabic. I studied Modern Standard Arabic for two quarters and really, it's so hard, but she just says "He needed it for his work" and I hesitate and say "What kind of work did he do?" and she says "Oh, he worked for different places" and it's such a weird answer that it summons the ghost of my mother who I hear say "Spook" with derisive finality and I almost laugh aloud because it's such a thing she would say, a judgment delivered upon anyone in an embassy whose role was not clearly defined. I decide not to press.

"Where did you go in Turkey?" I ask. She is silent for a while looking at a point past Honey. "First we stayed in the city, with a lecturer from one of the universities." She returns her gaze to me. "He had a beautiful wife named Gonul, I remember." "Gönül," I say reflexively, and years of vocabulary memorization kicks into gear like a tic (Gönül: *heart*; Gönüllü: *with heart, volunteer*). "It means 'heart,'" I say. "That suits her," the woman says. "She was very kind. They lived in a cold-water flat in one of those neighborhoods with the gorgeous wooden houses." "Ah," I say. "She had a little girl, I don't remember her name. That's who taught me 'seni seviyorum.'" She shakes her head. "Imagine remembering that after all these years." She smiles kindly at me, the first smile she has produced. "It must be something about hearing you say it." Honey is still staring at her stupefied which is downright weird and I poke her. "Can you say hello?" I say. "This is Honey. Well, actually Meltem. Turkish." "Pretty," the crone says.

Honey comes to life and starts kicking and wanting to be let out and as sometimes happens when I'm out with her I worry so much she's going to make a big scene that I get a fight-or-flight thing and say "You know I'd really love to keep talking but I should probably get her home for a nap," and the woman waves her hand toward the door and I say "I'm Daphne. What was your name?," which is a weird verb tense, and she says "Alice" and Honey wails and I say "Alice it's so nice to meet you, I hope we will see you again tomorrow!" and I fire the stroller out the door like a shot even though as soon as I leave I regret running from what is likely to be the most interesting conversation I have all day week month year.

I let Honey out of the stroller and she does her spunky little run down the sidewalk until her head gets the better of her and she topples over hard and cries and I hustle to pick her up and cuddle her before she wants down again. While we walk home I think about what we are going to eat and I think she had Cheerios this morning which means she could have an egg which is nutritious and protein-filled and wouldn't be a repeat and I think egg and berries and yogurt although that's the last thing that I personally want to eat and wonder if I could somehow get a burger and shake from the Frosty and eat it away from her prying eyes.

Finally we are home, or back at the house, and I scramble us four eggs and split them between two plates and I slice up strawberries and put yogurt in a bowl and set her in the high chair and set myself down next to her and think once she goes down for a nap I can eat the bag of Lays.

It takes her a very long time to go to sleep. I open the bedroom window so I can hear her outside and her shouts and moans echo around the deck while I eat the chips drink a glass of water and then smoke a cigarette. It's 12:10, early for her nap but I decide to wait her out and finally the sounds stop and after ten minutes it's safe to assume she's out.

Now I have peace and quiet but again it occurs to me that I don't really have anything to do and I think I should force myself to go in the garage and see what's there, all my parents', really my mom's, linens and books and art that I haven't been able to bring myself to dispose of but which would require some more substantial dwelling than I have to display. They are an adult person's things, rugs and engravings and whatnot, which would be absurd in our tiny apartment. It occurs to me briefly to unpack everything and just put it around the mobile home but imagining her things against the faux-wood panels makes me itch. Moreover I don't trust the town's youth—the meth kids imagined although in fairness not actually seen—to not eventually break in and trash the place. I collect

my cigarettes and phone and go inside and poke my head in at
Honey and she is sleeping with her cheek mashed against
the floor of the Pack 'n Play and her hands by her sides and
her butt up in the air, and I back out of the closet stealthily and
make my way to the pantry and out the back door into the heat
and down the steps and to the garage where I gird my nerves
and then hoist up the door and step into the pleasingly dim
cool space smelling faintly of something motor-related, or the
kind of oil I imagine you'd put on a baseball mitt.

And there it all is, my little Aladdin's cave, the beautiful
rugs piled in the corner on the side where the pickup truck
used to go, a love seat and Mom's prized formal settee beside
them shrouded in a blue tarp, some smaller lumps that I think
are a mother-of-pearl inlay coffee table and an ottoman
wrapped neatly in butcher paper. Art boxes lean up against the
Snap-on tools workbench, all the housewares boxed up into
pyramids on the side where the Buick used to live. My parents
had me late and there were eight years on the road before and
eleven years on the road after I was born; ample time for Mom
to collect treasures, the acquisition of textiles being almost a
formal perk of foreign service wifehood. I walk over to the rug
pile and run a hand over a deep blue and red kilim on the top
and give it an appraising sniff and it is pleasingly devoid of
damp. I pick one of the boxes and pull up its tape and open its
flaps and inside see what are obviously dishes of various sizes
wrapped up in tissue paper. Uncle Rodney and I packed up
Mom's bungalow in Sac and he uncomplainingly hauled everything all the way up here with his truck. I took their iron
bedframe, lugged it to grad school, and now it's in our apartment in the City. I unwrap the top dish and it's a jewel-blue

glazed ceramic ashtray, "Tunis" painted on its base in Arabic and the name of some hotel. I carry it over to the settee and throw off the tarp. Beneath it the strangely pristine white jacquard is protected by yet another nest of plastic, and I sit down on this and put the ashtray on its arm and put my feet on the ottoman-shaped lump and light a cigarette, relishing the taboo feeling of indoor smoking, even just in a garage. "Hi Mom," I say to the stuff. "Hi Dad," I say to the urn, which is perched where I left it on the top shelf of the steel shelving at the back of the garage, a terra-cotta number allegedly acquired in the village where my parents met in Corfu.

I take my phone out of my pocket and snap a picture of the garage to send at some future Wi-Fi-enabled point to Engin with the caption "çeyizim." This is a joke we made on his first visit, that all this stuff here in the garage is my dowry, my trousseau rather. Obviously it was a joke, although in Turkey it's not strange for parents to feather the nest for newlyweds—I guess they do that in America too, if you're lucky they just buy the whole nest. I do come to the marriage with an impressive hoard of housewares and no siblings to squabble over them, even though we have no grown-up-seeming place to put them.

Our wedding, or the grouping of events that I think of together as "our wedding," was dictated by procedural matters. His mother and aunt, with what was really extraordinarily good grace given that I was a foreigner and that we had only been together for a few months when we decided to get married—I mean we had been together before but as far as they were concerned I arrived out of a clear blue sky—threw us a sort of lite version of the engagement ceremony at his mom's house and then later a really nice dinner in a restaurant. Part of it was

I think they felt terrible for me because I had almost no family members and so everyone swallowed their alarm and conspired to make a fuss over us. And at least I spoke Turkish, not anything like flawlessly but I make an effort with my idioms.

The restaurant thing was supposed to follow a Turkish civil ceremony in a municipal hall, the official wedding ceremony. Originally when I found out I got the Institute job we were going to do a legally sanctioned thing and get married in Turkey and then apply for the U.S. K-3 nonimmigrant visa from Turkey, which is kind of a combo fiancé/marriage visa which would have let us start the process in Turkey and let Engin come to the U.S. with me and then do the rest of the applying there. But then we were advised by acquaintances and the Internet that this visa was basically nonoperational. And the K-1 fiancé visa takes eons, up to a year, and you can't be together in the U.S. while you wait. So then we decided that we would forgo an official Turkish marriage and just have a nice dinner and then commit what I consider to be mild visa fraud by taking advantage of a loophole in U.S. visa policy that allows you to apply for a fiancé visa as a sort of fait accompli. Your honey comes to the U.S. on a three-month tourist visa, and you get married right before the three months is up, the idea being that your passion is such that it can be satisfied only through immediate entry into the marital estate. You have only a few family and friends, which is conveniently how many family and friends I have, you take a few pictures, you file simultaneously the I-130 Petition for Alien Relative and the I-485 Application to Register Permanent Residence or Adjust Status for your spouse who has now overstayed the B-2 tourist visa, and you spend a thousand dollars in fees and throw yourself on the mercies of a sympathetic visa officer who asks you a bunch of invasive questions and wants to see your text messages and makes you swear up and down you had no intent to marry when your honey got his tourist visa, and then you avoid leaving the U.S. until the green card is secured. That's how Engin got his green card, the one which let us make a baby and from which it should have been a sure thing to move to citizenship. The miracle is that we got that one effortlessly, and then lost it basically through a malicious fluke. It's obvious from all of this stuff incidentally, that they don't want you to marry someone who's not from the fucking United States, all you have to do is read the reams of alphanumeric gibberish on the relevant websites.

Anyway although it was foolhardy from an immigration protocol standpoint we had a big dinner in Istanbul but we told everyone to assiduously avoid thinking of it as a wedding so we didn't get nailed by USCIS if they found for example a Facebook photo that appeared marital. The night before the dinner Pelin threw me a semi-ironic henna night in her apartment—a relief since like all once-traditional events in late capitalist urban environments the henna night sometimes takes the form of a giant boondoggle with hotel, caterers, costume changes, god forbid a belly dancer, etc. But this was just her and Engin's select relatives and friends and two women I invited from my teaching days and they all made jokes I didn't understand and sang "Yüksek Yüksek Tepelere" or "To the High High Hills" which has lines like "I miss my mother, I miss my village" and I got drunk and cried and everyone laughed because crying was actually the thing to do since historically you were facing the loss of your hymen the onslaught of your mother-in-law and the advent of family life and everything that comes with it. Then we went out to a bar and met Engin and we danced to a terrible pop song called "Married, Happy, with Kids."

I loved the nonwedding dinner. My godparents who had been posted in Nicosia with my parents were now posted in Tbilisi and they came all the way to Istanbul in honor of my mom and dad and discreetly avoided consular discussion. Murat, his gallbladder healed and in Istanbul for a sabbatical, came in spite of his reservations about the marriage and the Ph.D., and though he was obviously still grumpy with me, he and his wife were charming with Engin's dad who had been forced to buy a new suit and tame his beard for the occasion. Murat is married to a Dane and they are one of a handful of dual-national marriages I know, which all seem to follow one of two models, which is either both parties are super classy intellectual types who meet in some prestigious university setting, or summer-love style unions that take place between people who are highly mismatched class-wise, like a bluestocking and a villager, and are presumably predicated on very strong mutual attraction. Engin and I don't seem to fit into either of these models.

Anyway at the dinner I spoke English with my godparents and Turkish with everyone else and my hair was perfect and my makeup was perfect and my dress was an ivory shantung tea-length thing I extravagantly ordered from Neiman Marcus and had shipped to Uncle Rodney, who dutifully shipped it to me. When I was tipsy in the bathroom I looked at myself in the mirror and wondered if it was all real. And then I went back out and danced with Engin's friends from the bar and with Pelin and with my godparents and it felt real, sort of. People had spent money to fly in an airplane to sit at a table with us; logistics had been wrangled. Sometimes I look back and wonder whether I was so hell-bent on marrying Engin because I wanted to play at being a cosmopolitan, but I've met a lot of men Turkish and otherwise and never wanted to marry any of them and that's really the best answer I can give myself. It was real, if risky. Marriage is always a risk.

Rodney didn't come to this obviously but along with my dress he tucked a check for $500 into the package which made me sob like a child when I opened it, feeling so coddled by everyone. He officiated our official U.S. wedding, which took place in his backyard in Quincy at the very end of Engin's tourist visa. Two of my friends from grad school who spoke Turkish flew to SFO drove up rented a cabin and ate tri-tip sandwiches and I wore my dress from the Istanbul party. I cried a lot more at that one because my family's absence—Mom's absence—felt so pronounced, and because I was terrified USCIS was going to suss out the lie.

Sometimes I would feel the ground give way beneath my feet—on the henna night—or when we landed in SFO the first time and Engin was suddenly my responsibility as a U.S. citizen and wife to lovingly care for and squire around and make sure he was having a good time and secure the correct citizenship status for (a task I have so far failed dismally at). But throughout our various weddings and comings and goings, we would periodically ask each other if we were okay, and we were.

I pull on my cigarette and look around at my çeyiz and get the feeling that sometimes comes over me when I think of Engin, one that has nothing to do with Skype, when my brain can manage to slough off the impedimenta of logistics and access the feeling of whole-body contentment and gratitude and need, the obvious core of everything I feel about him and which I can only hope will continue to be there existing at some unseen level, shaping decisions and material outcomes until we both die.

I put out the cigarette. The smoke collecting in the garage has a soporific, mildly sickening effect and I stand up with effort and open a box full of what appear to be suzani pillowcases that I definitely want at some point but not now, having no decorative pillows to put in them, and another box with twenty-five different pomegranate things, glass pomegranates and ceramic pomegranates and actual dried pomegranates. For reasons unknown, my mom collected pomegranates. This box takes the wind out of me a little. I take one off the top, a rough-glazed rustic-looking clay one, and close the box. I'll put this one in my office. Or in our bedroom. Or maybe I'll carry it to Turkey. I don't know. I go back into the house and set it on the nightstand and lie down on the bed.

DAY 5   Today is Sunday and Honey is up at 5:40 which is excruciating but it is one of the mornings I love, where she can't stop kissing me and hugging me and laying her face on my face and her eyes shine with joy that is summoned just by my very existence. Normally when she wakes up so early and I try to get her into the bed for a cuddle there's nothing doing; she says "Nyo" in an indignant nasal tone and she windmills her body around so her legs jut off the bed and she inches herself off hits the ground and starts tearing around the house. But this morning I lift her from the Pack 'n Play get back into bed and kiss her all over and she laughs her little seal's bark of a laugh, the laugh of a person who hasn't fully learned how to laugh properly, and I lay her on top of my body and she is all love and melting hugs and rolls off me to rest her head on the pillow and put her arms and legs across the bed like a starfish, periodically doing little jumps and jolts as though making sure the energy filling her small body is evenly distributed, then letting me lay my arm across her and get cozy and think she is just such a nice little tiny person. I feel the greatest sense of well-being available for love or money and I think Thank you God or whoever for this moment. After forty-five minutes of more or less unbroken cuddles touching my face poking my eyes saying "DAH" into my mouth she scoots herself off the bed ready for the day and it is time for breakfast, an egg and a banana and when that is done it is 7:15. If we were at home this would be a very respectable time for us to have finished breakfast, and I might have a chance to actually bathe while she stood next to the bathtub holding the shower curtain and crying for me to come out. It might actually have given me a chance to select my outfit for the day with some modicum of care for the sheer pleasure of looking respectable or like an attractive woman in the waning years of her prime. Every day I envy Meredith her beautiful clothes, expensive clothes or unusual clothes she finds on her prodigious travels. But she is also eighty pounds, bird bones that can perch as they are meant to on precipitous heels, visible panty lines that look somehow louche and obscurely elegant but would look obscene on an ass like mine.

Twenty minutes for stories and milk on the couch, although Honey is increasingly reluctant to sit through an entire story now, even the ones she loves, and begins rifling through the pages faster and faster until I can't even rapidly paraphrase the illustration. I hope she is not hyperactive requiring treatment. Twenty minutes of taking all of the pots pans melamine bowls out of the kitchen cupboards. If we were at home leaving the house at five minutes to eight with my hair clean my minerals powdered across my face a little blush a cardigan and skirt and somewhat stylish sensible shoes we would be in excellent shape for an eight-o'clock deposit of Honey at daycare and a corresponding 9:30 workplace arrival. We would be off to a very good start, all things considered. But here we have no project for which this early waking and breakfast and stories-and-milk represents a smart and auspicious beginning, and no minerals to powder on my face.

So I decide we will go for a walk, a real walk, no stroller, while it is still cool and the birds are chirping and the heat of the day is a hint not a promise. We can buy a newspaper at the High Winds Market. I gather Honey put her into pants and shirt cover her face and chubby wrists and arms and hands and ankles with sunscreen and it gets in her hair and we set out on the move. The High Winds Market is closer than the Holiday but small small small and all the fruit is wax and shipped in from Ecuador and in the deli it's baloney city. We stop to watch two deer and two perfect fawns in the undeveloped scrub lot next to the original Deakins place. The mothers look at us and Honey shouts "Daggy daggy daggy" until they tense up and bound away, the fawns wobbling behind them. Then it's ten minutes before we've made it out of Deakins Park and that's with Honey hustling her buns. This land is made for getting across on your horse or your wagon or the railroad. My mother told me that my great-grandfather used to ride a horse two days west every time there was a Freemasons' meeting in Cassidyville, stopping to camp on the plains to break up the trip. That's the way to do it. By the time we've reached the railroad Honey is lifting her arms to be picked up, and forgetting always the slow rate at which ground is covered in the high desert I don't have the Ergo and so have to carry her on my own steam the rest of the way to the store. I hoist her up onto my shoulders and we stride through the scrub on the highway that leads to the market, and she puts her mitts on my head and sort of caresses my hair, what a funny thing she is. We are panting when we arrive.

I buy the *Recorder* for fifty cents and feel that a treat is in order so I also buy a Starbucks Frappuccino in a bottle and

Honey gets a string cheese even though she has twenty-six string cheeses at home and I curse myself for not bringing one but she holds the new one in her fist and gleefully bites the head off and smiles at me with a mouth full of cheese. I put her back on my shoulders to take the highway back to Deakins Park and the knowledge that we have seen what there is to see and there is no new route, no new view, adds length to the twenty minutes it takes to get back home. Once we leave the anxieties of the highway and the trucks that barrel down it I put Honey down to walk and I scan the headlines of the paper. The county supervisors are scheduled to vote on whether Paiute should join the fifty-first State of Jefferson and lobby the capital to secede, I read. I find it stunning that Cindy and her lawn sign are a viable political movement although I guess supervisors can vote on anything. What I understand to be the sentiment at the State of Jefferson's heart is that nameless legislating fat cats in big cities cannot properly represent the interests of the sparsely populated rural counties. Which is probably true. But it seems that this probably true thing is also what dooms this move-ment to irrelevancy, it's like if the Greeks and the Bulgarians started agitating to leave the Ottoman Empire but there were only ten Greeks and five Bulgarians. Moreover based on the way the main street looks it's hard to believe anyone is just waiting for liberation from the yoke of the state to rise up and prosper. "Casualties of Capital!" I say aloud in Hugo's pomp-ous voice, and Honey pats my head quizzically.

When we are safely back at the house it is 8:45 and I think given Honey's early start this morning perhaps she can be per-suaded into a nap and I can read the paper and have a cigarette and recover from the walk to the store. I look at her until I find a gesture I can reasonably interpret as a rubbing of eyes and I tell her very cheerfully lovingly but authoritatively that she is tired and it is now time for a nap. I carry her to the closet close the curtains in the bedroom toss the comforter over the un-made bed put her into the Pack 'n Play with minimal ceremony say "It's time to take a snooze" gently pass my fingers over her brow and in between her eyes and over the tip of her nose which sometimes makes her involuntarily close her eyes like a parakeet in a cage when you put a blanket over it. I crack the door and leave the bedroom and immediately her cries begin but I determine them to be a feint and not substantive. I pause to feel sad that this store of Honey-based knowledge I have been building up which is so insanely specific to this time and place and person will live and die with the versions of me and her that exist at this moment. And that Engin is missing his chance to amass this same knowledge, if indeed this knowl-edge has the same weight for fathers as for mothers.

I drink a glass of water collect the cigarettes from the top of the grandfather clock and go onto the deck with the paper. I scan the letters to the editor which are all Jefferson-related in honor of the upcoming vote. I note with a start that Cindy Cooper has written one.

Editor:

The people in the North State do not have any represen-tation in California legislation and we are trying to get equal representation and that's the long and short of it.

The truth is we are working to have less laws that keep us from living a better life, so our grandkids have a better life too.

People want the government to stop charging them taxes for everything they do. Los Angeles does not pay the fire tax and they are the ones that pasted it on us and building the train and tunnels we don't need or will ever use.

We are working hard to make the North State a better place to live and have support from a lot of the people in it.

Cindy Cooper, Altavista

I would not have pegged Cindy as a community activist necessarily as she seems grumpy but sort of placid and immobile. There's a dissenting letter:

They say it is all about representation, when really it is about regression, anti environmental protections, anti immigration and the end of all progress made in the last century. Splitting the state is drinking poison and hoping the other person will die.

This from Brian Hendricks of Fairmeadow, thirty-five miles west of us. Go Brian, I think. There are a few other Pros, Big Government, regulation, taxes, blah blah blah. And then at the very end I start to see a letter from by god my uncle Rodney and it is so terse and Rodney-like I wish he was here so I could give him a hug.

People have been talking about this since the 1940s but it was true then and it's true now that for every dollar the North State sends to Sacramento we get two dollars in services from the State.

Rodney Burdock, Quincy

I would be amazed if Rodney has ever strayed from the Republican Party in his life but I guess secession is a bridge too far. He does after all work for the Forest Service, which is the Government like the Foreign Service is the Government like the University is the Government, like every institution that has ever employed my family apparently. Honey's cries have subsided to the point where I can assume she is happy enough being where she is and I look through the rest of the paper. There's a rambling two-page op-ed from Davis Birge-neau concerning the benefits of letting cattle graze on a specific patch of scrub by a local water channel and the combination of the prose which is full of a cattleman's reminiscences and my agricultural ignorance means that it reads like a foreign language, I mean I can't even understand the basic terms of the debate at hand. But reading it, reading about the "Tour of Europe" night at the library and the hunting safety class and the Fourth of July parade gives me a comforting feeling, like things are happening and people know each other and do things and the social networks that hold the world in place are extant here even if I don't have access to them and don't know if I would want to if I could. There is a whole column of the paper for the churches and I'm astonished by the number of them relative to the size of the town, Mormon Catholic Baptist Seventh-Day Adventist and things with inscrutable denominations, Grace and Freedom etc. and this is not even to mention an actual full-fledged cult, not listed, that took over a neighboring town in the 1970s and started putting up life-size dioramas of biblical figures along the highway which are there still. Engin loved this town when we drove through and made me stop the car so we could take pictures.

I see the name of my grandparents' Episcopal church, where I was baptized lo these many years ago. Services Sunday at ten and for no reason I can name I think we should go and just see what it's like and pass the time. It will take half an hour to walk there so I think we can leave at 9:20 and stop at Sal's so that we can communicate to Engin that we will not be available for our scheduled call until later in the day. I pause for my daily feeling of annoyance at the difficulty of communicating overseas and while the difference between what is available now and what it used to be like for example when we lived in Nicosia it is somehow *more* annoying now, the Skype calls with an echo or video but no sound or sound but no video or work in one room but cut off when you wander into an electronic shadow or the Wi-Fi relies on ancient copper lines that don't really work. I should get an iPhone so we could Face-Time but my non-iPhone is half the price. I could theoretically get the Institute to pay for it; the Institute, meaning the taxpayers and the Saudis, pays for absolutely everything Hugo and Meredith put their hands on, but I don't like the idea of HR somehow listening to my phone calls and what if god forbid I wanted to send Engin a sexy photo, should that urge ever happen to arise. Maybe the thing really is that now we have these tools there's the expectation that you will always be in touch. Overseas we called my grandparents every two weeks and we wrote letters and that was it and it was just easier than doing this Skype dance with all its awful reminders that the person you want to be here is not here. But Honey has to see her father's face as much as she can while he's not here, I think, and start crying, and I'm proud of myself because I think it's been about two days since the last time I cried.

But maybe church will . . . do something for us. Maybe we'll have a visitation. If nothing else by the time church is over and we go back home it will be time for lunch and then a long nap and if I'm honest a drink and maybe in the afternoon we can drive out to Antelope Meadows where I seem to remember there is a dilapidated swing set and a view of waving grasses and a man-made lake surrounded by spiky grass and gopher holes. A nice Sunday evening just the gals, and maybe I can convince myself to go back to work tomorrow or the next day or the next or the one after that.

Honey is silent now and I take a shower and the feeling of hot water on my skin and solitude and respite is so enormous I have a sensation that borders on randiness and take the head of the shower which is removable and spray it between my legs at varying distances and think about Tom Hardy until thirty seconds later I come in a painful, spasmodic way that feels incomplete, a misfired sneeze but I guess a sneeze nonetheless. I dry myself brush out my knotted hair put on jeans and the shirt I was wearing when I left the Institute. I lay out Honey's hat and the sunscreen and clean diaper and pack away the changing pad into the backpack with a bag full of raisins and a sippy cup filled with water and two books and a spare pants and there are twenty minutes remaining to sit on the deck and be clean and fresh and smoke two cigarettes and stand up feeling light-headed and ethereal. There's a breeze and it rattles the goat bell my mom brought my grandparents from Cyprus. I hear its unmistakable goat-summoning sound and I have suddenly the strongest sense memory I've ever had, so strong I touch the arms of my deck chair to know I'm here. Mom and I were on Chios, before the Syrian war, before the refugee crisis, doing a kind of Dad memorial trip to old haunts. I was a teen. We stayed at a village outfit called Aphrodite Rentrooms, a damp, spartan affair with austere beds side by side. We woke up from an Aegean afternoon nap to the sound of a hundred goat bells in the olive grove below, and we sat on the balcony eating pistachios and watched a sea of goats return home in the pink afternoon light. I try to remember the light, my mother in a white nightie in the little bed across from mine. The breeze dies and the goat bell is silent.

I wash my hands and put on lotion to mask the smell of smoke which never really comes off and I remember on that same trip a Dutch couple from the hotel invited us to eat dinner with them and the man pounded on the table about immigrants. "They say I'm Dutch," he yelled. "I'm black as my shoe but I'm Dutch." I shake my head like my dad and go into Honey's room touch her hand and she stirs. I touch her cheek and she stirs again and I say "Did we have a nice snooze" and she blinks at me and then her face wrinkles as though she will cry but then settles itself into more of a look of assessment, a serious look, and then she smiles, the way she has of what I think they call self-soothing; she is always adapting to her environments.

I put on more sunscreen and the hat and attach the Ergo for wearing her on my back which is challenging to do by yourself. I sit her on the bed and then squat down before her and sort of scoop her onto my back and hold her there with one arm behind my back while the other arm fumbles for straps and despite an instant and stabbing cramp in my side I manage to feed the buckle through the safety loop and then snap it tight and I adjust her and we look in the mirror and she smiles a big smile showing all her tiny teeth and I jump up and down to get her straightened out and she laughs and I put the backpack with her diapers etc. on frontways and say "We're off!" and we set out for the long walk across town, all the way down Main Street almost to the other end. I hand Honey half a banana and we plod along until she says "Eh eh eh aaaaaah" in my ear and I give her the rest of the banana and there's banana in my hair. Sal's it turns out is closed at 9:40 on a Sunday but I huddle near the door and get out my phone and find I can still use its Internet. I ignore my flurry of WhatsApp notifications and open Skype. Engin is not logged on so I call his phone. He answers and I hear festive hubbub in the background. "Canım benim" he says, and I say "canım benim." "You're early," he says, and I say "We're, um, going out and so I'm calling you to say we won't be able to call you at ten-thirty." "Where are you going," he asks, and it takes me a minute to remember the word "church," so seldom have I used it. Like "ecclesiastical," like French église. Ikliz, I say but no, he corrects me, kilise. "It sounds strange I know," I say. He laughs. "Church! Why?" "I don't know, Engin. We're bored. You know I used to go with my mom." "American religious fundamentalism is influencing my wife," he says to someone, which annoys me. "Pelin says don't go," he says to me and I hear the voice of my sister-in-law in the background. "Where are you?" I ask. "We're having beers with Pelin and Savaş on the Kordon. We decided to go to visit Dad. Tomorrow we'll go to the beach." The fucking beach. Pelin is beautiful beautiful beautiful and I wither momentarily thinking about her in a bathing suit, a sight I've been subjected to previously in a harmful manner, although jealousy isn't quite right here since she is after all Engin's sister, but even if he cannot lust for her exactly she can acclimatize him to the way that women are supposed to look and I know I do not look, and Pelin is the mother of a teenager and still looks the way she does. "How nice," I say. "Let's talk tomorrow, then." Engin sounds bemused. "Okay. But I can still talk on the Kordon. How long is your church?" "I don't know, I haven't been in years. An hour probably." Honey begins squawking. "It's your baba" I tell her and hold up the phone by my shoulder so she can hear it from my back. She gets her mitts on the phone and tries to turn it to look at the screen as though to see his face. "No, sweetheart, he's not on the screen, just his voice, my love." "I've got to go," I tell Engin. "Let's talk tomorrow." I feel unaccountably desperate to get off the phone, the futility of conversation alighting on me suddenly like a stinking, malevolent seabird. "I love you I kiss you bye bye," and press the red button while he is still saying something.

We start up the march again and approach the street where we turn up for the church and I picture him on the Kordon, which I think must be the happiest place on earth or was the last time I was there, before Izmir became a way station for desperate people preparing to cross the sea. A wide patch of grass stretches a mile up and down the waterfront of the main part of Izmir, innocuously ugly concrete buildings faced by a strip of cafés and the grass, upon which families and young people and lovers sit and men walk up and down selling pumpkin seeds and collecting empty beer bottles for recycling. It's obviously not Engin's fault that he is having a beach day while I'm lugging a sweating toddler to a rural church service—it's my fault for ensnaring him through marriage in the bureaucratic web of the evil empire, my fault for putting him in a position where his only chance to work was to go back to Turkey, my fault my fault. I know all these things but I am still full of fury.

I should look for a job in Turkey; I have no idea what is out there besides teaching English for which I have zero aptitude and hate doing and which does not pay well unless you do have aptitude, which is as it should be. I don't want to float like an expat spouse, start some offensive blog, "My Life Among the Turks." I want to make money, to have money. I don't want to dig for bargain clothes in a seedy pasaj. And it makes me feel so mournful to think of Honey not speaking English at school, not to mention what they would teach her. Although why should I be suspicious of what she would learn in a Turkish school? God only knows what she would learn at school in Altavista. These are all problematic thoughts to parse at a later time.

We walk the roads off Main Street to get to the church and some of the houses look okay but some of them are obviously hoarder houses, faded curtains pulled up at a corner to show dusty knickknacks and piles of nothing. I wonder if this is some specifically American disease or whether other places have it too. I have never met a Turkish hoarder to my knowledge. As we turn onto Second Street I consider the wisdom of bringing a child Honey's age to church. It has been probably fifteen years since I attended a church service, around the time of the Chios trip probably, and I strain to imagine what the experience is like vis-à-vis babies. I assume that St. Mark's follows the liturgy of my youth, although I imagine it will be less well attended by an order of magnitude. On the one hand, it seems unlikely that Honey will be able to cope with the mandate of spending one hour in silence. On the other, who will care if we get up and go?

The church is significantly less prepossessing than I remembered, a small L-shaped ranch building built of cinder blocks like the Golden Spike. The yard is torn up, just cratered dirt with small piles of rubble here and there. It's on one of the last blocks up against a dirt hill that crests up to a rocky out-crop looking out over the scattered houses of Indian Town. I'm sure it can't be called that anymore. I wonder if the church is functional and this possibility opens a door to turning back and going home and I desperately want to slip through it. There is a sign on the actual door that I hope says Church Closed but really says Pardon Our Dust so I open the door and it looks as I distantly remember from many years ago. One side of the L formed by the building contains what I think is called the nave, rows of neat wooden pews, all of them empty, leading up to a very respectable little altar area with pulpit flags crosses etc. The sun shines brightly down the aisle through the modest stained glass. The other side of the L is a mingling slash rumpus area with a large table and chairs and an open kitchen toward the back. There are tidy bookshelves lining the room and a bulletin board and a low-lying gray wall-to-wall carpet covers the concrete slab which is perceptible in the balls of your feet. It's all very nice-looking.

I know, although I don't know how I know, that for years the priest has been itinerant between three towns in the county, since the number of Episcopalians these days is such that one rural congregation could never support his care and feeding. The Mormons seem busy according to their parking lot, and the evangelicals too, out there on the road between Altavista and a hamlet called, incredibly, Brother's Keeper. There appears to be no one else in the building. I knew the number had dwindled but I had not considered the possibility that we would be the only people here.

I see a basket on a stand where you can write down people to pray for and I write my mom and my dad on one slip of paper feeling sentimental, and I put them in the basket, and then I write Ellery Simpson and family and Maryam Khoury on another slip and put that in the basket and I shake my head to disperse the stinging fog generated by this act and also feel guilty that I haven't thought of Ellery and Maryam for a number of hours. I squat down unclick the Ergo and gently lower Honey to the floor and she takes a few investigative steps and then tears off down the aisle, tripping over her own feet and falling headlong onto the carpeted concrete. She wails and I rush to pick her up and as I'm patting soothing stroking squeezing the hot head and sticky hands I hear the sound of a toilet flushing and a door opening and from beside the kitchen a tall, rather stooped brown-haired man in his forties emerges and visibly starts.

"Hello" he says. "Hi there," I say brightly, as if it were the most normal thing in the world to be attending a Sunday church service in an empty room. "I'm Daphne," I say, extending my hand. "Benny," he says, and shakes. I proffer up Honey, who gives him her signature and highly alarming come-hither look of downcast eyes sweeping lashes tucked chin and perfectly timed look up, it's actually gross how cute and coy it is—nazlı, the word is in Turkish. "This is Honey." "Hi there, little Honey," he says and gingerly grasps two of her fingers. "Are . . . we going to be the only ones here," I ask him. "Well, usually there are seven of us," he says. At this the front door opens and a slightly ruddy wren of a woman rushes in, clad in flowing skirts and sleeves. "Everyone is sick," she says, answering a question she didn't hear me ask. "Randy is sick and can't do the music, the Gates girls got heat stroke at the fairground yesterday, and I don't know who-all." "Hi," she says and looks at me. "What a delightful sight the two of you are." Honey begins kicking and I put her down to tear around again. "Yes, hi, well, I'm not sure how she'll do. It's the first time she's been to church," I say ruefully, as though our attendance were recorded in a central database. "Well that's even better, then," the woman says. "It's a blessing to have you both. Do I know you?" I say my name and the name of my grandmother and she nods. "Yep, knew your lovely grandmother," the first person I've met, I think, who has remembered her. "My name is Sarah and I'm our Worship Leader when Father H is out." Two other women walk into the church, not old, but one walks with a cane. We are all white in the room. "Gladys, Mary," Sarah says. "I'm thinking this is going to be it today." I look at the rows and estimate that they could comfortably accommodate eighty people. Benny, Gladys, Mary, and I shuffle toward the pews and distribute ourselves as evenly as we can, Benny in one quadrant, Honey and I in another, and Mary and Gladys in a third, with the fourth quadrant empty. It looks like a plague has come through and we are the last people on earth and we are praying for deliverance.

Honey has toddled off and is squatting near a rack of ecclesiastical magazines at the back of the rumpus area and I think that might work and I move back to the second-to-last pew so I can keep an eye on both the pulpit and the child. The nave is lined with big open windows that make the building seem more spacious than it is. It is very clean and bright and airy, an illusion of bigness within relative to the squat brown building without. In my pew I set the Ergo the diaper bag the liturgy printout and a pencil I find in the bag. "Daphne," Sarah says to me from the pulpit. "If you could just get behind you to the keyboard and press Play on the digital box." I find the keyboard and a little box on it with a screen and buttons and I press the one that says "Play." The canned organ of the processional sounds through the air and we assembled begin to sing. Honey pauses for a moment to marvel at us then runs down the aisle and climbs the stairs to the altar area. I run after her and scoop her up whisper "sorry" as though there were a hundred other people in the room rather than four and we trot down the aisle back to my pew where I put her up in a seated position and hand her the liturgy and the pencil and she stands on the bench and starts tearing holes in the liturgy with the pencil.

We didn't have any kind of service here for Dad. He wasn't religious and his family was Catholic, a suspect faith, and he wasn't from here and it would have been utterly strange to have any kind of thing for him here in this building. But we did have one in our Anglican church in Athens, when we finally left Altavista and braved the reentry, the wives from the embassy ladies' group flanking Mom as she unlocked the door of our apartment. I sit in the pew and try to put myself back inside that church, a beautiful stone building near Syntagma Square. A place for travelers and pilgrims since the nineteenth century, it advertises itself—for Philhellenes, for drifting colonials. I remember sitting in the pew thinking how strange it was that Mom and I were sitting there without him like we did every Sunday, but that this time it was his very absence that we were commemorating, marking that absence permanent. That we wouldn't swallow cake and lemonade and make the hot walk home and find him waiting back at the apartment doing a puzzle. That he was just . . . absent. I close this window in my consciousness and think how odd it is that Honey has never been to that church with me. She's never seen Syntagma, she's never roamed the warren of the National

Garden with its permanent fug of cat pee, its rusted playground equipment, the clamor of peacock screams and maybe a brass band sounding through the dusty foliage. She's never been anywhere that matters to Engin or me, except here.

We are onto the Confession of Sin now and Honey scoots down off the pew and is again running toward the rumpus area which I feel is fine except she is holding the pencil sharp side up and I run after her and take it away and she issues a "NYO" that echoes through the building. I return to the pew get her sippy cup trot back out hand her the water and she flings it and is back down the aisle, with a detour into Benny's pew to pat winsomely at his knee and although I have misgivings I allow this to happen as it lets me get out the prayer book and hymn book and uncrumple the liturgy and try to figure out where we are.

We are in a Psalm and I see Benny handing his *Book of Common Prayer* to Honey as though she might follow along and then looking bemusedly at Honey while she tears a page from it and I spring across the aisle to his pew to collect her and say no no no and smooth the page and whisper "sorry" again to the room over the sound of Sarah's incantations. I carry her into the rumpus area and set her down and give her a plastic cup from a sleeve of plastic cups on the table. I return to the pew. First Lesson is read by Benny. During Second Lesson read by Gladys or is it Mary I see Honey zip up the aisle and again begin climbing the stairs to the altar and again I zip down the aisle and grab her and whisper "sorry" and we have reached a point where I feel it would be equally rude to leave and to stay. I want someone to say something like "It's all fine!" or "Bless the children," but the service is proceeding with what seems like a lot of ceremony given the size of its congregation. Sarah asks me to press Play again for a hymn. Honey joins me in the pew and begins pulling things out of the diaper bag. Sarah begins her sermon which I listen to with one ear as Honey heads back to the rumpus area and I hear something about the troops but then I also hear things about American Exceptionalism and I think Huh, interesting, and I want to hear more and whether or not American Exceptionalism is something we support in the congregation—I don't think I have ever heard the phrase used to connote something positive and I would be glad to know the spirit of dissent is alive in the small-town church, but Honey falls down and cries and I take her outside the building and then we come back in and I let her run in circles making small squawking sounds for the Apostles' Creed and the Lord's Prayer which is the prayer I used to say every night before I went to sleep. I recite the words and rather than a balm on my soul or the breath of God or something I just feel the relief of knowing the words to something without even having to think about it, knowing the beginning the middle the end, the way I want to speak Turkish, the way I want to raise my child, knowing and assured. In Turkish "fluent" is from the verb meaning *to flow* but I guess if I think about it that's true in English too. Anyway, Dear God, let me be the one who flows.

I hear banging and run to the rumpus area and find Honey pulling bowls out of a cupboard. I collect her and return to the pew and Benny in my absence has been called to press Play for the Offertory hymn and I'm mortified to remember that offertory means offering and this is the time for the baskets and I don't have even spare change to put into one. It feels so tacky to come as a guest to this moribund congregation and let my child wreak havoc and not even leave a dollar and I see with deep shame Benny pulling twenty dollars out of his wallet to put into the basket that he himself is carrying around. Mary and Gladys put their contributions in, even Sarah the Worship Leader, and when he comes my way I whisper "I'm so sorry, I forgot about this part," and it seems clear that Benny has no children because he holds the basket in front of Honey as though it will be a fun diversion for her and Honey of course grabs the money and I have to wrest it from her and put it back into the basket and she begins her chorus of "NYO NYO" and kicks and writhes and I know that it is time to go.

I wave ruefully at everyone and scurry toward the door and I see Sarah look questioningly and put a hand up but I don't stay long enough to see whether she is going to say "Wait" and we are back out into the heat of the day and I feel suddenly choked by the smell of juniper and I think I'm glad my mother my grandparents my grandparents' grandparents aren't here to see how small the church is now. I put two blocks between us and the church and then I sit down on a crumbling curb off Main Street and wrench another muscle deep in my side trying to get Honey onto my back into the Ergo.

We walk toward home, Honey sweaty and limp and heavy on my back, and I worry about how hungry she must be since it is lunchtime and I try to pick up the pace to the extent possible in the heat. But halfway there I feel the buzz in my pocket that means service and I look at a photo of Engin and the gang on the Kordon at dusk and then I think I ought to call Uncle Rodney back and tell him how much I liked his letter but I decide I'm not up for it, favorite uncle, only uncle though he may be.

We straggle the rest of the way home and I'm ready to collapse, it's so hot, but finally we mount the steps to the screen door and I lay Honey down on the floor turn on the AC take my shirt off and rub the red grooves of my flesh. I decide against frozen pizza because of the oven and make a quesadilla instead even though that's basically another fucking string cheese sandwiched between carbs and I stuff her full of blueberries too and try to get her to eat some browning avocado. She goes down docile for her nap and I stretch out on the bed and fall into a sleep so deep I wake up with drool on my chin.

Honey wakes up at the same time and I decide against Antelope Meadows because I don't feel like getting her into the car seat but then I think the light is turning pink and it would be nice to go for a drive. That's what my mom did with Rodney and her parents when she was little, she told me—they'd get in the pickup and drive out to someone's ranch and drop in unannounced and be received with coffee and a piece of cake and normally that would sound horrible to me, that's the one thing about Turkey I can't really deal with, there's a lot of visiting, but right now it sounds so so nice and I wish I knew someone to do it with.

I'm rummaging in a cupboard looking for nuts when I find Grandma's cocktail napkins printed with cattle brands and delighted with this discovery observe her sacred five o'clock cocktail hour on the deck, where Honey is more or less penned in with the books I set down for her. I can't find the nuts but I have two petite screwdrivers and the better part of a bag of Lays. I would like to have a cigarette out here in the thin air but I do not smoke in front of Honey because that is the worst thing you can do to your child according to experts. I am not used to drinking liquor instead of beer and I thrill a little at the heat it sends across my limbs and then when I think about dinner I decide we might as well just walk over to the damn Golden Spike again. The bank account must be closer to $200 now, but I vow that I will do a thorough investigation of our finances in due time. This is a kind of emergency, I say, and norms are set aside during an emergency.

"We're going out," I say to Honey, and I prattle cheerily to her as I tote her around the house, squatting down to pick up her changing pad and put it on the table and pick up her diapers and put them on the table and pick up her wipes and put them on the table and pick up her two sections of *The Very Hungry Caterpillar* which she tore in half the other night when she was damp from her bath and put them on the table, and then put all the things into the bag. She chortles every time I squat down and say "WHOA" and stand up and say "WHOA." And then I get her string cheese from the fridge and put it into the bag, and find her socks on the floor and set her on the counter and put on the socks and shoes and then we are finally ready to go and I think about what drink I am going to get when we get there to keep the festive feeling going.

Honey is reasonable on the walk over, holds my hand over the hillocks and listens when I tell her we have to look both ways crossing the train tracks, so I am cautiously optimistic that there is no fractiousness on the horizon and we can have a nice dinner.

The restaurant has a dark bar off the main dining area through a beaded plastic half-curtain, one I've only ever been in for my grandmother's wake. Tonight I hear a cheery "Hi" from its depths as I wait at the hostess stand and look through to see Cindy Cooper and a big be-mustached man I don't know sitting in one of the leatherette easy chairs in the bar area. She waves us over. "On Sunday they've got Picon punch for four bucks," she tells me, this is a horrible Basque drink with almond liqueur but four bucks is four bucks, and she says "Sunday" like Sundy too. I ask her whether she thinks it's okay to have Honey in the bar area and the bartender looks at me like This is America ain't it so I pull up a chair and Honey sits on my lap and I give her a string cheese from my bag and she smiles happily at Cindy and the man who it turns out is Cindy's boyfriend Ed van Voorhees, who I've heard about from Uncle Rodney and I realize must be the brother of Sal, she of the café. Ed comes from a big ranching family but is I think a Pepsi distributor spreading Pepsis across the west so there's got to be a story there, gambling or whatnot.

"I read your letter in the paper," I tell her. Ed slaps Cindy's back and hoots and Cindy looks defiantly at me even though I think my tone of voice is neutral and she says "Well I'm not really one to write a letter to the paper but I just felt it was right now that the supervisors are gonna put it to a vote." "You know my Grandma Cora worked for the BLM," I tell her, intending it as a mild rebuke. "Damn near everybody worked for the BLM in this town," Cindy says. "But the head honchos don't live here and they can't keep telling us how to run things." "My uncle Rodney wrote a letter too," I say. "He says the North State needs a lot of government support." "Well Rod works for the Forest Service don't he," says Ed, just as Cindy says, "If we had some industries up here we wouldn't need the state's money." Ed nods. "We can't all be pencil pushers," he says, which is unjust to

Uncle Rodney who is outside or in his truck about half of most days. Ed must see me narrow my eyes because he then says, "Hey—I love Rod. We go all the way back to kindergarten."

Everyone's sense of propriety spurs us to move on. I ask Cindy where she's from intending it to be a courteous neutral question but she's from San Bernardino, way south, way way south. Flatlander, I think, with the tiniest tribal thrill, and she obviously is sensitive to notions of authenticity herself because she adds, "Been up here ten years, though," and I say, "Ah," and she says, "I came up with my ex. He's gone now but I knew this was home as soon as I got here" which strikes me as remarkable, to have that reaction on your first visit.

Ed asks me what I do and Cindy tells him that I work at the University. "You teach down there?" he says, which is what most people justifiably think might be the primary activity at the premier public university in the state but is not in fact the case. "Not exactly," I say. "I work at a research institute for Islamic societies." "Like ISIS?" he asks me. Which, Jesus. At the University it is basically considered indecent to mention ISIS unless it is in the form of a question like "Whither Transnational Movements in the Age of ISIS?" "No," I say. "You know, like any country where there's a shared Islamic past. Like Turkey or Morocco or, uh, Jordan," trying to name places where there will be fewer bad associations. "Or Indonesia," I add, since this is technically part of our mission along with manifold places in sub-Saharan Africa which are all horribly underrepresented in the Institute's programming due to the many swirling complex currents of religious studies area studies history anthropology political science and how they do and do not interact and do and do not reflect and refract aspects of scholarship and society.

"Well what do you-all think about ISIS?" he asks. I wish we were on campus and I could defer to Hugo or Meredith since it is really against protocol for me to talk about Issues as opposed to Programs. I am supposed to plan and find funding and administer, not have Ideas, although paradoxically I would never have been hired without a demonstrated interest in Ideas, since Hugo and Meredith are terrible snobs about credentials and need someone to write their research proposals and keep them company and Karen was a marketing major and has never left the country. That said I don't really know anything about ISIS, what I do know is a hundred Turkish verbs that begin with *k*, but I have half-listened to many lectures and panels that I try to recall now. "Well, a lot of people don't think that ISIS really counts as an Islamic group," I say as I suck down my drink, quickly because the taste of almonds makes me gag. "They kill a lot of people who are Muslim." "But they're running a whole country on Islamic Law," Cindy tells me. "That's the whole thing they want." "There are a lot of different interpretations of what Islamic Law means," I say. "Some people think they are actually operating more like a nation state, like they decide what they want to do and then they find the justification for it later. Like, the uh, U.S. does."

I can feel the booze zip like a friendly fire through my veins. "It's kind of like if we want to blow up some person in another country we do it and then we do some law thing to make it legal afterward." This feels like the wrong tack. There is a litany anyone who is interested in the "Muslim world" aka a huge swath of the known world knows: Without Islam we wouldn't have algebra or astronomy. Or Plato, whom the Arab scholars brought forth from obscurity for the Europeans to froth over.

Not to mention we wouldn't have Hafez or Rumi or Yunus Emre or Ibn Khaldun. We wouldn't have the Registan or the Dome of the Rock or the Umayyad Mosque—well, that's gone now I think. I go with "Muslims consider Jesus a prophet too, you know." Cindy rolls her eyes but Ed says "Well, that's interesting. Huh. I did not know that." But I'm not done, I'm drunk and I must now issue my verbal Facebook meme. "There are over a billion Muslims including my husband's family and the majority of them don't want anything to do with ISIS or even know what ISIS is about," I say, with a pang as I picture again his wounded expression, his onetime Barış Manço mustache or maybe it's Erkin Koray who had the mustache. But what I know from my deceased dad is that diplomacy is hard and requires dissembling and betrayal.

Ed also did not know this and it prompts Cindy to give him the rough and basically sympathetic outline of Engin's visa situation during which Honey begins kicking. She squirms off my lap and I give her half of *The Very Hungry Caterpillar*, the half with the one apple two pears three plums four strawberries five oranges. She sits next to my right foot and turns these pages and sticks her little index finger through the holes that the very hungry caterpillar made. I order a greyhound. It's nice to be in a bar, it's nice to talk to people, even these people, it's nice when your baby is sitting nicely behaved on the floor of the bar.

"So what do you think we should do about ISIS then?" Ed asks me and Jesus, ISIS, ISIS, ISIS, what fear we're all living with. "I don't think anyone has a good answer," I say. "Sometimes I think we should just hammer the shit out of them and Bashar al-Assad too" and Ed laughs and we all cheers and I feel savage and parochial and bad, all this activated so quickly by $4 punch. Why do Americans always go back to the bomb. I feel my face bloom into a glorious Irish sunrise.

Honey is on her feet and halfway out of the bar before I register her absence, mostly from Cindy's expression, and I turn to see as she trips and falls over the hummock where the linoleum of the bar ends and the patterned floral wall-to-wall of the restaurant begins. She pops up like a top and begins brushing her hands anxiously the way she does now when she falls down, but I sense immediately through the Irish sunrise that something is different. Unlike with most of her falls she starts yelling, one anguished yell followed by a silence that I know portends real screaming. I lunge for her, knocking the table with my ass and sending the greyhound onto the seat where I'd been sitting. I run across the bar and squat down and try to wrap her up in my arms but she is frantically wiping one hand on my chest and screaming like I've never heard. A streak of blood appears on the placket of my white shirt and my stomach becomes a lump of plutonium. I cannot get her to hold her hand still. I see the hostess and Cindy hovering in my peripheral vision, the hostess holding out a napkin which I take without looking at her. "Oh my sweet baby my sweet Honey, show Mama your finger," but I still cannot get her to hold still and finally have to grip her wrist very hard to see that the fat part of her tiny middle finger, her little grape, has torn open. Her sounds are no longer supported by the scaffolding of crying and are just awful rhythmic shouts. I look up and the hostess points to the corner and the bathroom. I bundle up the baby and smash her hand to my chest and run through the dining room where there are about five tables of people. I stumble on the way and hear the clatter of silverware as a man in a cowboy hat swiftly stands to intervene, but I right myself before he can take my arm and I say "Thank you" and keep running. I shut the door behind me and lock it set Honey on the counter and turn on the faucet. "Amee-amee-amee" she says, which I think is Mommy, and she looks at me with an expression that is equal parts puzzlement and pain, and she cries again and continues to wipe her finger on my chest as blood wells up again and again, and my body tenses as I imagine the flap tearing further through her agitation and I know that if I do not get a hold of myself I will throw myself around this bathroom like a terrible screeching missile and I have to settle and suddenly I do, I am calm, and I say "It's okay." "It's okay, baby." "It's okay." It occurs to me that she has never seen blood in quantity before, never had any kind of bleeding injury, and I see that after she wipes a new red gout onto my shirt she uses her other hand to try and wipe it off. I have to angle her body down and forcibly hold her arm straight to get it under the cold faucet and droplets of blood spatter as she flails. Someone I think is Cindy knocks on the door and says "I've got a first aid kit here" and I open the door with one hand on writhing Honey on the counter and take the proffered kit. Cindy muscles in and raises an eyebrow. "Think she needs stitches?" she says, looking at my shirt. "I . . . think with a cut like this you are supposed to do cold water and then see if the bleeding will stop." The toilet paper mechanism rattles as I snatch a long trail of toilet paper. "I have this toilet paper," I tell her moronically. I hold Honey's arm hard enough there will certainly be a bruise and I endeavor to isolate the wounded finger from its mates, and see that blood continues to well out of the flap. Cindy puts a stabilizing hand on Honey's shoulder and I twist the toilet paper around the finger in a lumpy, inelegant turban.

I survey the blood on the counter and in the sink and the drops on the floor and point out to myself with the impeccable logic of the drunk and frazzled that there is more blood because I have been drinking and drinking thins the blood, before I remember that it is in fact Honey's blood, and Honey hasn't been drinking, only me. "If . . . if you could just bring me my bag I have some hand sanitizer and some wipes I can use to clean up." Cindy looks at Honey, who has, thank sweet God above, restored some of her natural composure and is pointing at the little puddles of blood on the counter and saying "Dah! Dah! Dah!" and backs out of the bathroom. The sound of Honey's cheery normal voice leaves me rubbery, the adrenaline flowing out like blood down the drain of a slaughterhouse. I perch Honey on my hip and hug her and say "What a good, brave girl, what a scary thing, so good and so brave." She begins crying again but in a more controlled way when I try to look at the toilet paper to see if the blood has soaked through. A bird's-eye inspection shows a bloom of blood on the inner layers, but none have breached the integrity of the outer layers.

I say "shhhhhhhh" to her and I smooth the damp hair down at the back of her head and across her forehead and she puts her head against my neck and then rears it back to smile into my face and say "Eeeeh," pointing at my chest and the blood all over my shirt and the skin of my neck with a tiny adult kind of concern, as though she's saying "Oh dear, Mommy, you've soiled your shirt." I look in the mirror and I see a murder victim, a mugshot, my hair a nest and blood everywhere.

I wish Engin could see. I want to take a picture but it would be too cruel to send him. But just for me to remember, I fish my phone out of my pocket and take a gruesome portrait of mother with daughter.

Cindy is back at the door with the bag in one hand and the half of *The Very Hungry Caterpillar* in the other. I take the book first and set it on the counter away from the blood. I have been working to compose my face and as I reach for the bag I look at her and say "I'm so sorry—we crashed your and Ed's date and then made this big fuss." I smile with the corners of my mouth turned down ruefully and hope for an answering smile but she just says "Kids are hard" and I realize I don't know whether she has any. I set Honey down on her feet and she holds on to my legs and puts her face between my knees. I get out the wipes from the bag and the hand sanitizer and I wipe away the blood and then squirt little plops of sanitizer down onto the counter. "You oughta think about a tetanus shot for her," Cindy says, which unaccountably annoys me, of course she has had her damn shots, I even know the exact date because that's the kind of thing I remember. "She had her second TDAP shot on the sixteenth of last month," trying to sound authoritative. Honey raises her little arms to me and begins making her "heh heh heh" want-want-want sound and I pat her head and swiftly wipe away the last smear of blood from the bowl of the sink and run the faucet and pack away the wipes and the sanitizer and the half of *The Very Hungry Caterpillar* and pick up Honey and put her on my hip and kiss her hand and put her backpack over my shoulder and brush past Cindy who holds the door open. "Thank you," I say. "I'll just settle up." When I exit the corridor into the restaurant the tables of patrons and the hostess look in my direction and I remember that I am covered in blood. The martyred Honey smiles a big smile and waves her wrapped-up mitt in the air and there is scattered applause for the baby. I want to disappear from the surface of the earth, I want soft merciful darkness to envelop Honey and me both. "Sorry about that," I say to everyone, "We're okay!" and walk in measured steps to the hostess stand where I give her my debit card and ask if I can pay for one Picon punch one greyhound and Ed and Cindy's drinks plus tip, approximately thirty dollars down the slaughterhouse drain too. "Better stay out here, ha ha," I tell her, because I am not setting foot back in the bar. Ed waves kindly from his seat. "They got a carpenter's nail sticking out of that carpeting," he says. "Must have snagged the finger on that." "Did we get a little booboo," says the hostess, who is a majestic figure of a woman nearly six feet tall with broad shoulders blond hair and weathered pink skin. Honey is now in full lover mode, smiling and then ducking her face toward my neck and peeking up through lashes. Thank God. "That's what I get for bringing her into the bar, haha," I say, and scuttle out after signing my slip and putting my card into my pocket. "We'll get Emilio to hammer that down, anyone could just trip over it, imagine me and my sandals!" says the hostess to my retreating figure. "You okay to drive, hon?" Cindy calls from the table. "We walked here—it takes five minutes. Thanks for your help!" Big smile, big smile and wave to Cindy and Ed, big wave to the folks.

I pause in the anteroom with the little piano and put my back against the wall by the door, out of sight of the main dining room, and slump, a slump that translates itself to Honey, who puts her head on my shoulder and her injured paw on my other shoulder and inspects her new appendage. I smell her hair which has its puppy smell and then put her down to pack away my wallet her diaper shit and prepare us for maximum efficient travel on foot.

I carry her out the door down the concrete steps and into a vast lavender sky and hot dry air that saps the remaining vitality I had counted on to carry us home. We walk through the parking lot and stop at the road while a truck barrels past. My heart suddenly starts pounding. I picture myself and Honey under the wheels of the truck, all her bright red blood outside of her body, her limbs mangled, and start crying. She puts her hand on my face with her toilet paper mitten and I walk fast, nearing a run as we pass the railroad tracks. My arms are beginning to falter as we round the circle toward the house and I'm gasping for the last twenty-five yards and then finally we are inside and I've illuminated every lamp before I realize neither of us has eaten anything. After debating with myself for three minutes about how best to approach the wound I find Band-Aids in the medicine cabinet and steel my entire body and wet the toilet paper and ease it off, during which Honey screams, and more blood oozes. I wipe the flap with a Beta-dine wipe and she screams more and starts wiping the finger on my chest again, and the blood streams. "I can't fucking do this again," I say to the empty room, to no one. We go to the sink and wash the finger again, and she cries. But then, mira-cle, as though she's already grasped the basics of what needs to happen, she actually holds out her finger for me to look at and wipe with some gauze and dab on some cream and more or less wrap a Band-Aid around it. What a smart baby. I put Saran Wrap around the mitt and affix it with a tiny strip of Scotch tape. I fix scrambled eggs. I cut an apple. Honey, smart baby, knows to eat with her other hand.

I give her a warm washcloth bath and take the Saran Wrap off. I hold her tight and we read *The Little Blue Truck*, which is about a truck that stops to help a mean dump truck when a bunch of farm animals leave the truck stranded in some mud. "This is not a good message," I tell Honey. "Really we should help people even if they don't deserve it." That's what Little Blue Truck was doing; whether the farm animals absorbed this lesson or not is unclear. But maybe Little Blue was just helping a fellow *truck*. I put her in the Pack 'n Play. I go on the porch to smoke a cigarette and remember for probably the third time today that I am married.

Honey looks so much like Engin, came out looking so much like him in the way that children are said to resemble their fathers for troubling evolutionary reasons. And even though I carried Honey and gave birth to her and nursed her and pour my life into her sometimes I look at her beautiful small face and wonder if I'm her mother. Then I try and feel for one moment what it would feel to be almost seven thousand miles away from her and I wonder that Engin has not boarded a plane and fought his way through a battalion of U.S. Citizenship and Immigration Services officers to be with her and a fury settles like a cloud of horseflies on the image of his face before I think this is a horribly unfair thought to have.

Here are the ways I have imagined Honey dying: she stands up on a chair and the chair tips back and crashes through the window and the glass shatters and pierces her throat. She stands up on a chair and the chair tips back and crashes through the window and she falls two stories and shatters on the pavement. She darts out into the street like a panicked cat and gets crushed by a bus. She strangles in the blind cords. We fly to Turkey and someone blows a hole in the fuselage or the pilot reaches the nadir of a years-long spiritual torment and drives the plane into a mountainside or the pitot tubes freeze up and the inexperienced pilot who knows something is wrong is overruled by his imperious boss who was in the bathroom and has no idea what the fuck is going on but always has to have the last word and the plane speeds into the ocean. I give her a tortilla and she folds it up and crams it into her mouth all at once and stops breathing. The ceiling fan comes loose from its 1920s moorings and crushes her skull while she eats breakfast. We visit my father-in-law and he doesn't pay attention and she is swept away by the sea. We go anywhere and I don't pay attention and someone spirits her away. I go to work and forget to bring her to daycare and she roams the house screaming until she falls down the stairs and breaks her neck. I go to work and the Big One hits and I can't get home to her and she dies in the wreckage of her daycare with all the other babies. We go to Istanbul and some demented widow from Dagestan blows herself up and Honey is scattered across the pavement. We stay here and she goes to school and some demented teen takes his dipshit mother's unsecured assault rifle and fires rounds and rounds of bullets into her body and her classmates' bodies. She rides a bus across Bulgaria and the bus veers off the road and flies into a concrete barrier. Her cells suddenly decide to murder her with mad replication. She gets in a taxi outside of Diyarbakır and a van crosses the median. Why did I have a child? To have a child is to court loss.

DAY 6   For some reason I wake up on my own at 5:00 a.m. exhausted but alert. I go in the closet and look at Honey who is sleeping peacefully with her hand over her head, the Band-Aid brown with dried blood, and I go onto the porch with a cigarette. It is a breathtaking Paiute morning, the air is so cool, so thin that the call of a bird or a human voice would carry the hundred miles to the place where the mountains rise out of the plains. The sky is streaked with pink and the smell of juniper is tempered with some other freshness, some hint of a cooler season to come. There are three deer in Cindy's yard, picking their legs through the damp grass with grace that belies their witless expressions. I sit for a minute and feel the whole-body feeling of place-love, and the smoke from my cigarette lingers discreetly in the morning air.

But then I come back to earth and it is Monday and obvious that I am going to have to do something regarding my place of work and explaining why I am not at it, in addition to my potentially lost income of $69,500 which is my family's primary income. What is interesting is that under normal circumstances examining our finances and being hyperaware of every sum available to us is one of my primary interests and hobbies in life but in the past six days I have assiduously avoided thinking about it at all, namely the fact that $1,700 is due for our apartment and $1,100 for daycare, both of which are far below the

market rate and contingent on the health and/or goodwill of
the price-setters, which could change at any moment, and if
we go to Turkey after all or Engin makes his way back here
that will be $900 for the plane ticket if we are lucky which will
have to go on the credit card. I lug out the laptop and log on to
the banking portal and take stock which is $268 in checking
with $176 available after two nights at the Golden Spike.

It is nearing the end of the month and I can assume that the
University has not gotten wise to my job abandonment and thus
that my full monthly salary is forthcoming on the first which
after my mandatory retirement contribution taxes healthcare will
be $3,316 which after daycare and rent leaves $516 which is
never quite enough for phones and utilities and the food we are
all three eating on two different continents and hopefully
Engin will get one of his periodic but not totally reliable pay-
ments from Tolga et al. And there is the mobile home obviously
with its current list price of $80,000 down from $99,900 but
it's not something to bank on although Christ that would be a
windfall. I read in the news that some huge percentage of Americans can't find $400 in an emergency so in the grand scheme
of things we are really doing astonishingly well, a thought that
both bolsters me at the intimate nuclear family level but demor-
alizes me at the citizenship human family level. I'd wager some
huger percentage of Altavista residents can't cobble together
$400 but then again Cindy Cooper owns her own mobile home
and goes to the Golden Spike every Sunday for $4 Picon punch
with her lover so maybe she's sitting pretty, who knows.

It occurs to me now in full force that if I do in fact abandon
my job I will lose my gold-plated university health insurance
and I conservatively estimate that whatever alternate mecha-

nism I take advantage of if I do not resume the job will be $700 per month if we stay here, and what if one of my dire nighttime imaginings comes true, what if we are sickened or maimed, what then?

I look at the Institute e-mail and see 165 unread e-mails which is actually better than I expected, it is 5:32 a.m. and I could conceivably read through all of these before Honey wakes up. I have the brief and insane idea that I could just work "from home" here in Altavista and not have to pay rent in the City but there are several reasons why that won't work one being that Hugo would never allow it, he likes to have as many attractive and competent women bustling around his person as possible, and I'm still highly competent at least and Hugo assures me in his ludicrously inappropriate way that I will return to myself as long as I don't have any other children. Two being Internet which is needed in order to access the VPN that will get me on the network drives. The final and most important thing is Honey because I obviously can't sit in front of the computer while she just rolls around on the floor all day, although I often stare at my phone while she rolls around the floor. If I am going to work anyway and Honey is not going to have my attention she may as well go back to daycare and I may as well go back to the office and we may as well wash all the bedding and fold it up and sweep the floor and mop it and vacuum the carpet and make Grandma and Grandpa's bed and tape some cardboard over the soft place on the bathroom windowsill and turn down the thermostat and set the timer on the lights and lock and close the doors behind us.

Or we could go somewhere else. There is something almost sexually pleasing about this thought. I could take thirty-five dollars from the checking and go to Joie de Vivre which is the town's sole beauty establishment and have my hair washed and blown out and I could moisturize my face with the ancient cold cream in the bathroom cabinet and iron my white blouse and put on Grandma's jet-black fur coat from Gray Reid's in Reno circa 1972 and put Honey in her overalls and we could polish up the Buick and hit the road and go somewhere where we will step out and really be somebody.

I am feeling deeply criminal about my absence from work but the truth according to my lizard brain is that it is nearly impossible to be fired from the University, I mean various Vice Provosts are always groping their colleagues and it takes years before any action is taken. Moreover Hugo and Meredith are so divorced from the Deep Administrative State, HR and Purchasing and so forth—a sort of parallel army of administrators with less education who all the specialized administrators like ourselves loathe and condescend to—and since both Hugo and Meredith often contravene every employment rule by having me fill out their HR paperwork for raises promotions etc., not to mention my own performance evaluations, it's highly unlikely they could get it together to file the piece of paper that would for example inform Payroll that I was gone.

When I think about all this some muscle in the exact center of my body constricts. I do not want to fill out any more paperwork of any kind. I do not want to be referred to as Assistant in anyone's e-mail. I do not want to look at the CV of a stranger and google them and write a letter of recommendation based on this information and sign someone else's name to it, someone who has known this person and read their papers and met with them privately and in classroom settings for

seven years. I do not want to deal with THE CONFER-
ENCE for weeks culminating in having to stand in front of a
room full of people sweating trying to make someone's Power-
Point work because they didn't let anyone know in advance
that they needed audio. I cannot manage both my own sense
of being over- and underutilized and that of Karen who shares
my every grievance but makes 40 percent less money. I cannot
hear Brad our central campus fundraising guy exclaim "Salam
Alaikum" with his arms flung open in wide embrace whenever
a rich Muslim visits the Institute. I cannot escort the Al-Ihsan
guy around the campus with his hand on my elbow. Crucially,
I cannot go in and meet with the Office of Risk Management
to give my testimony regarding the Simpson and Khoury
families' pending litigation regarding the taxi to the Fidan-
lik Park refugee camp outside of Diyarbakır. Another brain,
not the lizard, tells me that this last one is the one thing that I
actually have to do.

It is already 7:15 when I have done a rough inventory of
e-mails and Honey will coo any minute so I go inside and wash
my hands and slice a banana into very exact half-inch slices and
get out two eggs, so many eggs we are eating, too many eggs,
and fly around the house picking things up. We didn't bring
very much stuff up here but what we did bring has multiplied in
the way of children's things and there are single socks and stuffed
animals I don't even remember packing and books and the
ubiquitous halves of *The Very Hungry Caterpillar* and the many
bibs and wipes I use to wipe her nose which is always runny
but which the pediatrician assures me is no cause for concern.

She wakes. Breakfast. Change the dressing of her finger, a
circumstance to which she has already adjusted, the lamb.

Every time I get used to something with Honey it changes, which I am told by BabyCenter is normal, so I do not have a real sense of when her naptime is anymore—it used to be very regular back when she had two, but now I don't really know if she has two still or wants to have them. Sometimes I put her in and she talks to herself for an hour and sleeps for thirty minutes and sometimes she sleeps for three hours. I don't know. On our morning walk to Sal's I put her in the Ergo frontways, she's almost too big for this configuration and dangles off me like an overgrown appendage but I love carrying her like this, I feel so secure with her right on my front, and she rubs her eyes and rubs her eyes and yawns and looks grumpily drunkenly up at me and by the time we arrive at the hotel she has actually gone to sleep. I don't want to deny her or myself this bonus nap so I wonder if I sit gingerly I might open the computer and see if I can't answer one of the 165 e-mails. The crone is not yet here, only a tidy-looking man who looks exactly like my uncle Rodney with a beard and a tucked-in T-shirt and cell phone holster and definitely a gun somewhere, reading the paper and eating a muffin. I order coffee and a glass of water.

My phone buzzes to life in the Wi-Fi enabled sanctuary. Daycare writes to me on WeChat. "We were worried about Honey," she says, and I feel a pulse of shame so strong I worry it will wake the sleeping baby in her pouch. "I'm so sorry," I type. "She is fine. We went on a trip to my grandparents. We will be back hopefully next week," I say, which I hope is true. "Please do not worry, she is fine." She sends me an emoji of a cat holding a rose and a checkmark that says "OK."

I decide to address Meredith and Hugo. I find the last of each of their e-mails and see something from Hugo about can

I deal with getting his honorarium expedited from someplace where he went to give a lecture about Casualties of Capital which is not my job but Karen is on vacation. "Dear Meredith and Hugo," I write. "I want to apologize for my absence of the last few days—Honey and I have been ill and now to compound this my grandmother is also very ill, so we are in her hometown trying to sort out her medical situation. There isn't reliable Internet so I have been a little out of reach. I will of course be taking these days as sick time but will check over my e-mail and take care of anything that is urgent. Please let me know if either of you need anything at all." I hope Karen is having a nice vacation from constantly upgrading Hugo's flights against all state and institutional regulations and fighting to get justification signatures from the relevant authorities after the fact.

I think the lie will fly—I have never to my knowledge mentioned the deadness of my grandparents and in fact Hugo has already written back. "Take as much time as you need" and I feel an embarrassing surge of gratitude and shame. They are actually always very nice and accommodating to me. Then I just feel relieved about my reprieve, as though I have already absorbed my right to this caretaking time for a grandmother who has in fact been dead for years. When my grandmother actually died it was a relief because she had been married to my grandfather for almost sixty years and when he died it was obvious she had no reason to go on. The thought of Engin and me being married for sixty years and dying of grief at the other's passing seems vanishingly small but I close my eyes for a moment and try to picture it, we are in our stone shack by the Aegean, Honey is there, she has a family, is her family Turkish?

Is she? Do we have any other kids? I open my eyes, momentarily overwhelmed. Better to just picture an ancient version of Engin and me on a bench under an olive tree not saying anything at all. I briefly picture us on the couch in the mobile home and then I'm done daydreaming for the time being. I put my chin gently on the top of Honey's head for a moment and give her hair a sniff.

The crone has come! She scoots the door open with one whole side of her body and is in by the time I make a half-hearted move to stand up and get it for her. She takes one very slow step at a time, holding a cane before her. Her back is ramrod straight, and she is very petite and wearing a white turtleneck and a navy skirt and white Reeboks with an ample sole. I am transfixed by her but when she reaches the table next to us I snap from the reverie and half-stand and pull a seat out for her. "The little one is sleeping," she observes. "Normally she's squirming around." This seems like a promising acknowledgment of our past interactions. She goes up to the counter and orders something and shuffles back and sits down. "How old is she?" "Sixteen months last week," I say very brightly. "Sweet little Turkish baby," she says. "Well," I say. "Half Turkish, half Californian!" She sits down at the table next to the one where I'm standing and I seat myself taking care not to jostle Honey who is still doing her little-big baby snores in my chest.

"Where are you from?" I venture.

"I'm from a little town in the Rockies. But now I live on a farm near Lake Michigan."

"By yourself?" I wonder aloud.

"More or less. I have some friends who kind of look after me. Family friends." She looks down at her hands and there's a long pause. "They are in a snit with me about this trip. I drove all the way out here myself, if you can believe it. They didn't want me to do it." This genuinely shocks me, and it registers on my face which is always registering things and she gives a kind of harrumphing laugh.

"How long did that take you?"

"Something like two weeks. First I stopped in my home-town."

"And why . . . here," I say, I mean of all places.

"During the war my husband worked not too far from here, in a forestry camp." I must have looked quizzical. "He was a conscientious objector. A pacifist, you know. They had camps for them out here." "Huh," I say. The only camp I know of that is near here is the Tule Lake internment camp where they put Japanese-Americans which nobody here ever talks about I don't think. Honey stirs but then settles back in, her body dragging down on the straps of the Ergo.

"I visited him one time before we were married, before our kids. It was maybe the nicest trip we ever took together. I just got a yen to see the place again, I guess."

"But your friends didn't want you to come."

"No," she says. "It took me weeks to convince them. They have medical power of attorney, so they might have been able to stop me, but we finally came to an agreement. I'm supposed to take my medicine and call them every day," which seems fair to me. She looks over at the counter where Sal has produced a coffee and a hideous slab of brownie. I stand and trot up to get them, taking care not to jostle Honey. My new friend spears a corner of the brownie with a fork and brings it to her mouth with an incredibly gnarled but reasonably steady hand. I wait. There is something odd but not unpleasant about what's going on. She doesn't seem to care whether I'm there or not and for once I have no anxiety about divining whether that is the case. Honey is asleep and work thinks I'm bereaved and things seem just fine in this particular moment. Sal comes around and wipes a table adjacent with a rag and as she passes by I smell vinegar from the rag.

"There was a while when driving a car was the only thing that didn't hurt," the crone says. I want to ask how old she is but that seems rude. "I'm ninety-two," she says, as though I had spoken aloud. "I went to the library and had the librarian search the Internet for 'old people' and 'road trips' and she found an article about some hundred-year-old fool jogging across the country. I showed Mark and Yarrow the printout." I laugh aloud. She looks disdainfully at the rest of the brownie. "Those are my caretakers," she adds. "Mark and Yarrow."

"Like the flower," I say. I must know that from my mom. "Yes, just like," she says. "They have a little boy named Rain. They are hippie types, you might say." She chips more of the brownie off and pushes the debris onto the tines of her fork.

"I'm kind of stalled out now, though," she says. "I seem to have run out of steam for getting in the car. It hurts a lot more. So I'm here taking a break before pushing on."

"What a place to take a break," I say. "The end of the earth!" She looks around at the café.

"It has changed a lot from what I remember. We would have been here around forty-five."

"That's what everyone says," I say.

The door to Sal's opens and the teens I saw walking a few days ago come in and elevate the level of noise in the place and Honey stirs against me.

"What brings you here?" she asks.

"My mom was from here. She's gone now and I inherited my grandparents' house. I just came up to see how everything was looking."

"My hometown was kind of the same way," she says. I love the extemporaneous way she talks, she's like an Oracle breathing fumes from a vent. "I knocked on the door of my old house—a woman was there living with her son. It was a mess, pizza boxes everywhere. Slatternly, my mother would have said. There had been a tree out in the back that I just loved, I used to sit on a swing tied to its big branch, but it was gone." She pushes the plate with the brownie toward me and says "You can have this if you want" and I pull it toward myself because I always need a treat. "They seemed very unhappy in the house. I guess my family wasn't very happy either, but my mother always was one for housekeeping." She dabs her mouth with her napkin. "What's the line, 'Unhappy families are unhappy in their own way'?" I scan my brain. "Tolstoy," I say. Or Dostoyevsky? I should know. She nods. "Anyway, I saw the house and I just decided to keep on going till I got somewhere I wanted to be," she says. "Westward ho!" She grins a surprisingly vital and grin-like grin for such an old person. She's beautiful, I think.

"Where are you staying?" I ask.

"The Arrowhead Motel, it's called." She raises her eyebrows. "It's passable."

Her eyes focus on me. "Where do you live when you aren't here?" she asks.

"We live in the City—San Francisco," I say. Honey is suddenly awake and squirmy. Her body is strong enough that she can put considerable strain on the Ergo when she decides she wants to be free and I have to stand and dance and hush her.

The crone reaches a hand out to touch Honey's foot, which Honey swiftly kicks away, and I grab it and hold it tight and say "Gentle" and the crone's hand stays hovering in the air, grasping at nothing. Then she pats around her person and her hair and then very slowly and stiffly stands up and says "Well, I'm off" and starts to shuffle away without so much as a by-your-leave. Normally I would wonder whether I offended her but there is Honey to deal with and I take Honey out of the pack and give her a string cheese and set her down, and she stumbles and puts both hands on the ground with her butt in the air and comes up with hair and fuzz all over the cheese. I dip a napkin into my water glass and wipe it off more or less and return it to her. We open the computer and Skype Engin. He clicks on and I see he is somewhere not his mother's, appears to be smoking a cigarette on an unknown balcony with café lights and I wonder whose balcony what balcony and then I think Jesus he gets to have *fun*, and feel momentarily so pissed and bewildered that someone could be out there having fun at a party instead of drinking with Islamophobes and dealing with torn baby fingers but his face lights up when he blows kisses to Honey and she looks at him and waves furiously and they babble to each other and I again say a small prayer of thanks that she doesn't break his heart by being indifferent to the sight of him on the screen. Then he looks at me and says "My love." And I say it back and then he says "I was hoping when you opened the computer there would be some news but based on the view you haven't gone home yet." "No," I say. "I'm paralyzed. I'm the nymph who turned into a tree."

I don't remember the Turkish word for nymph so I say the latter in English and he looks puzzled but I decide not to clarify
and say "I just need a few more days to make a plan."

"The church was depressing," I go on. "Only six people.
We left early."

"It's depressing there," he says. "You should go home." He
looks exasperated and despairing and I feel like screaming and
I ask where he is and he says Sema his friend from high school
is having a party and then I remember again how much he gave
up to come and marry me, a whole life lived in one city and all
the dense social webs thus accumulated, and what it must feel
like when they are severed and now what it feels like to try and
repair them all. "I'll go back this week," I say, and he communes
a little longer with Honey and asks what happened to her finger
and I tell him she fell and that's it and then I let him go back to
his balcony party, the lights of the city glittering behind him.

I allow Honey to run around a little outside Sal's on the wide
empty sidewalk and then I hold her hand and we slowly walk
to the little town park which is farther down the road from the
hotel, just before the turn to the Desert Sunrise casino and
which I had forgotten about until now. She runs into the grass
and back in the trees is lo and behold a tiny playground and she
screams, actually screams with joy and runs clumsily toward it
and I laugh at the transformation and then immediately
think Christ what an asshole I am that we haven't just gone to
the damn playground. I get her into one of the baby swings
and push her and first she looks thrilled but then as she feels
her stomach drop her face crumples and she cries and strains
her arms toward me and I feel sad that she might be a physical
coward like me consigned to hate amusement parks and I give

her another little push to see if she will acclimate but she wails and I pick her up and hold her close and we stand together looking at the slide and agree we will try that one next time.

I put her back in the Ergo and we start the walk home and I remember the library, a teeny-tiny cheerful brick-fronted building near the cemetery, and we detour there. An elderly woman with short white hair is sitting at a cramped desk inside and she greets us pleasantly and asks what we are looking for. I ask whether I can use my San Francisco library card and she says she'll have to make up a new one for Paiute which takes five seconds since it's a piece of paper she fills out with a pencil. I scan the bulletin board with notes about job placements and the "Tour of Europe" evening program. I check out some board books for Honey, so worn they feel like fabric, and I find *Anna Karenina* and check the line and I was right it is Tolstoy and I get that and *Jurassic Park* because I want something my brain can just kind of ooze over without effort.

We get home and I want to give Honey a nap but she had the weird morning nap and she appears now to be full of beans so I let her run around the yard, and I sit against the base of the deck, immobilized by boredom and desperate for a cigarette. I remember my new books but I'm not feeling up for the unhappy families different in their own way so I start in on *Jurassic Park* darting my eyes up at Honey now and again and then I see Cindy come out of her house looking unusually spruce in a jacket and purple blouse tucked into her jeans.

"How's the baby's finger," she asks me, and I point to Honey on the grass, proof of life. "It's fine. We cleaned it out and she has a nice Band-Aid. She's being a big girl." Cindy nods. "That's good," she says. "Nasty cut."

"Thanks again for helping us with that," I say. "I was terrified," and she just grunts.

"Where are you off to looking so nice?" I ask. "Board of Supervisors," she tells me. "It's the vote today."

"Are they actually voting to leave the state of California today?" I was too interested in the letters in the paper to apprehend this fact. "No," says Cindy. "This is the first in a series of steps," sounding like she's reading off a cue card. "It's not a resolution or an ordinance, just basically the Board saying they will support our efforts this way and take it to the legislature and hopefully get them to pass a bill."

"And so they're going to vote to see if they all agree to do this?"

"That's right."

"Down at the courthouse?" The courthouse is a rather incongruous temple on a street parallel to Main Street in the middle of town, visible from the playground we grumped around in earlier.

"That's right," she says. I feel flickers of curiosity and concern. I have the rogue thought that I'm a property owner and thus have rights in this decision. Then I feel unconsulted and obscurely furious. "Maybe I'll come too."

She looks impassive. "Well, I'm driving and I don't have much room." She's so rude.

"Oh, I don't mean with you. I'll just wheel her in the stroller, it's only twenty minutes."

"Well okay then." I do not feel any particular warmth from Cindy and wonder if it's the drinks and the blood at the Golden Spike or my crypto-Muslim husband or if she's just not a very warm person or if it's a reflection of the warmth that I am directing at her. I always forget that I am walking around and can be seen and heard just like everyone else. I remember how Sal said "She's not nice but we love her anyway."

I get Honey into the stroller and it only takes us twenty-two minutes to get to the courthouse moving at a brisker pace than I can really handle. I'm panting when we get there and worried we're late but I behold Cindy again, seated on the front steps smoking and looking impassive.

"Hi again" I say, with the feeling of being at a party and clinging to the one person who will talk to you.

"Smoke?" she says. "Later," I say, gesturing at the baby. Honey wants to get out of her stroller so I take her out and set her on the lawn in front of the courthouse and give her a string cheese, how many string cheeses has it been today, I try to figure, too many in any event. She toddles and bites hunks off the cheese and then lets the macerated pieces tumble out of her mouth into the grass, from which she retrieves them.

"Are you going to give a presentation?" I ask Cindy, who has the look of someone who is getting ready to give a presentation. "Not me," she says. "Bruce McNamara's supposed to say something. We've been writing 'em letters and I don't know what all for weeks, as you know." "Like your letter in the paper." "And to the supervisors, and everyone else."

People are coming up the walkway now, and Cindy trails off. More people than I've ever seen in one place in Altavista—more people than I've seen, total, in the whole time I've been here. There is a group of elderly women with very short hair, and a group of middle-aged women with very long hair. Most everyone is white, there are four or five people who are brown but no one who appears to be black. Cindy nods hello to a clump of three gray-haired men in cowboy hats and mustaches who seem in a hurry to get into the courthouse.

"There are so many people I don't know here," I say, because I can't think of anything else to say.

"Well, you know," says Cindy. "Not everyone lives in town. Lot of ranchers came from Rigby and Sundown and those places"—tiny towns beside which Altavista is a metropolis.

"Also I doubt you'd know many people in town now," she says, not unkindly. "Haven't really seen you up here that I can remember. Since your mom died, I mean."

"Yeah," I say. "I guess you never met my husband's family when I brought them up last year."

"Can't recollect I did," she says, sounding awfully like a cowboy for someone from San Bernardino. She pulls on her cigarette.

A Ford truck pulls up and discharges a very tall, very thin woman in a red blazer with a sportswomanlike braid down her back. "Goddamn," Cindy sighs, "it's that cunt" and I visibly startle. "Sorry," Cindy says.

"What cunt?" I ask superfluously, just to feel the word, the little charge of tongue meeting teeth as the word goes out into the air. "She's from way over the coast, big ranching family." "Why is she, uh, a c-word?" I ask.

"She was helping us to get organized for Jefferson but she won't stop talking about the UN and some agenda they have that they are planning to do that she says is gonna have us all in chains by the year 2030. Don't get me wrong I hate the damned UN but it's a distraction when we need to be talking about *our* state." "Oh," I say, idly wondering why she hates the UN, my mom looked askance at the UN because the UN representatives

always had the nicest house and biggest car of whatever post-
ing they found themselves in. Honey runs toward me laughing, a sunburst, a comet, barking her shins on the first step
and falling into my knees, still more or less laughing. I pull her
up into my lap and kiss the top of her head with the puppy
smell that she has after a while with no bath. She is writhing
to get down and play again. She coughs and Cindy holds her
cigarette up over her head. I'm desperate for a puff.

The Cunt walks up the steps and into the courthouse, nod-
ding coolly at Cindy who raises a surprisingly regal hand in its
purple sleeve. "Hi, ladies," says the Cunt. "Howdy," I say for no
reason I can name. "See you inside, Cindy?" she says cheerily.
I gather Honey and hold her wriggling like a big trout while
I collapse the stroller which doesn't fold over the diaper bag so I
have to unfold it get out the bag throw it over my shoulder collapse the stroller while Cindy heaves herself up from the steps
and straightens herself out. We walk up the stairs behind the
Cunt, who strides purposefully up to the imposing paneled door.

"Is she gonna do a presentation?" I ask Cindy. "That's what I'm
worried about," says Cindy. "She doesn't live here and she wasn't
at our last meeting when we planned out who was supposed to
say what. I'm not good at public speaking so it was never gonna
be me, but McNamara's real good, and Donna Elkins, and
Chad Burns." I don't think Cindy is really even talking to me—
she's muttering, and I don't know who Donna Elkins is and have
only the faintest awareness of Chad Burns, someone's cousin.

The courthouse is nice and cool under its friendly little rotunda. I unfold the stroller and put Honey back into it and wheel
it after Cindy into one of the beige rooms in which municipal
business is conducted and we see already fifteen or twenty people

seated. Cindy spots her group and goes to join them. "We'll just sit over there," I say, gesturing to the back of the room.

Honey is the only small child here except for a very young baby sleeping in a Snugli, and Honey is starting to rustle and moan. I do my customary calculation of suffering whereas X is the suffering of those around me and Y is the suffering of Honey and Z is the suffering of me, and I assess each component suffering as it is affected by the available scenarios, where A is taking her out and wheeling her back to the house toward the looming dark to sit on the porch under the enormous purple sky with her morose mother drinking screwdrivers, and B is staying here and observing democracy taking place as is her and my constitutional right. I find yes, another string cheese in my bag, and peel it open and give it to her and pick her up and bounce her and together we cast an eye at the Board of Supervisors.

The Board is six people, four men and two women, white like the assemblage of people filling the space in front of them. One of the supervisors I recognize; she was in Rodney's class in school I think and then went down below to get a business degree and start some kind of import-export thing with her husband in one of Sacramento's sprawling suburbs. At some point she came back up home and took up residence on her family's ancient ranch, where she breeds border collies. I am considering what might have compelled her to leave her Granite Bay McMansion her local-interest fundraisers her cardiobarre to come back to Altavista to live. Her name is Cheryl Clabbers and I only know anything about her because Mom used to get the *Paiute Recorder* even in Sacramento and they ran a profile thing when Clabbers came back, wherein Clabbers said she was "born Republican" and talked about her dog-breeding concern. For some reason these tidbits killed us. All the way up until Mom died I could say "Seen Clabbers lately?" and she'd laugh helplessly.

There is a lot of shuffling and clearing of throats and one of the male supervisors ventures a modest joke. "I wonder what the big crowd's here for," he says, and everyone laughs but particularly Clabbers, who has a laugh like a brass bell being struck. "So let's go ahead and get started," he says. "I'm sure we're all eager to get to the main event.

"First I want to make sure that everyone has a chance to speak. We're going to do things the right way here and everyone is going to get a chance. If you do want to speak you got to fill out one of the comment cards. Everyone has three minutes and we do have the clock here to keep track." Honey is grabbing at my thumb and pulling it up to her mouth as though to kiss it. I smooch back on her and she hugs my neck and there's some preliminaries I miss and then Bruce McNamara strides up. He's a nice-looking man, a man's man, the upper end of middle age with trim hips and a slight paunch and aquiline nose bristly hair and jeans and plaid shirt impeccably tucked. He says "I was born here in the North State in the forties and anyone who was here knows it was a paradise back then. There was no better place in the entire world to live. We had booming industries. We had wonderful schools. We minded our own business." Honey, who has been rapt since he began speaking in his big rich voice, starts pointing and saying "Hey! Hey! Hey!" and the room looks at me and I do a little wave and try to appear worthy of a modicum of indulgence and pity.

Clabbers is sitting up at the podium with her fake smile, very coiffed, very white teeth and power suit along with her colleagues, who are all over fifty and don't seem to be suffering from the general physical and spiritual malaise as the other residents of Altavista I've seen here and there on the streets. Maybe they live out of town, in big spreads out in one of the valleys where the grasses are green and the air is sweet. They drive down below to Reno once a month to do their big shop at the Costco and they go over the border to Oregon for their above-standard health care and they have life insurance and homeowner's insurance and boats to put on the lakes and snowmobiles to put on the winter snows, and they are rooted and prosperous and friendly but apparently mad as hell about something.

Based on the quality of her noises which are calm but rising in volume I feel that Honey is in the vanishingly rare frame of mind and body when she might actually go to sleep in the stroller rather than just lying there gaping up through the stroller window at the sky or the fluorescent light until she panics and screams and struggles to get out. And people have been flowing into the room and the crowd has actually become so large as to encroach on our patch of territory at the back. So I take her off my knee where she is still "hey hey hey"ing and put her back in the stroller, and while another man is at the podium saying "We are an island now, controlled by a foreign government" I wheel her out whispering "'Scuze me 'scuze me sorry pardon me" and the people shuffle aside and smile at the baby and we wheel down the accessible ramp to the side of the courthouse stairs which is hey a federal intervention from which I am now benefitting.

We go three circles around the courthouse which lets me admire what a beautiful little building it really is—they've painted the dome an odd bronze color but the rest is white and polished, probably some kind of veneer because underneath

I'm guessing it's that porous volcanic Paiute stone. And it's got nice lines, neoclassical, short without being squat. Just the right size to stand out of the high desert as an edifice of colonial law and order. Things take a turn for the worse in its immediate environs with those too-wide streets. Somehow up here we missed the narrow Victorian niceties of the gold country, we've got no cozy saloons and our main street is so wide you can see two tumbleweeds ambling down it at the same time. The land is always trying to reassert itself or the people always trying to spread out.

I have done one loop looking at the wide streets listening to something that is probably a frog and feeling the waning heat of the day but I see that Honey has her eyes closed and we head back to the ramp and haul open the big door of the courthouse and stand just outside of the meeting room from where a woman's voice has slipped out to echo around in the dim hush of the rotunda.

I see it's an older woman, classic Altavista, short hair western shirt nice white pants, she could actually be my grandmother back from the dead, except that my grandmother loved being a Californian, loved going down to the cities, loved eating Crab Louie in San Francisco and tacos in San Diego and going to Los Angeles to visit her cowboy friends in the film lots. I can't in my bones believe that she would support any of this but then again she was a Republican her whole life and maybe this is where that ends up now. I'd also like to think my grandmother wouldn't say "Barack *Hussein* Obama" like a curse. I realize it's a luxury, not to know.

This lady says "We're just having a terrible time up here. Our economy is hurting. My husband and I were looking at property recently and the number of foreclosures—we just couldn't believe it. Like the gentleman said, we've lived here all our lives and this was just a paradise. We had all the industries we needed and we were providing food to the whole nation. Something has to change, I don't know what but it seems like this is the closest thing to an answer we're going to find. I just hope we can do it in time." *In time for what?* She leaves the podium very straight back very fine paper skin on her hands and her forearms and makes her way slowly to her husband who is older and has a walker in front of him, darker skin like he might be Native although why a Native American would support this movement is a mystery and is I guess unlikely. I wonder how many people here in Paiute County can say they are Paiute let alone in this room. The old-timers' accounts in the historical pamphlets sometimes have some loyal character named e.g. Indian John who helped out at the ranch and was like a brother to them in all ways but the most important one. Maybe the malaise, all the rotting homes and sagging enterprise, are punishment for taking the land. Maybe nothing good is ever happening on this land again for anybody.

There is a very young woman making her way to the microphone, she is beech-tree slim fair-skinned straight strawberry blond hair and can't be more than fifteen I think, and how awful that her parents are trotting her out like this when she can't even vote etc. etc., and she begins speaking. "I'm not even from Paiute County," she says confidingly. "I live down in Shasta, but I wanted to come up here to tell you that we are with you. Other counties are with you. The next generation is with you. I've lived in the North State my whole life, all twenty-three years, and I tell you now as a wife and mother myself"—impossible,

I think to myself—"the State of Jefferson is the kind of place I want to raise my baby son now." A hooting sound, and a blur of happy motions around a sturdy good-looking man with a beard, who is wearing the Snugli with the infant. "We didn't have the problems of the rest of the state," she is saying. "We didn't have drugs, or gang violence, or those types of urban problems." There it is, I think. Suddenly I have a vivid memory of someone at my grandfather's funeral cornering a pregnant blonde near me and asking apropos of nothing if she was "gonna give it one of those names like Sharniqua," an interaction I didn't quite grasp. Maybe this is about Urban Problems. But she is going on. "We don't need to pay a tax for a water tunnel or a bullet train we're never gonna use, we don't need to send our water down south, and we know we've got everything we need right here. Anyway, we're with you," she says, so confident. She heads back to her little tribe and cups her baby's head in her hand and her husband puts his arm around her. *Bitch*, I think. Clabbers leans forward into the microphone and says "I'm not supposed to say anything but I just have to tell you it's so nice to see a young person in here today," and there's more quiet hoots and affirmations from the audience and I want to throttle this smug interloping teen with her intact family and her burly husband and her white panic. Until now I have regarded the proceedings as something of a side-show because obviously the fucking Union is not going to get a fifty-first state and obviously California is not going to accept being split in two, not to mention part of Oregon, but Clabbers who is an actual elected official appears to be affirming everything that's being said here.

The supervisor who called the proceedings to order leans

forward into his microphone again and says, "Like I said we're gonna do this the right way, so anyone who still wants to say anything, I really encourage you to come up to the podium. You'll have to fill out a comment card, but you can do that after you speak—we don't always need to follow the rules just exactly as they're spelled out! So come on up, folks." I have a brief insane thought that I will go up and say something about, I don't know, my grandma and how she was in the historical society and how she ate Crab Louie and bled California gold but the impulse dies in its cradle. From the doorway between the cool dark air of the rotunda and the fluorescent buzz of the room I see the Cunt stand. I look over at Cindy and feel a little wave of almost fondness for her as she shifts in her seat and turns down the corners of her mouth with admirable economy of expression.

"Hi everyone," the Cunt says, looking around the room like a beauty queen, flicking her braid from her front to her back. Her skin is flawless ivory. "I know a lot of you in the room already, and I'm so honored for this opportunity to address the Board of Supervisors. I've been working with the North State counties now for, let's see, my whole life." She laughs. "Five generations of my family have ranched and lived off and enjoyed and stewarded the land," she says. She looks like she would be cool to the touch, with languid veins peeking through thin skin. "I don't need to tell you all that the state of California has lost touch, and that the Federal Government is imposing policies on us that are actively harmful to our way of life. This is the same government that wants to tell you how to educate and take care of your children, who are *your* property." I have never thought about Honey being my property, it's such an odd way to put it. Do I feel like Honey is my property? I ask myself, and the answer comes back yes and no. The Cunt continues. "You want to talk specifics and facts and figures I'll tell you that the Federal Government is currently in the process of taking away four good dams that are providing water for our agricultural lands in the North State by the border. These are good, clean, renewable energy dams, folks, and they're replacing them to 'steward Coho salmon'"—this with her long fingers forming air quotes—"that you can, this very day, buy in Whole Foods for eight ninety-five a pound. An allegedly endangered fish that the government needs to save by taking away the sources of water for families and farms. I know I've only got a little time here, but I want to encourage you all to watch one of my presentations on the UN Agenda 21, which is so tied up with the future of our state and our country. Not if, but when, these reforms take place, we are going to wish we took action, if we don't take action now, while we can. And that means supporting that State of Jefferson." She looks around again. Something is crackling in the room. "In conclusion I want to leave you with one of my favorite passages from the Bible" which, what the fuck happened to Church and State I wonder. "'If my people, who are called by my name, will humble themselves and pray and seek my face and turn from their wicked ways, then I will hear from heaven, and I will forgive their sin and will heal their land.'" I roll my eyes all the way back into my head. "This is our land, that we *love*, folks," she says. "We've got to do what it takes to protect it. Thank you." Mad applause and she waves at everyone and swishes her braid again and sits down with Cindy's group, who put hands on her shoulders and she puts her hands on top of their hands and whispers things I can't hear.

A last guy gets up, probably in his fifties, camouflage base-ball hat, tucked-in polo shirt in a nice currant color. "I'm Larry Elkins," he says, "and that's a tough act to follow." Everyone laughs. I wonder if there is anyone in this room who felt the crazy emanating off the Cunt besides me and apparently Cindy. *This is California*, I think, feeling a little hysterical. "I've got a quote that I wanted to read too, from our greatest president. And that's President Lincoln. 'You cannot strengthen the weak by weakening the strong. You cannot help the wage earner by pulling down the wage payer. You cannot further the brother-hood of man by encouraging class hatred . . . You cannot estab-lish sound security on borrowed money . . .'" What a fucking pedant I think but the room collapses into whoops. Honey wakes with a cry and furiously struggles against the restraints keeping her in the stroller. The noise in the rotunda is tremendous. I bend to free her and put her on her feet, where she is immedi-ately charmed by the novel sound of her small shoes slapping unctuously on the marble floor and starts running in ragged little circles.

I peer back into the room, where a small, soft, be-sweatered woman gets up to speak. "I'm Cathy Lindstrom and I just want to say in my opinion any elected official in Paiute County who publicly supports the State of Jefferson is violating the oath of office he or she took to uphold the Constitution of the state of California and the Constitution of the United States of America." There are some boos here and a man's voice calls out "The Fed-eral Government is violating the Constitution of the United States of America" and a supervisor intervenes. "Everyone gets their three minutes, Bert." I want to whoop for the woman but I'm too anxious to draw attention to myself and while I'm

standing there equivocating Honey falls flat onto her face and
unleashes a ghastly howl. I run to her and pick her up and
cradle her and I see that everyone in the room has turned their
face toward the door. I see Cindy's eyebrows arch and I wave
at the room and with one hand steer the stroller out the door
into the afternoon, doomed not to hear the rest of rebellious
Cathy's three minutes or the vote itself.

We maneuver down the ramp and by the time we are at the
sidewalk Honey has recovered her equilibrium and I see that it
is nearly five o'clock so time for dinner bath milk book brush
teeth bed since we need to preserve the sanctity of our routine.
I think it would be so nice to go somewhere else to eat, but not
the Golden Spike obviously, where I never want to go again,
just somewhere where I don't have to try and make the most
of whatever pitiful shit we have on hand. I have the same or
better tools as my grandmother but for some reason I can't
re-create any of her efforts. "Fix," she would say, instead of
"make," as in, "I'll fix us some tuna fish sandwiches," and the
sandwiches were tidy little squares on white bread I would
never buy, with a lot of mayonnaise I would never buy, and a
piece of iceberg lettuce I would never buy, but I loved them
loved them loved them, with chips on the side and a glass of
sun tea, everything so tidy and symmetrical on the plate. At
night she would make tuna noodle casserole, or side-of-the-
box lasagna, or steaks she would do in the frying pan with
lard, and afterward a bowl of yellow vanilla ice cream from the
box, with Hershey's sauce on top.

We get to Main Street and look up the road in the slanting
sun. I think well we could go to the Frosty but Honey shouldn't
eat burgers and fries and besides last time we were here I

learned the new owner is an evangelical with a stack of unsettling magazines about the Holy Land. There's a Chinese place in a big drafty room that was once a Curves gym which closed after two months, and there's a diner past the Holiday Market that as far as I can tell is never open, and a pizza place that for some reason I just feel too sad to go into. Last, and I mean literally, it's the only other place, there's Reynaldo's which is actually just about fine, and which my grandmother liked, "Mexikun," she pronounced it, and I'm thinking about her tonight so that's where we go. It is five minutes up Main Street in what I think was once a Black Bear diner and has the advantage of being sort of warmly lit and the slightest bit cozy and sometimes has real live groups of people eating there and I say, "That's what we'll do, Honey, we'll have tacos and rice and beans and guacamole and Mama will have one beer." And I push the stroller and Honey seems soothed by the cooling night air and the sound of the bugs which have started up sometime without my noticing.

We arrive at Reynaldo's and I'm disappointed to see it's almost empty and only one car in the parking lot. But I wheel in the stroller, which catches in the door since there's no one to hold it and Honey says "Uh-oh" which she has just this month started to say, adorably, when something isn't right. A young woman with piteous acne, who is not white, maybe a daughter of the eponymous Reynaldo, slouches over a podium looking at her phone and she rallies and shows us to a table. Before I get Honey out of her stroller I see the crone, no, must call her Alice, in a booth in the corner of the empty restaurant. I'm so desperate to sit at a table with someone that I wheel over. "Hi there!" I say. "Well hi," she says, like she's not surprised to see us. She's tucking into a giant trough of rice and beans. "You can join me if you like," she says. And I say "We'll do that, thanks!" And I take the high chair from the hostess and I say "We'll sit right here" and lug it over and arrange Honey in it. Alice reaches over to my surprise and chucks her under the chin with a gnarled finger and Honey looks shy and moves her chin into her shoulder and looks up at Alice through lashes, and then smiles her coy little ray-of-light smile and I want to die with pride again.

"She's a beautiful little girl," Alice says and I say "thank you" rather than make a thing about it. I inspect the menu, a massive laminated sheet covered with smears of ancient salsa, and select a combo platter with one soft one crispy taco one enchilada rice beans sour cream and guac and I think this is just what we need to get back on our feet and I'm feeling good about what's happening, Honey is chewing a chip she has fumbled from the red plastic basket before us and Alice is looking at me not unkindly and the window is open and the light is yellow and warm inside and growing purple outside.

I catch the teen's eye and I ask for the platter and a Dos Equis. "Thank you for letting us join you," I tell Alice. "We were getting a little anxious for company." "I know how that is," she says. "We just went to a really weird thing," I decide to say because I feel preoccupied by it again. "They are voting right now on whether the county should secede from California." She raises an eyebrow. "Why would they want to do that?" "They think the cities run everything and don't understand them," I say. "And they are right-wing 'live-free-or-die' types."

"It's a strange part of the country," she says. "My husband always talked about it, long after he was up here."

"And your husband is no longer with us, you mentioned."
Why do I talk like this? There is no euphemism I won't use.

"Gone almost fifty years," she says.

"Wow," I say, because what else are you going to say.

At this moment Honey catches sight of her own reflection
in the glass and says "Baby!" with friendly recognition. I have
never heard her say this word and I am overjoyed. "Yes, you're
a baby!! That's a baby! She's never said that word before," I say
to Alice. "Really any words for that matter. I was starting to
worry that she wasn't going to talk."

"I remember that," she says.

"Was it the same with your kids?" I ask her, relieved that
she has brought them up, I'm always scared to ask about
people's children. And she says "Well, they died young," which
is exactly why I usually don't fucking ask.

"I'm so sorry to hear that," another platitude thrown futilely
down a deep well.

"Well, it was a long time ago. Almost twenty years for the
third one."

"*Three*," I can't keep myself from saying. She sort of laughs,
a sound like leaves scattering across an abandoned basketball
court. She holds knife and fork in knotted hands, poised above
beans smothered in oily cheese. "It does seem like a lot for one
person, doesn't it."

Normally I am Miss Questions, I mean this is where I
shine. The worst thing about modern society is that people
don't understand that conversations need to be stoked by both
parties to keep going. I usually try to stoke hard enough for
everyone, but there is always a moment when I suddenly feel
the effort, when I'm consumed with anxiety that it's just not

going to Go, that the conversation is going to founder and it's going to have been my fault for letting it die. It feels like a grotesque wrong to let a conversation fade away into nothing. But there are no questions that feel right to ask Alice after this, and I feel suddenly so low so tired so fed up that my spine telescopes down a little farther into the seat and my shoulders sag and I actually put my elbow up on the table and prop my head in my hand. It's not only the bad news that Alice has delivered about her own circumstances, which I haven't really begun to index—were the children sick did someone take them did someone hit them with a car—but just the weight of the day, the weight of duties and time that suggests itself periodically since I had Honey, first I will cut up the enchilada I will be polite with this old woman with her unimaginable bereavement I will wipe Honey's hands we will pay the bill I will put Honey into her stroller and we will leave the bereaved one and walk all the way back to Deakins Park and probably Honey should have a bath and definitely she must brush her teeth even though she hates hates hates it and then we will have milk and story and crib and it's an hour away at least and then night and then the day begins and we do everything over again, and somewhere in there I will have to make decisions earn us money find my husband and at the same time absorb that this woman's three children are all dead, and Ellery Simpson is dead and countless children all over the world I'll never know about are dead.

I hear the soft prangs of Alice's silverware on Reynaldo's scratched-up old platter.

The thing came along that breathes some life into you and I have lifted my head off my hand and smiled at her. She looks at me a little owlishly, but kindly.

"It's so funny to meet you here," I say to her. "Since my husband's from Turkey and everything." "It is a strange coincidence," says Alice. The teen brings our food and Honey begins rhythmically banging her fork on the edge of the plate. "No, please, Honey, we don't bang," I say to her. She reaches her hand out toward my beans. Our beans. I spoon them onto her small plate.

"I loved going to Turkey," she says. "I always loved going places. That's why I joined the navy." "The navy!" I say. "I thought your husband was a pacifist." She smiles. "Well, he still served. He worked harder than I did, manual labor type things. They put them in Roosevelt's old camps, from the what's-it-called, the Conservation Corps. And anyway," she says, "I didn't do it for patriotic purposes. I just wanted to get out of town, and there was the navy saying it would take a woman and put her at a desk for a decent salary."

"My grandmother was in the navy too," I say. "It was the first time she ever left the state." She keeps talking like she doesn't see me.

"I know that young people now are used to living all over the place but it wasn't the sort of thing my parents did or their friends or anyone they knew did. I don't suppose anyone dies in the town they were born anymore but that was the idea back then."

She puts a forkful of rice into her mouth with the gnarled hand. I try to picture her behind the wheel of a car.

She looks at Honey eating her beans.

"Good eater," Alice observes. "Yes, thank god," I say. "She gets it from me."

"Well, you're still pretty trim, at least," Alice says. "You should get rid of that baby weight before it settles in, though."

I am stunned by this remark but it's also so oddly familiar. It's not just Hugo; women are birds of prey. I mean you are sitting minding your own business and then they descend on you from a clear blue sky with their talons out. I pray I won't do this with Honey, please god don't let me do this. In Turkey it's considered fine to note if someone has gained weight but since all the women I know there are svelte and gorgeous the custom does not feel like a toothless observation. And observation is violence, anyway, as any Orientalist knows.

"It's true, Alice. I've got some weight hanging around," I say a little more drily than I intend. I spoon beans into Honey's mouth, Honey the good eater, may it never bring her extra weight.

The girl brings the check and Alice reaches for it while I'm gathering up a spoonful of beans for Honey. "Let me," I say when I notice and she shakes her head with authority. "You can't take it with you," she tells me, and rummages in a serviceable black leather purse with a single strap.

"You know, I'm sorry I said that," she says next.

"It's all right," I tell her.

I think bizarrely that it might be nice to say hello to Cindy over the deck, we can have a cigarette and be soft around the middle together, despite the events of the supervisors' meeting and her ideological shortcomings.

I am wiping up smeared beans from the table with a napkin and Alice reaches out and puts a dry hand on mine. "Really, I'm sorry," she says. "You and Honey remind me a little of being around my own girls again."

"What happened to them," I say.

"They were all born sick. Two died in childhood and the third one died later," she says. "Oh god," I say and she just says, "Yes."

She shrugs. "A doctor told me later it's a one-in-a-billion chance that two people with that set of genes would meet and have children. And those children have a twenty-five percent chance of being born with the gene. But if they do, they don't have a chance. Unfortunately we didn't know that. And he was the only man I ever wanted to be with."

Honey is turning her body into a board straining against the back of the high chair starting to yell and I lift her out. I try to think of what else there is to say but she says "You go on. Get that little one to bed."

"Will you be at Sal's tomorrow?" I ask her.

"Inshallah," she says. I laugh. Engin absolutely hates it when I say this but it's like the first thing that foreigners learn in Turkey and it covers such a multitude of scenarios.

"Inshallah," I say. "Well, God willing Honey and I will be there around ten-thirty."

I wheel Honey out and up Main Street. I am thinking about how you could have three babies and all of them die and my brain worries the thought a little like a dog with something between its teeth and I have the thought I always have first that there must be something extenuating something that makes it less sad what thing she could have done that made her deserve it what thing could they have done what way could they have died that would make this situation acceptable, but there's never anything like this and I wonder if that's the source of all the world's sorrows, that everyone assumes everyone else did something to deserve it because otherwise the things that happen to people are just too horrible to bear.

But now I'm selfishly mercifully distracted because the air has that indescribably wonderful summer feeling that used to make me feel like I could go anywhere, do anything, have sex with anyone. The thing I miss most about a city is the feeling that something is always happening, a festivity at all times, a restaurant with people eating, a place to hear music, even if I'm not doing any of those things, maybe I could be. But now that I have Honey the possibility is functionally zero and when she is old enough to be left alone for days at a time assuming I could ever find someone I would trust to watch her for days at a time I will be too old to go to a rave meet someone at a bar look really good have sex with a stranger, not to mention that I am married.

But on balance I have been so lucky, not only did I once meet an objectively beautiful man at a bar in a beautiful city but I married him and he gave me a beautiful child who will speak two languages, maybe more. And maybe one day when his papers are sorted and our finances are more in hand I will go and do yoga lose the weight around my middle and get a good haircut buy some nice makeup have someone put it on me buy a good dress and Engin will think *Aman what a beautiful woman I married* even if she is a neurotic woman from a benighted country.

Thinking about Engin gives me the customary pang of guilt that I am not speaking Turkish to Honey; not speaking Turkish at all. She's got those dazed half-open eyes she gets when she's rolling in the stroller and she's had hardly any nap today and I think it's a good time to try and let her take in her father's tongue. "Honey my love," I say to her in Turkish. "Your mama is going to speak to you in Turkish a little." She cranes her head back to look at me.

"Since your daddy is a Turk he speaks Turkish," I say to her. "Your mama is American but I am speaking Turkish. She speaks Turkish rather.

"In Istanbul live your grandmother and your paternal aunt and your uncle. In Izmir lives your paternal grandfather." I hope I have these right, there are parent-specific names for relatives which seems excessive although I guess in English we spend a lot of time saying "My mother's sister," etc.

"In the summer we will go with Daddy to visit your paternal grandfather and we will sit on the pier and have Coke and pumpkin seeds. Won't it be nice?" I say.

"Your paternal grandmother in Istanbul misses you very much. She wants us to come visit her. When we go your daddy will take you to get a fish sandwich and to see Miniatürk."

I am floundering. The distance between myself pushing a stroller along the side of the road in Paiute County and Ayşe and Mini Turk World feels apocalyptic.

"Your daddy loves you very much," I tell Honey, and then in English for emphasis.

"And your daddy loves cats very much. He likes to draw and cook and he makes delicious salami and cheese sandwiches. When you were in my womb"—gross but I love that word, rahim, must be Arabic, no vowel harmony. I pause to think if there's a more modern word than this, and then realize that's a problematic way to think about it, latent anti-Arab prejudice rising forth, rahim it is—"I ate one almost every single day." We cross the railroad tracks with a bump.

"He loves to watch movies and when we watch them . . ." I stop here to parse the grammar because in Turkish you have to know what you are going to say before you start speaking, since the end comes first, or what is the end in English anyway. I think about trying to explain this to Honey but feel exhausted. ". . . when we watch them if I get either scared or bored and look at my phone he gets mad." It takes me nearly two minutes to get this out. I can't believe that something once so relatively easy is deserting me now.

I wonder if Engin is bored when he talks to me. Learning Turkish is no less than what's expected if you are for example a Chechen and you immigrate to Turkey but it's a bonus if you are American, Americans having managed to forge a dual impression worldwide of hopeless stupidity and national superiority that exempts them from learning other languages. Turks are also convinced that Turkish is an impossible language to learn, although English is the one that has no inherent logic and is all irregular verbs and phantom letters and bizarre plurals. Engin doesn't ever talk to me in particularly complex English sentences and that doesn't bother me so hopefully the reverse is true too.

Before he was deported Engin developed a rapport with the elderly Chinese women who come by our house on Monday evenings to collect the cans from our recycling and who speak significantly less English than he does. One of the ladies gets on my nerves because once I was walking into the house with Honey in my arms and she indicated via hand signs that I needed to go inside and get the cans and I said "I'm sorry I've got my hands full" and she said "No English" and I thought For fuck's sake and went inside saying "sorry" and then felt bad and barricaded Honey in her bouncer and went outside with the cans and she was gone and I felt worse. Engin would set cans and bottles into a separate bag and put them by the large can well in advance of the appointed hour and would sometimes be outside smoking a cigarette puttering with the succulents when they came by and they would exchange greetings. Once I looked out the window and he was exuberantly trying to shake the hand of the one that I let down. "My auntie," he said when he came inside.

I have trailed off in my Turkish conversation time with Honey while I remember this and now we are at the gate of the house and I wheel her up and rush through all the things that were prophesied at Reynaldo's, diaper jammies milk story teeth bed and it takes forty-five minutes and she lies down like a good girl as though she's been yearning for her bed and finally at the end I am on the deck with my drink and my cigarette and it feels almost as good as a bar.

I am halfway through my cigarette looking up at the stars and down at my phone and sending Engin a loving WhatsApp message and feeling virtuous for not having spent hours scrolling through BabyCenter even though it's only the Wi-Fi situation that has prevented me from doing so and not any abstemiousness on my part. I hear the sound of an engine in the distance and it grows louder and closer until a truck materializes in front of Cindy's house and discharges Cindy and Ed. It seems decades since we were together in the courthouse.

"How did it go," I call to her as they make their way up the cement walk next door. "We did it!" she says with un-Cindy-like enthusiasm, something like glee. "Five to one in favor."

I feel big and full of love to spread around so I say "My goodness!" with a faint sense of secondhand victory on her behalf until I absorb the import of this, one small step gained for a crypto-racist dream of separateness and economic independence for what is probably the poorest county in the state and the largest per capita user of social services. At what point does neighborliness become capitulation cowardice etc. Too late. "Congratulations, I guess," I say to them. "I'd, um, be sad if California split up, though, personally." Cindy shrugs and Ed nods sort of sympathetically. "Well, we don't know what's going to happen," Cindy says, and they go in the house and then five minutes later they are out again. "We're heading down to the Golden Spike if you want to come," Ed says, I daresay almost hopefully, or maybe I'm imagining it, and I point to the house and say, "Got the baby." "Okay then. Have a good night." "Good night, good night."

I know that I have to be careful vis-à-vis my water intake relative to my screwdriver intake and I go inside and have two glasses of the airless mineral-tasting water that comes out of the tap. I get the Diamond ice cream out of the freezer and the Hershey's out of the cupboard and I fix a huge bowl, making dense scribbles of syrup across the ice cream's uncanny yellow. I carry it back outside and eat it while watching the videos of Honey from daycare on my WeChat app. I have videos on this app from her first weeks at daycare after Engin left for his course, when she was eight months old and at the peak of babyness and they are precious precious precious but I cannot figure out how to get them out of the phone and onto the computer where I might feel more assured that they will last and I spend a lot of time worrying about this. In the first one she is wearing a onesie I bought her at the consignment store that is covered with tiny planes trains and automobiles. "You are going to be a baby who goes places," I told her, when we put her in it for her first day, although her dad is the one who was going places and so far she has mostly stayed right where she was born. In the videos Honey is wearing the onesie and sitting on a play rug next to another baby of about the same size. "Baby Bianca!" I say aloud as that is the baby's name and now like Honey she is a rangy almost-toddler, with a little ponytail of black hair sticking up in a plume from her head. She speaks Chinese with her mom and maybe one day with Honey, I hope. Honey has a beatific smile on her face. The video is a fourteen-second loop and I play it over and over again while tears run down my face.

By and by the ice cream is finished and I want to have a cigarette but know from experience that the fatty dairy scum on the inside of my mouth will be inharmonious with the cigarette and I think I can sluice it out with a final screwdriver to cap off the evening. I sashay inside and prepare this and come back outside and take a big swig and then see that the ashtray is brimming over and this is upsetting to my sense of orderliness because truly there is nothing worse than an overflowing ashtray on the deck of a mobile home and I set down my drink and pick up the ashtray and walk around the deck to the back of the house where the trash can lives.

But somewhere along the three short steps off the deck I pitch forward and land with the full weight of an adult body in motion on my eyebrow and right shoulder. My head bounces off the concrete path that leads to the carport and I see black and hear rather than feel some concussive force inside my head. It is the kind of fall where people would normally surround you and hasten to pick you up look in your face dust you off hold up fingers and ask if there is someone to call but there is no one to call only a riot of stars that I see across my vision against the riot of real stars in the sky above me when I roll over onto my side and then my back, gripping my brow and wondering if there is blood. I lie there for a minute then roll back onto my side and then onto my front and I put one knee up and one hand, and then the other knee and other hand and I stand very slowly with one hand over my throbbing eye. There is a lot of pain and I stand there feeling it and I feel my wits shaking themselves off and swimming against the current of alcohol in my blood and after a minute or two they slowly congregate and say Well here we all are and what are the signs of concussion and shouldn't we stay awake in case we should never wake up again and then I feel reassured and then I feel afraid.

I slowly get up and take another moment to steady myself and on wobbling feet make my way up the stairs and back into the house and turn on the light in the other bathroom and inspect myself, a very white face and red weal around my eyebrow, but all in all the lack of evidence of what has happened is surprising given the clamoring inside my head. I go back outside to the corner of the deck where I can get Cindy's Wi-Fi and google "what to do in a concussion" and apparently it is wait two hours before you go to sleep which is two hours I can spend reading about the percent of people who develop brain bleeding and blood clots and never wake up. What's her name who was married to Liam Neeson fell down from a standing position and a few hours later she was gone. I consider what will happen in this contingency and it would be Honey trapped in her Pack 'n Play screaming and screaming into an empty room and I put my head in my hands.

The problem is that if this happens no one will know for a very long time because Engin will give me a couple of days before freaking out and Uncle Rodney won't think anything of

it if I continue to not call and Meredith has no idea about ge-
ography and I am not in very good touch with my small assortment of friends from high school college grad school scattered
across the earth. Cindy and Ed are out carousing. I could leave
a note for Cindy but what if she doesn't come home and spends
the night howling at the moon with Ed. I could call the police
but I don't want to put it in anyone's mind that I am an unfit
mother a drunk etc. There is a dinky little medical center here
thanks to a parcel tax of $200 a year that all the live-free-or-die
types were persuaded to vote for because otherwise there
would be no hospital for three hundred miles, but you can't
deliver a baby there or have anything but the most rudimen-
tary of surgeries and it's closed now anyway. Suddenly something emerges from the depths of my throbbing head and I
consider Alice. Alice the crone.

I look at the time on my phone and it is 10:30 which is
egregious but hopefully not unforgivable. I remember she is
staying at the passable-is-all-you-can-say-about-it Arrowhead
and I take the chance that I can use Cindy's Wi-Fi to make at
least a voice call. I look up the number of the Arrowhead and
copy it and then paste it into the Skype keypad, my right eye
closed and my hand over my eyebrow which I feel forming a
knot. I hear the click as Skype kicks into gear and the sound
of a phone ringing. "Arrowhead," someone says curtly. "I'm . . .
trying to reach one of your guests, her name is Alice. An older
lady. Really old. I know it's late. I don't know her room
number . . . if you could just put me through. It's a little bit of
an emergency."

"One sec," the man says and I hear another ring and another and another and I think of course she's asleep and not

going to answer a ringing motel phone but then I hear a click and clattering and a croaking hello.

"Ms. Alice," I say, and start rushing so I can get to the end of this mortification. "I am so very sorry to bother you—I'm Daphne, from the restaurant tonight, with the baby, Honey?"

I wait two beats for her to say "Oh, hello" and rush ahead.

"I am so, so embarrassed to say this but I've had a fall and hit my head and I'm concerned about the possibility of a concussion and so while I'm sure everything's fine I'm wondering if you could maybe check on me in the morning since they say you shouldn't sleep with a concussion. I mean, that's what I've read." There is a pause.

"Don't you think you ought to call 911?"

"Well I considered it," I say, "but I actually feel okay and think I'm probably fine, this is just more of a contingency plan in case the worst should happen, I like to have all my bases covered and I don't want to upset the baby with an ambulance, which would have to come all the way from the next county over probably." A longer pause.

"Okay," she says.

"Oh, thank you thank you thank you" I say. "I'm at Three Paiute Way in Deakins Park, the one with a Buick and big birch tree out front." "Hold on," she says, and makes me repeat it, which I think is a good sign.

"What time do you want me to come?"

"What time do you usually wake up?"

"About six."

"Well I think if you were to come at seven that would be good. I'll leave the door unlocked so you can get in."

"Okay then."

"I'll, um, leave you some instructions on the very off chance that something bad happens."

"Okay."

"I really can't thank you enough for this, Alice."

"Okay. Take care of yourself," she says, and hangs up. I wonder whether she will really come.

My head swims a little and I light a cigarette which I remember now was the precipitating factor and now the ashtray is out in the yard somewhere with cigarette butts strewn everywhere but I don't dare brave the steps again to find it. I take a long drag to anchor myself to the bench and my head throbs. I will need to write the number for Uncle Rodney as he can take Honey if I die until Engin can get her but how he will get her is another question. I have to assume hope pray that there will be some way the U.S. Citizenship and Immigration Services can find their humanity if Honey is left motherless and her father needs to come and get her even without his papers in order but I'm sure they won't. I google "mother dead father no green card" and after some grinding on the part of my phone an answer appears in the form of an applicant whose sponsoring sister died and evidently something exists called "Humanitarian Reasons" but it all hinges as usual on the submission of new and different forms and I think how the fuck will he ever be able to get through on the telephone to a person to say "MY FUCKING BABY is there in CALIFORNIA" and I just have to hope he has the good sense to go to the U.S. consulate in Istanbul and throw himself on their mercy and I think I need to make this list as simple as possible I need a process chart a job tree an org chart like I make at the Institute so first Alice calls Uncle Rodney and then he'll need to come up from Quincy and get Honey and I guess he should be the one to call Engin and then Engin will need to call the lawyer and the consulate about what to do to get Honey and I realize I don't have a will and wonder if I should make one and briefly hysterically I think that Engin's only conduit to his child will now be a forest ranger in Plumas County who calls him "Engine" like fire engine even though it's Engin more like Angler and I don't bother to correct Uncle Rodney anymore because it's like he just cannot do it no matter how many times he hears you say it. I consider that if I really thought any of this was going to happen I would be crying but then I think no one ever really expects these things, you physically can't anticipate them, so how I feel has no bearing on what will actually happen and I need to just make sure everything is organized and at least I have some life insurance through the University.

I pour some of my melting ice on the cigarette and hear it hiss and put the butt on the windowsill and I go inside to find the small notebook I use to scribble Hugo's various instructions in during our conclaves. I tear out several sheets and I consult the contacts list on my phone and I number one sheet "1" and write "In case of emergency please call my uncle Rodney Burdock at xyz. He should call my husband Engin Mehmetoğlu at xyz and our attorney at xyz." I laboriously write out the link to the site explaining what to do about Humanitarian Reasons for the green card and I put all the pieces of paper in the middle of the dining room table and I unlock the front door and go outside and finish the screwdriver and smoke what I consider might be the last cigarette of my life so I try to make it count.

DAY 7 I wake up to the cooing of Honey and as soon as I achieve consciousness I feel my head in the hands of an unloving god and my mouth full of acid and ash despite a clear memory of brushing my teeth in the fluorescent light of the bathroom vanity and helplessly swallowing three expired Advil against the knowledge of what was coming. The red numbers on the hotel-style clock on the nightstand read 5:45 a.m. and I think please Honey, please Jesus, please go back to sleep, but her coos are becoming squawks and caws and I sit up and feel a wave of such profound dread that I have to lie down again and close my eyes. What unforgivable things did I do last night, I wonder, and try to still my pounding heart with the true fact that there is nothing unforgivable I could have done apart from the simple folly of drinking to excess at high altitude and falling down the stairs. Whatever devastation I've wrought I've wrought quietly in the privacy of my own mobile home. The pounding isolates itself to the upper-right quadrant of my head and I feel the egg on my eyebrow and think "I'm alive." And then I think "unfit mother unfit mother unfit mother," one of those word pairings of the sort my brain likes to get stuck in its gears.

"Shhhhh," I say to Honey in her closet wondering whether she might lie back down and soothe herself to sleep. "Shhhhh," but the position of the tongue to produce the sound allows me to taste the full ruin of my breath. Her caws become shrieks. "Dadadada," she says. I force myself up and place my legs over the side of the bed. I am wearing only underwear and I look down at my slack white belly and the long thin hairs growing around my bikini line. I lie back down; I sit back up. I shuffle around the enormous bed and into the bathroom and see my eyelid is so purple it is nearly black and it becomes red radiating out from my eye. I drink the glass of water that is sitting forgotten by the sink. I know I have but it feels like I have never had a hangover like the hangover I have now and I can only propel myself out of the bathroom by hunching forward sagging my shoulders like Early Man. Honey's noises are insistent and I shuffle to the closet and see her bright face like a little night-light in the dark. "Ameeeee," she says, and lifts up her arms to me. I have heard her say "Amee" before but she's said it to several people and I've never been positive she is referring to me. But this seems very clear and my heart starts bleeding and I pick her up and she is incredibly heavy and I carry her back to the bed and lie down, trying to clutch her to my bosom while she squirms and writhes to sit up stand up try and jump on the bed and my stomach is full of water and baby bees. My head pounds so much I have to sit up and put it between my knees. She stops her frenzy and puts her arms around me and her cheek against my back.

"I'm sorry," I say from between my knees. "Mommy isn't feeling very well." "Ameeee," she says and rears back and yells with laughter. She scrabbles around to my knees and I lift my head and she puts her hands on each side of my face and gives my mouth a big open-mouth smack and smiles so warmly and brightly that I say "Oh thank you my dearest one," with genuine gratitude, and then she starts rifling her hands through my hair, grabbing hold of a big hank and yanking down. "Ouch," I say to her. "Ouch ouch ouch" and I find her hands and extricate the hair and hold them very tightly. "We DO NOT pull hair," I say, and she flails out of my reach and tumbles sideways off the bed with a loud thump. I spring off and around to the other side and she is trying to get her breath, her mouth open in preparation for what I know will be a tremendous cry. I pick her up and hold her against my body and lean my ass back against the bed and try not to throw up from all the jangling of my body parts and she screams. "My poor monkey," I say to her. "Poor poor monkey. We got a bad bonk. Yes, that was a very bad bonk. Mommy has a bonk too. Poor lovebug sweet monkey, my little peach blossom." I lean back to see her face and tears are running down and I wipe them away and wipe her nose with the scratchy white sheet and hug her again while she cries and wonder with desperation rising in my throat how in the loving fuck I will survive the morning. Soon she wants to get down and I set her on her feet and she takes off running from the bedroom into the kitchen.

I follow her with my hominid shuffle my head throbbing at every plodding step and when I get to the kitchen I look through the door to the dining room and see Alice standing there, Alice, utterly forgotten, called in the night, Alice, holding one of the chicken-scratched "In case of my death please call this number" papers I am now mortified to remember spreading across the dining room table before smoking what I believed would be the last cigarette of my short span on earth. She looks at me and I cover my breasts and turn around and shuffle quickly back to the bedroom. "I'm early," I hear her say. "One second," I manage to cry out and I'm fumbling around the closet for a T-shirt and sweatpants which I pull on and then emerge. Honey is holding on to Alice's leg.

"I thought I'd find out sooner rather than later whether you were alive," she says.

I lunge to the kitchen sink and vomit up the water I drank. Alice stays where she is. I run the faucet and remove the hand sprayer and spray water ineffectually to wash the mess down.

"I'm hungover," I say helplessly. "I'm sorry."

"I thought you might be," she says. "You sounded a little keyed up on the phone."

I see her looking around the house presumably to see whether it's a safe environment for a child. The essential tidiness and coziness of my late grandmother's home overcomes the detritus of Honey that is strewn around the linoleum and carpet.

"You know you have to be careful at this altitude," she says mildly.

"Can I get you some coffee," I say and look around for a coffee machine filters coffee any of the things I would need to make the coffee, and she says "Tell you what. You are good for less than nothing right now." She gently takes Honey's hands off her leg and walks carefully gingerly frailly over to me and takes the dish towel from the handle of the refrigerator where it is tucked and opens the freezer takes out ancient frozen peas wraps them in the dish towel and says "Take this to bed with you and lie down."

"What are you going to do?" I ask her, holding the peas to my burning eyebrow.

"I'll mind the baby." I look at her and somehow telegraph my concern that she won't be able to corral Honey at her advanced age.

"I don't move very fast but I think I know how to take care of a sweet baby," she says, and looks down at Honey and says "Don't I know how to look after a sweet baby?" and Honey shrieks "Daaaahhhhhh!" Alice looks at me with an eyebrow gently raised.

"I don't get the feeling that you could move any faster than I could." From my roiling stomach I am trying to muster up the will to be polite say no thanks I've got this but some slumbering self-preserving instinct wakes and I gesture at diapers on the coffee table and bananas in the fruit bowl and say "There are eggs in the fridge" and there is really nothing else for me to do but go into the bedroom close the door take off my clothes get into bed curl up on my side put the peas on my burning face pull the covers all the way over my head and cry until I fall asleep.

Sometime later I open my eyes and I'm under the sheet in a foul-breath-smelling pocket of warmth and the peas are a big wet spot on the sheet beside me. I have such a serious feeling of badness that I have to just submit to it, curl my knees up to my chest and let it wash over me like waves, waves that will ideally recede after they've spent their energy on my supine form, giving me a chance to stand up catch my breath. I have had a hangover in my life more times than I care to admit and so there is a part of me that knows that this particular body-mind-heart-spiritual-level, ethical-level feeling of badness is just the hangover and not a permanent state, but I also know that this hangover badness like all hangover badness is latching onto preexisting badness. Surely the tide of badness rising steadily higher over the last eight months is a sign that there is something to which I cannot acclimate. Engin's green card, my job, Hugo and Meredith and the breast pump in the basement of Oberrecht Hall. And Maryam. And Ellery. Now instead of waking up to see a stranger's back next to me as I might have done in the past and thus ushered in hangover-specific badness it's the feeling of the grave injury I've done to my face, the egg on my eyebrow, being an unfit mother, not just to my own child but any other child that might cross my path.

If I have learned anything from my twenties it's that rather than fight against hangovers you have to let the badness wash all over you, this is bad, this is the worst, this is the worst feeling, things are bad, and then perform a quick reckoning and giving of thanks. I am of sound body reasonably sound mind I have a treasure of a child who is healthy and loving and makes eye contact I have $1,847 in savings a loving husband and all that's standing between us is some administrative bother some paperwork and it's all going to be fine. I get myself into child's pose on the bed which is the only thing I can remember from my brief tenure in yoga but then I think of the pictures of the little children on the beaches I used to visit with my parents, the little boy in the red shirt in a pose just like this, and the badness is back but now it's world-historical badness, all the dead women and children on every continent on the planet and I have to stuff them all back with apologies so flaccid and pointless they become their own source of badness in the room. I lie flat on my stomach with my legs straight toes pointed and clasp my hands together under my chin and my chin to my chest and I say the Lord's Prayer making sure palms touch, a remnant of my childhood marked by ritual gestures conforming to specifications mandated only by myself. Then I smell toast and hear the sounds of cupboards opening and closing and have such a strong sense memory of being in my mother's house that I try and place the child I hear until I realize it's my own.

I'm simultaneously desperate to cuddle and unable to deal with her so I lie there for a while longer and doze until the absence of sound wakes me again. I sit up. The room swims but the awful clamoring of my head has died down to the point where the pain of the fall speaks louder than the noise of my parched and alcohol-wounded brain cells. It's 1:10 by the nightstand clock which means incredibly that I have been sleeping for around six hours and I wonder what in god's name she can have done with Honey all this time. I stand up and slowly maneuver around the bed to the pile of clothes outside the closet door and I put on my stained white shirt my pants and pull my hair into a bun and shuffle to the bathroom splash water on my face brush my teeth and look at my mangled eyebrow again. I slowly move out of the bedroom into the kitchen and from the kitchen I see the back of Alice on the couch, and Honey's feet stretched out beside her. Miracle of miracles, my child is sleeping on a lap, something she has not done since she was just a small baby.

"Hello," I say to Alice in a whisper and she cranes her head around to see me, smiling faintly. "This little one was very tired," she says. "I can't believe how long I slept." I raise my hands in an odd rueful gesture and let them drop limply. "Has she been putting you through the wringer?"

"Not too badly," she says. "We read stories"—pointing to

the pile of books on the floor—"and we learned nose eyes mouth fingers toes and we went for a walk around the front of the house." What, I think to myself. How. She looks me up and down. "We walked very slowly" and I nod.

"Are you better now?" she asks.

"I feel more like a human being," I say. "Thank you so much for doing this, you really don't know what it means."

"I know what it means," she says. "Didn't I tell you I had three small children and no husband to help me?"

I want to ask what happened to her husband but I feel very raw and tender and wish to spare myself further bad information for just a little longer. So I just say "You're an amazing woman," which seems likely to be true even apart from the amazing favor she has done me by coming here to care for the child of a potentially dead stranger. Her hand holds one of Honey's hands; Honey's other hand is flung out and dangling off Alice's knees.

"I made some tuna fish if your stomach can take it," she says, and behold there is a sandwich on the kitchen table with a little pile of chips next to it.

"Bless you," I say. I pour myself some coffee from the pot and take the coffee and the plate gingerly over to my grandfather's La-Z-Boy, facing Alice on the couch.

"Why isn't your husband here?" she asks me. I sip the coffee and it's thin but it's coffee.

"After Honey was born and much agonizing we decided he should finish his certificate in video postproduction so that his employment prospects would be better, and it was going to be cheaper and easier to do it in Turkey, so he went back to Turkey for what was supposed to be a total of six months, but when he came back to see us midway through, under sinister and it turns out illegal pressure he was made to relinquish his green card at the San Francisco International Airport and go back to Turkey and is now waiting indefinitely to obtain a new one, a process which has been slowed by bureaucratic incompetence."

"That sounds bad," she says.

"It is bad," I say.

"How long has he been gone?"

"Eight months, more or less." When I say the amount of time I am struck anew by its longness, it's an amount of time that if he had left me for example and was not hanging out on his mom's couch in Kadıköy would mean it was time for me to move on find closure start trying to make a new life. As it is I am getting the distinct impression from Meredith and Hugo and everyone at work that they think he is an imaginary man, or at least one who isn't planning to come home, which is really rotten of them.

"And you're on your own with the baby."

"Yes."

"That's not easy."

"No."

"But you earn your own living."

"Well, I was. I guess I still am. I'm not sure, actually. I walked out of my office a few days ago and I know I've got to go back but I just can't stomach it for some reason."

"Must be why you drank so much." I laugh. "I guess so."

"And the house?" She looks around and I follow her face, trying to see it as it is, and noting how odd it is that neither Mom nor Rodney nor I ever found it within ourselves to change a single thing about its interior, to divest it of any of its furnishings, dismantle the world that my grandma made.

"Ah, yes, this is my house, technically." I wave my hand around the expanse of the living-dining room. I catch a glimpse of my pale arm in the reflective glass of my grandmother's hutch housing her milk glass treasures.

"My grandparents lived here and left it to my mom and she left it to me. It's been for sale for years but no one seems to want it. How long has Honey been like that?" I gesture at the sleeping cherub.

"Only about twenty minutes."

"We can move her into the crib if you want." Alice looks wounded by this. "I mean, only if you wanted to be on your way," I say. "I'd love for you to stay forever!" I say brightly, just to make sure she doesn't think I'm trying to get her to go. I desperately do not want her to go.

"I don't have anywhere to be," she says.

"I'm really sorry to impose further but do you think it would be okay if I took a shower?" I venture, and she says "Go ahead." I creep slowly back to the bathroom. First, brush teeth, I think. Clear away the scum so you can think clearly.

I come out of the bathroom feeling as fresh as can be given the circumstances, some of the badness washed down the drain and I find a clean white Engin T-shirt and look sorrowfully at my aching eyebrow. Honey is still asleep, the woman must be a witch.

"Thank you," I say again, running out of ways to say it. I bring her a glass of water which she accepts and sips and I sit back in the La-Z-Boy. "So what's your plan?" I ask.

"I'm trying to get to a place called Camp Cooville, that's where my husband was. It isn't very far, somewhere over the Oregon border. I've been there before, I think I told you. We always wanted to get back sometime after the war but never got to it." A fly buzzes against the window, trapped between the glass and the tweedy beige curtains.

"When are you going to go?"

"I should think the next few days. I've been trying to get up my strength a little. I thought maybe if I ate some real food instead of the hundred pounds of banana bread Yarrow made me bring."

"Ha!" I say. "You've come to the wrong place for that."

"I like the Mexican place," she says. "I can't say I care for the Golden Spike."

"Yeah, we're maxed out there, I think."

"The fellow at my motel says you can get a prime rib dinner at a place called Antelope Pines." The site of the ratty swing set and the man-made lake.

"That's right. Antelope Meadows. I forgot about them," I say. "They have an ice cream bar. I mean it's just a machine but they have a variety of toppings to go on the ice cream."

Normally when I am interacting with a stranger I want it to be over by a certain point so that I can avoid the inevitable moment of giving or taking offense or feeling bored or boring someone else but it feels so unexpectedly nice to "visit with" someone as my grandmother would have said and to have someone else smooth my child's hair while she miraculously sleeps in a lap that I try to prolong it.

"We could go for dinner," I venture. "If you aren't busy. I mean I don't want to impose," which I realize I've already said.

"I'd just like to buy you dinner or something to say thank you for coming this morning and taking care of us."

"Okay," she says.

"Okay," I say.

"I'll have to have a nap myself," she says, looking down at Honey. "I guess I'll go after this one wakes up and then we can go early, say about five."

"That sounds perfect," I say. "Would you like me to bring you a newspaper or something? I have yesterday's."

"That might be nice," she says, and I bring her the paper and I get *Jurassic Park* but the sentences make my head spin so I just curl up and kind of stare into space and remember that Engin will want to know where we are and why we haven't Skyped yet.

"I have to go outside where I get a signal and try to call my husband," I tell Alice, and she nods, and I surreptitiously get the cigarettes and the lighter from the cupboard and head outside to the deck corner and try Engin on a voice call. He answers right away and the first thing he says is "What's going on?" and I say "I tripped and fell," pointing to my forehead even though there's no video. "I hurt my eyebrow pretty badly." Then I wonder why I told him this since it will just make him worry.

"Where's Meltem?"

"She's inside with a nice auntie I met here. Sleeping."

"What auntie?"

"Just an old lady we met in the coffee shop. She's a stranger here too. She's my new friend, I guess." "Great," he says, and he sounds sour. "She's been to Turkey," I say brightly as he says, "Did you go to the doctor?"

"No, it's fine."

"I'm worried about you."

"I know," I say. "I'm sorry. I think I'm just having a melt-down," I say in English. I start crying. "I'm also sorry that every time we talk I start crying," I say to him. "I don't know why we thought this would be a good idea, to have you leave to take the course." I realize how much of the time he's been gone that I've been trying to assure him that everything is going really extremely well. I think I can feel him starting to ruffle, preparing to launch into "So I could get a better job and earn more money" but he stops and just says "Biliyorum." I know.

I have the feeling which never fails to destabilize me, a sudden reminder of the faith I've placed in the strength of in-visible bonds, ties stretching across the ocean like the fiber-optic cables or whatever it is that allow us to Skype. Spending the summer in Turkey, abandoning my Ph.D. program, mar-rying Engin, these were not so much decisions as they were realities that quietly but ecstatically asserted themselves at the time. Every so often this thought comes and knocks me on my ass, that we're just building this whole castle on such a flimsy and hastily constructed premise that we love each other and want to be together raise our child together grow old together and how easy—how wrong but how easy nonetheless—it would be to walk away from it all, with nothing changing ex-cept I could stop worrying about the progress of a lot of ex-pensive pieces of paper through a vast administrative machine, although I'm sure it would come with its own tortuous admin-istrative processing. But then again I have Honey and if Engin feels even a tenth of what I feel about Honey he'll never live without her.

Badness washes around my ankles on the deck, rising swiftly. I'm just crying into one hand and holding the phone with the other hand and Engin is silent on the other end. I have the distinct impression that we have entered a definitive moment, when Engin or I can say the thing that will snip apart the whole nest of skeins that tether us to each other. Now in this moment it seems incredible that such an apparatus, a child, all this paperwork, could have been born of something so careless as two people deciding to spend the night at the bar and never again be parted. But at the time all obstacles seemed to melt away with no resistance.

I wait for the word that will highlight what a disaster it's all been. But he just says "I love you," in English, and I say "I love you too" and I know it will carry us forward another day. "Listen," I say, when I stop shuddering. "This is a Humanitarian thing, they have a category for it in Citizenship and Immigration. Maybe the lawyer can push it through on those grounds."

"Okay," he says.

"Are you mad at me?" I say in Turkish.

"No, my love. I'm not mad at you." I want to ask what about your mother what about Pelin what about Savaş what about Gökay what about Özgür and Sema and everyone else you know but decide to stay with the answer that matters, the one that feels good. We stay on the line just listening to each other breathe and I take out a cigarette and light it and he says "Öfff" which is a sound expression that conveys all the frustration of the world and I say "Fucking hell" in English and he says "Fucking hell" too.

"I'm sorry that I made you do this," I say.

"What are you saying? I'm the idiot who gave the immigration guys my card and signed that fucking paper." While we talk I think suddenly of a thing I saw in a BabyCenter comment, a random flash of true insight imparted by a stranger. It was about the "culture" of your family, that only you and your partner can make and which dictates the things that you do and enjoy and the way you raise your kid. I think the remark was delivered in the context of making your baby go the fuck to sleep or something like that. But I think of how it is when Engin and I are in the Buick together or sitting on the couch each doing our own thing or when we talk throughout a TV show about where we should buy our stone shack or how much of an idiot Tolga is or the nature of Hugo's essential being or what new bizarre baby behavior Honey is exhibiting. When Rodney and Helen visited when Honey was born she told me "Just remember that these are the good ole days" which seemed kind of sinister but now I understand. I have always just liked to be around Engin so much and it occurs to me that I am denying myself and Honey that opportunity, that I am robbing us of the good ole days, that I am stymying further opportunities to build our singular familial culture, and I get pissed all over again.

I remember too that I have been feeling very sorry for myself and not that sorry for Engin which is unfair because he is the one who had the god-awful demeaning interaction with the two men resulting in his being turned away from the United States and put back onto a plane and not being able to see his infant daughter and then discovering that his compliance with their demands, his signing of the dreaded fucking form I-407 meant that he is on record as voluntarily surrendering his green card and he like me must look back at that encounter and want to literally murder everyone involved, as I do, poke them with a knife, except that he can actually picture it and see the scene in his dreams whereas I rely on stock footage of various bland consular rooms I have known and every beefy male movie villain to fill in as the Homeland Security guys and every day I ask myself why I didn't warn him to be careful why I assumed good faith on the part of these people why I pictured all the kind friendly consular officers of my childhood helping me renew my passport or giving my mother her terracotta urn, and not the people Engin had to see, people who took him away from his child because they vibrate with some higher mandate about securing our fucking borders. I feel so much hate and I wish I had somewhere to put it, that there was some decisive action to take.

"I'm so sorry," I repeat. "I'm so sorry we did this to you."

We sign off and I light another cigarette smoke it down to the filter staring across the road at the scrub beyond the split-rail fence, where some quail are making their coordinated swarm through the sagebrush, and then I wipe my face off and go back inside. I feel clean, somehow. Or neutral. It's like the hangover and the anguish of the morning has wrung out sentiment from me, I am a dishrag that has been squeezed and placed over the rack to dry. Alice is there on the couch, petting the head of Honey, whose eyes are heavy but open, her rosy little lips pursed into a kiss, her hand reaching up toward Alice's face.

"Well, this one's awake," says Alice. "Probably needs a snack."

"Hi baby!" I say to Honey. "Did you have a nice nap on Alice's lap?" and she kicks and strains to roll off Alice saying

"Amee-amee-amee." I kneel down to meet her and need to put my hand back to steady myself from mild spins. Alice stands up with effort, I can almost hear her back clicking, and then briskly straightens her skirt.

"Well, then. I guess I'll go and get my nap."

"Are we still on for dinner," I say rather than ask, feeling bereft at the prospect of her absence.

"Oh, sure, I guess," says Alice.

"I'll pick you up at five at the Arrowhead," I say. "We'll go have the prime rib."

"Okay," she says, and walks slowly to the door. I scramble up from Honey's level and intercept her and lay a hand on her bony shoulder and she flinches and looks at me with what seems almost like hostility.

"I just want to say thank you again, for what you did."

"Well," she says. "What else was I going to do?" Honey tugs at my knees and raises her arms to be picked up. I reach down and bring her up, using her as a shield against some faint but perceptible disapproval I suddenly feel in the air of the mobile home.

"Say bye-bye, Honey," I say, waggling the baby's hand. "See you soon."

Alice exits the screen door and makes her painstaking way down the deck stairs and I watch her get very slowly into a Dodge that I note with some concern is parked partially up on the curb, although in fairness to Alice it's a rounded curb and easy to glide up onto. I feel very lonely and very unable to cope. It's 2:20. I have the thought that I could put Honey down for a nap and then realize that she has just had one. So that's two and a half hours to pass, my head faintly throbbing my eyebrow throbbing the residual rivulets of badness still lapping around my ankles poised to rise at any moment. The only good thing is that Engin and I seem to have restored somewhat the ideal of our life together, the mirage winking into something corporeal even if it's just through Skype. I change the Band-Aid on Honey's finger which she is mercifully still for and then I sit on the couch to gather strength and watch her run to and fro; into the guest bedroom and the little tiny study then back into the living room bashing into my knees laughing hysterically, then staggering back and spinning all the way around on unsteady little legs for what I think is the first time. I see suddenly how the little stores of fat that formed the rolls on her wrists and ankles are melting away and the slim lines of a child are starting to assert themselves in her body. She was never one of those gloriously fat babies with huge dimpled thighs but she had the minimum mandated squoosh that babies owe us, and hands that made dimples when they clenched into tiny fists. I want to take her out of her onesie and set her loose in the diaper so that she will read like my baby again, and not this lanky, wild-headed hoyden spinning around the living room. "Come cuddle with Mama," I say to her, and try to grab her as she rushes past, and hold my head to her head but she struggles free and says "NYO" and is off springing. I lie down on the carpet and wait for her orbit to bring her back to me. She runs over and laughs and starts slapping my face, hard, and pinching my cheeks with her little talons and I have to say "NO, HONEY" and grip her hands and she struggles and moans and I've ruined it all. I remember the guidance of BabyCenter about demonstrating the positive rather than censoring the negative or something like that and

I say "Nice, nice, gentle, gentle," and mime stroking my face with her hands firmly in mine. She smiles and begins to do it herself and I say "very nice, very gentle" but then she's pulling my hair with all her might, and I yell at her and pry her fingers off hard and stand up and my head throbs with renewed vigor.

"How about a snack," I say, and she says "Tsseeeee" and we go to the fridge and I pull out a string cheese and unwrap it for her and then she's off running with the cheese waving like a floppy baton in her mitt. We need to go for a walk, I think. For once I am dressed and ready at the moment I have the impulse to go and I decide that Honey can wear her pajamas and first walk, then ride on me and we will walk a good long way. But then the prospect of covering the somehow interminable stretch required to get out of Deakins Park is so unappealing that I think no, we will drive the car to another location and start the walk from there. But then we'll have to get in the car and get out of the car and Honey will scream when I put her into the car seat and I can't bear to hear her scream right now and I scrap this idea and so we find ourselves on the pavement of Deakins Park again, taking big long strides to try and get out and over the railroad tracks and onto the road to somewhere.

Honey seems to have entered a stage where her only direction is forward, fast, and yet she lacks the coordination to really run. So she does a sort of swift headlong forward walk as though she is running against a great wind, her arms mostly staying at her side, her head and shoulders leading as she moves forward forward forward, falling frequently onto her hands and knees and moaning and holding up her hands for me to dust them off. She hates to have mess on her hands and she's not sure how to dispatch the mess, but I'm here and I wipe off the gravel bits and dust and kiss her palm and she's off moving forward again until we finally cross the railroad tracks and I scoop her up and put her in the Ergo which has been hanging off my back like a tattered cape.

I decide we have to do a loop. I think like I think every time we leave the damn house that the thing that makes me really crazy about being up here is that it is so draining to walk a great distance and then you have to just turn around and do it over again, reliving the same monotonously grand landscape in the same high heat and hot buffeting winds, with the same curious effort of moving your body at high altitude, the same slap of your flat feet on hard asphalt under the pale empty blue, the same nowhere to go.

"We need a horse," I say to Honey, strapped to my front and sitting heavily. "Horse." "Hone," she says. "That's right!" I say. She is lulled by the heat and silence and motion of my body and I wonder like I wonder every time whether it is harming her that I keep putting her in these long-walk situations where she has no verbal stimulation, just her mother, a big silent broody anchor that she is attached to like a barnacle. But it is hot hot hot and my head and my eyebrow throb and I turn us back around and finally we are home and it is 3:45 and I give her milk and put her into the crib to see if she will take another nap and she seems to be thinking about it and I go on the deck and smoke a cigarette and collapse.

Cindy emerges onto her deck with a terrible look on her face and then she sees me and we say Hi.

"What happened to you?" she says, "My god, your face is all busted up."

"Took a little tumble down the stairs," I say breezily. "Nothing serious!" She shakes her head. "What's new with you," I ask. "Did you all howl at the moon?"

"We went over to Manny's."

"You don't look too happy."

"They arrested Chad Burns over that eighty-six grand." There are so many things about this I don't understand that I just say, "Wow." "He's sitting in jail right now, they're trying to humiliate him." "That's too bad," I say.

"It's fucking criminal, is what it is," Cindy says. She puts out her cigarette and moves inside the house purposefully, the conversation disappearing with our smoke in the hot still air.

"Can I ask how your husband died?"

We are in the car with Alice, having navigated with reasonable success and minimal badness the end of the nap the dressing the loading into the car of Honey and the drive to the motel to collect her. She looks over at me with a peculiar expression and says, "He wrote a long letter, packed up his briefcase, took the bus over to the city courthouse, sat down in front, opened his briefcase, poured kerosene all over his flannel, and set himself on fire."

I am stunned and I swerve the Buick as I look over at her and then back at the road.

"Jesus," I say. "Was he . . . protesting Vietnam?"

"No," she says. "Then . . . why," I ask, and she says, "No,

I mean, no, what I said isn't true." I glance over at her again and then back at the road.

"Okay."

"He just died," she shrugs. "His heart gave out when he was a young man."

"That's so sad," I say, and immediately start misting up because there's so much sorrow sloshing around the world. "But why the new version?"

"He was so good, it seems sad to me that he didn't go out in a blaze of glory. He just worked and fretted himself to death." I can see her look over at me out of the corner of my eye. "He was a very special person." I make a sort of bullshit sad smile where your mouth extends flat across your face.

"Anyway, there's no one left now who knew him or the girls. I can test out all kinds of wild stories." I look over again and she has an owlish expression.

"I could see that," I say. "I know it's not equivalent but that's sort of how I feel in Paiute. Everyone's dead or moved on and I don't trust the people who stayed behind with the historical record."

"But I can't do it," she says, as though I hadn't spoken. "The things that happened, happened." I feel brave enough to ask what I have been wondering.

"And your kids?"

"Oh, they really died." Okay. Honey blats in the back.

To get to Antelope Meadows you drive out past the bird refuge out past the dump to the side of town where the rim rocks grow. Big brown rock formations shot through with pale and glimmering veins, they pop dramatically out of the flat earth here and there, sometimes a mantle of soil and grass draped along the top of them. I point at them to change the subject.

"Rim rocks," I say. "Pretty," she says.

"Somewhere around here there's a set of them called Squaw Rocks"—I feel suddenly obligated to provide some kind of local representation and look around the horizon helplessly for the rocks in question, which I don't think are actually anywhere close to here. "There's a legend that the Pit River tribe came over and menaced the Paiute tribe—or maybe it was the Modocs, or maybe it was the other way around, the Paiutes menacing the Pit River—anyway the chief of the tribe that got menaced turned the opposing warriors into rocks as punishment." Not only have I bungled the story like a horrible colonist but I am not even selling the bastardized version. But I liked the story because it's sort of like Daphne and Apollo and the laurel tree, ostensibly without the rape, although I'd like to know why the rocks are "squaws."

"Hmm," she says.

I remember as we pass the first set of rim rocks that this is my favorite route out of town, but one you would only really take to get to Antelope Meadows since it doesn't lead anywhere else I would want to go. I wish I hadn't waited so long to drive out here when the trip could have eaten up just one of the blocks of time spent slapping my heels on the asphalt heading out of Deakins Park and sweating under the straps of the Ergo.

I consider what Antelope Meadows will have on offer. The wine will be challenging but probably $5 or less. Beer will be Coors or Bud and Sierra Nevada if I'm lucky. I will have to make one count because I'm driving. The thought flits through my mind that I am thinking like a person with a Problem, a

LYDIA KIESLING

thought I dismiss, preferring not to add the challenge of achieving sobriety to the resolution of our immigration difficulties, the finessing of my job abandonment, the disposition of my mother's household effects, the raising of Honey. Especially not with a lingering hangover and a black eye. I kindle a little flame of pleasure thinking about the food, such as it is, which like the Golden Spike is possessing a kind of awful majesty. I am fully intending to get the $21.99 prime rib dinner and damn the expense, and Honey can share this with me and eat the damp wrinkled foil-wrapped potato and reheated broccoli florets and crinkle-cut carrots that will accompany the slab of meat. The meat will have a lot of fat in it and they bring you a little dish of very hot horseradish if you ask for it and it makes my mouth water to think of it.

The road that passes through the rim rocks is on an incline so slight you don't feel it until you approach the turnout for Antelope Meadows and see a gentle valley spread out before you, the scattered houses of an ill-starred housing development that every year seems to recede further from the possibility of one day becoming a thriving community. There is, of all things, an overgrown airstrip in the vast basin, I have no idea why, maybe for the cattle gentry who were supposed to settle here and never did. Around all the structures plants and native grasses assert themselves, California fescue and Idaho fescue and a lot of other things I couldn't name, soft and spiky and glinting silvery green in the late-afternoon light, covering the homes of mice and marmots whose holes and mounds are in evidence every few yards. Here and there Indian paintbrush glows red amid the green. In the spring Paiute is a riot of wildflowers, but now it's more subdued.

208

"Isn't it beautiful," I say to Alice, because it really is.

"It reminds me of where I was born," she says. "Our mountains are more impressive but your light is more interesting." Like the Orientalists of yore I have a bad habit of categorizing, taxonomizing that I am trying to break myself of, to not say things like "That's so Turkish," etc., like someone after their first summer abroad. But now I feel a rare flash of possibly legitimate familiarity: women who have returned to the stony west for obscure personal reasons.

We make the turn onto the long drive for the Antelope Meadows lodge, which is a wooden A-frame surrounded by some ratty log buildings. I feel a little thrill to see that there are cars in the parking lot. I look at Alice.

"I'll drop you off in front and park" and she says "I can walk across the darn parking lot" tartly. "I ran around after your baby all morning, didn't I?" "Right," I say, and park next to a behemoth pickup. Honey, who had fallen into her traveler's meditative state, immediately starts clamoring to be released from her car seat. Alice struggles with the button of her seat belt but I don't help her. I get out and get Honey out. I heft her up onto my shoulders and she laughs and shrieks and we monitor Alice as she steps effortfully out of the car. When she's on her feet she straightens her skirt and adjusts her carriage, her shoulders just brushed by her dense and immaculate blunt-cut hair.

She sees me staring at her and says, "What," sourly.

"Your hair is so beautiful," I say to her without thinking.

"Well, thank you," she says. "It was always my pride and joy," she says, and begins walking slowly around the car.

As we approach the door to the lodge I glance at the assortment of bumper stickers in the parking lot. "Save a tree.

Wipe your ass with a spotted owl," says one. "Muzzle Pelosi," says another, with a photo of the U.S. congresswoman in a Hannibal Lecter mask. They both have the State of Jefferson sticker with the flag with its stupid two crosses denoting being "double-crossed" by the Government according to the last *Chronicle* article I read. Whatever generosity of spirit the golden light and fragrant air have stirred in my breast snuffs out and I feel myself droop, looking ahead to a meal with a grumpy old woman in a room full of hostile good ole boys.

I hold the wooden door for Alice and stoop to bring Honey down off my shoulders, and discover that she has taken hold of a fistful of my hair. "Ow ow ow," I say and try to extricate it from below while holding the door open with my hip. Honey grunts as she yanks and Alice says to her, "OH miss! You had better let go of your mommy's hair," and pinches the top of her thigh with a gnarled hand and Honey lets go and is first silent in shock and then puts her hand theatrically on her thigh and cries out and I set her down on the floor and pick her back up. I think Alice ought not to pinch my baby but that's an awkward conversation to have.

The interior of the Antelope Meadows lodge has an air of abandonment notwithstanding the cars out front. There is a bulletin board with laminated informational sheets about the variety of floor plans available for anyone who might still wish to purchase a plot in the development. There is a separate bulletin board for current residents, with yellowing cautionary notices about water scarcity and bears. A few dusty animal heads gaze out from above a cold fireplace. To the left of the main room is the bar/lounge with pool table and a sour smell that extends faintly to the lobby and to the right is the restaurant. I lead Alice to the hostess stand where there is a pretty peaches-and-cream-complected youngish woman in a T-shirt and ponytail with a rose tattoo peeking up near her collarbone. "Two adults and a baby," I say, and she looks questioningly at me.

"I know I recognize you," she says, "but I'm trying to think from where."

"My grandparents used to live here," I say. "Frank and Cora Burdock, over in Deakins Park." Her face lights up.

"We used to ride bikes!" she says. "My folks lived behind them on the other side of the circle for a few years." "Kimmy?" I say after a moment of silence, remembering being five, seven, eight, eleven on home leave, and riding bikes with a moon-faced, smiling girl around and around the park.

"I remember," I say, marveling at how completely that tie had been severed over years of sporadic visits. I don't know her last name; we aren't Facebook friends. We ceased to exist to each other when we were teenagers and I'm surprised by how clearly her child's face returns to me now. We hug around Honey and I say "Can you say hello to Kimmy" and she squirms against me. "This is Honey," I say.

"My goodness, how beautiful," she says to the baby. "What is she, year and a half?"

"Just about," I say. I always feel impressed by how easily other women can do this. I don't think I have any idea how old babies are from looking at them yet.

"I've got three," she says. "My oldest is twelve if you can believe it." We are the same age or thereabouts, thirty-one, thirty-two, thirty-three. "Amazing," I say, feeling truly amazed.

"I know, I'm crazy! But we have a lot of fun." She laughs. "I married a local boy, we live out over on the road to Rigby" and motions east. "I'm just helping out my sister tonight, so this is a real coincidence!" I shift Honey to my other hip and smile broadly wondering what I should say. She saves me the trouble. "My folks are down in Chico now." "Great," I say.

"We always missed your grandparents so much," she says kindly. "They were real good people."

"Thank you," I say. "I miss them too."

"Your mom was in Sac . . ."

"She's gone now too," I say, and she nods. "I heard that. I'm sorry. Are you up here to stay?" she asks, with seemingly genuine interest.

"Just visiting, you know, showing Honey the place. We've been trying to sell the house but it's just sitting there."

"Yeah, the market's no good right now, unless you got a land parcel to go with it. Where are you living now?" She darts her eyes over my hand and then her gaze moves and lingers on my face and I remember suddenly my ghastly eyebrow and how it must look. I put my hand to it and say "Ugh, I know, it's awful—I tripped last night and banged it on the front walk." And she says "Yikes" and I answer her question and say "Down in San Francisco. My husband is Turkish—he's over there now finishing school. We had some mix-ups with his green card that we're trying to deal with." I hate how much of a shady business this makes it sound like our marriage is, not to mention my fucked-up face and the fact that she probably thinks I married a foreign wife-beater even though this makes no sense because I just said he was back in Turkey and I feel irrationally angry at Kimmy and her local boy and three children.

"I remember when we were kids you always lived somewhere over there . . . was it Greece?" "Yeah," I say. "Good memory!" Alice shifts beside me and I realize how rude I've been. "Uh, I'm sorry, Kimmy, this is Alice, my friend" and Alice nods and Kimmy says "Pleasure" with a huge smile.

"How long are you here? We should get together. My kids love little kids. And they're homeschooled so we love getting together with other families." I feel equal parts suspicion and guilt at the word "homeschooled" but I say "That sounds really good" and it actually sort of does. She's so cheerful and nice. She picks up a pen to take my number and I consider giving her the number which is functionally useless but then I think that's hostile and I say "My phone doesn't work that well here, and we cut off the landline. Maybe we ought to just pick a time."

"Gotcha," she says. She looks inside her mind with the look all women get as they tally their forthcoming obligations. "How about Tuesday lunch?"

"Great," I say weakly.

"You want to just save my address on your phone? It's out on County Road Twelve" and rattles off a number that I type into a draft text message. Honey is still resting limply against my body and I am feeling so fatigued from this interaction that I start rocking from one foot to the other in my impatience to exit.

"Well, see you then," I say. An elderly man in a trucker hat hobbles up to the hostess stand.

"Well, let me get you seated," she says, and she puts us in the corner by the huge window looking over the swing set and the lake and lugs over a high chair for Honey.

"Can't wait to catch up," she says, and I say "Yes, yes" and she goes back to seat the old man. I get Honey in the high chair and Alice slowly eases herself into her chair.

"You found a friend," Alice says drily.

"It's so strange. I hardly remember anything from when I was a kid," I say. "Like I deleted most of my memories somewhere along the line. But I remember her face."

"They always come back when you least expect it," she says. "Prime rib, rib eye, T-bone, New York strip, lamb chops, pork chop," she reads. "Not an easy place to be a vegetarian."

"Oh god, I'm sorry," I say. "You didn't say." I scan the menu. "There's, uh, a Caesar salad. French fries."

"Oh, I'm not a vegetarian anymore," she says. "It's too hard on the road. Especially here in cow country."

I am distracted by Kimmy walking back to the hostess stand. "Three kids," I say absentmindedly. "I literally cannot imagine."

"Well, some people take to it better than others," Alice says and I feel a little resentful at the implication.

Honey takes a soft gold-wrapped square of butter from the bowl next to the basket of dense white bread and mashes it onto her salad plate. I'm suddenly aware of the lingering upset of my stomach and the pounding of my head. "What am I going to do," I say to Alice helplessly.

"Order your prime rib," she says kindly.

A teenage boy comes to wait on us and we order. I ask for the inevitable Sierra Nevada which I am suddenly desperate for and Alice asks for a glass of red wine.

"So how much longer are you planning to be on the road," I ask Alice, while Honey tears up her bread and stuffs it into her mouth.

"Well, the map says it's just a few more hours to the place I'm trying to get to."

She looks out the window. "I've been stalling. It hurts so much to drive honestly, I'm not sure what to do."

"And then you're supposed to drive all the way back once you've gotten there?"

"Something like that," she says. Honey grabs a fistful of the polyester tablecloth and yanks, and I put both hands on the surface of the table to stabilize it and say, "We don't do that," while keeping one eye on Alice.

"The last day before I got here I could hardly stand an hour in the car." She looks at her little bird wrist and gnarled hands. I remember that I left my child unattended with a ninety-two-year-old woman all morning and the chorus unfit mother unfit mother resumes in my head. I pull Honey's hand away from her mouth into which she is trying to stuff a piece of bread. "Slowly, please," I say, and she pulls free and jams the bread in.

"Ha," Alice says drily.

"What are you going to do, then?"

The food arrives, the expected enormous slab of prime rib hanging off my plate, run through with stringy fat. Honey starts flapping her arms and saying "Heh heh eh eh" and lunges over to scrabble her fingers across the surface of the meat. "Wait just a minute please, Honey. Please be patient. Please do good listening," etc. etc. I cut some little tiny pieces and put them onto her plate and she starts shoveling them into her mouth forming a meat wad and then spitting it out. A really uninspired salad is set down in front of Alice, cubes of cheese and kidney beans from the can on iceberg lettuce.

"So really, how are you going to get back?"

"Well," she says. "Mark and Yarrow and I had talked about one of them flying out to drive me back. Or fly me back. Or some combination of things." She rummages around in her leather purse and pulls out a burner cell phone.

"I call them every day with this," she says. "Tell them where I am and assure them I'm eating and taking my medicine." She rolls her eyes.

"Makes sense," I say. She begins pulling little orange pill bottles out of the bag, and one of those Monday Tuesday Wednesday AM/PM pill boxes with flaps like my grandparents used to have.

"Maybe you could help me, actually," she says. "I wasn't supposed to be gone this long and all the pills they set up for me in my box are gone. It's a little difficult for me to open the bottles."

"Well sure," I say, delighted to be useful to someone, and reach for one. Honey is very interested in anything that has other things inside it and she lunges for one of the bottles and shakes it vigorously before I wrestle it away. I squint to read the instructions.

"This one says take with food," I say.

"Yes, yes." She sounds irritable. "There are three that I need to take now."

"Okay," I say, feeling some instinct of care and competence spring into action. I reach across Alice and take hold of the pills, briskly lining them up in front of me. "No," I say preemptively to Honey, and deposit some bread and potato and broccoli and carrots next to the chewed gray wads of meat on her plate. When was the last time she ate a green vegetable, I think, my brain scans the calendar and it was broccoli sometime in the preceding week and that's not so bad but obviously could be better, although she did have a sweet potato and that is fibrous and nutritious at least. I read every label and isolate the meds Alice is supposed to take now into one group and the others in another, both out of the reach of Honey. She reaches both arms out in front of her and I make a move to stop her but she grasps with two sure hands my water glass, which I'd unthinkingly moved closer to her to make way for all the pills. She slowly brings the glass to her lips and slowly tilts it up until her lips meet the ice and water. She flips the glass up a little too swiftly and water sloshes out and fills her silicone bib. "Uh-oh! Uh-oh!" she says, looking at me with concern.

"Good job!" I say to her. "What a good girl!!!!" I leave Honey to splash more water over her bib and return to the pill counting. I put three pills in front of Alice to take and carefully dole out the rest into her box.

"All set," I say, and look to the wet ruin of Honey's outfit. Water pools around the pieces of prime rib on her plate. I tilt it back into my glass. Alice slowly pops pills into her mouth and swigs her wine. A wet spot creeps from under Honey's plate.

"So Mark and Yarrow," I say. "Are they your relatives?"
"No," she says. "I don't have relatives to speak of. I'll probably leave my money and things to them. They already bought my house, I think I told you that. I live in a cottage on the property now. It's sort of a commune. My husband and I wanted it to be that kind of place, when we bought it. But he never got to live in it."

Honey starts pulling at her wet seat and caterwauling. I shhhh her and get her bag from under the chair and pull out a pair of baby pants, congratulating myself on having the foresight to bring a change of clothes. I reach over and pull her out of the high chair and onto my lap, and hold her legs together to keep her from kicking. I take up the patter of talk that I've convinced myself works to soothe her. "Don't worry big girl we're just going to put some new pants on, we don't want to be a cold wet baby sh sh sh" and I tug the pants off over her shoes and wiggle the new pants onto her, wipe up the damp on her high chair with my totally nonabsorbent green napkin and set her back in place. Alice is chewing meditatively on a piece of the airy nothing bread.

The hum of conversation in the dining room is broken by big guffaws, and I look behind to see two enormous red-faced white men, not fat, just huge like tree trunks, in matching camouflage hats, their heads thrown back, forks gripped in big fists. Nancy Pelosi and Spotted Owl, I think to myself, perhaps unjustly. Honey looks too and one of them sees her and lights up and starts waving and then peekabooing behind his paws, and she looks up through her eyelashes and puts her chin to her shoulder and I roll my eyes.

"How do they learn this," I say to Alice, who looks confused. "She's so flirtatious with strangers." I point to the baby. "I just wonder where that comes from."

"Mine were like that, the twins at least, until they got sick. Before the little one got sick too she needed attention so bad she didn't flirt so much as throw herself on people."

"When did they get sick," I venture.

"They were a little older than Honey." I want so much to ask what it was how did they get it what were the symptoms and I notice I've put my hand on Honey's curls without realizing. I hadn't even considered that she might already have an illness that will kill her.

"Sorry," she says. "I don't mean to scare you."

"That's okay," I say. "I think about bad things happening to her all the time." Honey is looking over her shoulder at the big men. "I mean I spend a lot of time trying to be prepared for something awful to happen." She shakes her head. "You can't prepare."

"I know," I say. "But I still try. Hedging, I guess."

"You can't prepare for seeing your children wasting away. Or when they're gone, but you're still their mother, with all that love and nothing to use it on." Her nose wrinkles and my mustard fog immediately gathers behind my eyes.

"I'm so, so sorry," I say, pointlessly. I want to do a laying-on-of-hands, but where. Her hand sitting forlornly on the table? Her ax-head of a shoulder blade? There's no right place. I keep my hands on my silverware.

"How old were they when they died?"

"The twins were young," she says. "Their sister was grown, a little younger than you. I was already old." We just sit there together in silence. She looks ahead, out the window at the swing set at the edge of the lake, the series of black mole holes that dot the expanse of dried grass.

With whatever emotional intelligence she has Honey looks bemusedly at us but stays quiet.

"I'm so sorry," I say, again.

"You'd think there's an age when you get used to it, but you don't." What to say here? I understand, I don't; I imagine, I can't; so I just say "I believe you." I blow my nose into the napkin.

"It's nice, actually," she says in a creaking voice. "To be around Honey. I remember things I forgot before, about taking care of little children." She takes her fork and spears a single bean with shaking hand. "Today I thought about the twins being born. I remembered being pregnant again when they were just Honey's age, right before we knew they were sick." Honey drops her fork on the carpet and moans and I pick it up and wipe it off and hand it back without looking. "If I could freeze a moment I think it would be that one. We took them on hikes every weekend, a pack and a baby on each of our backs." I stifle a sob and she looks almost affectionately at me.

"My husband always wanted a whole bunch of kids. I just wanted one who wasn't sick, even though I felt bad to think about it that way. But he died before we could have another. And it probably would have been sick anyway." She puts a single kidney bean into her mouth. "I was a teacher, you know."

"How long did you do that?"

"Only got to do it for two years. Then I had my babies and that was just about it for me for a good long time."

I shake my head to disperse the little cluster of thoughts her report has brought on. Alice placidly chews salad. Honey is occupied with her bread. The burly men clink their forks. A thought announces itself and as is usually the case whenever I have a charitable thought I decide to immediately say it and regret it rather than stop to consider and then talk myself out of it.

"What if we took you on to the camp?" I say. "You said it's just a few hours. We can leave you there, or bring you there and come back here, or whatever you decide to do." She frowns. I wonder whether I've offended her, and remember anew that any ship of that nature has sailed, since she saw me half naked this morning after having agreed to announce the news of my death should the occasion require. She has seen my boobs and held my baby. I forge on.

"I can talk to Mark and Yarrow if you think it would help them feel less anxious." Her hair is so smooth, it's like gray onyx or something, if onyx can be gray, my eyes keep going back to it. I want to touch it, a bridge too far.

"What about your job?" she asks.

"I think as long as I keep e-mailing them they can't accuse me of job abandonment." I swallow another piece of prime rib. "So what do you think?"

"I think it's odd that you aren't more worried about my plan. Mark and Yarrow were ready to have me committed. I have to admit the fact that you aren't makes me wonder if I really am crazy." I catch the implied rebuke and have to decide quickly whether to reveal some sign of how much it wounds me or whether to laugh it off.

"Well, given my behavior since you met me that's a reasonable fear, Alice," I say, deciding to take the high road. "I probably seem like a nutcase."

"I don't think you're a nutcase," she says. "Just highly strung." I take Honey's sippy cup full of milk out of my bag and give it to her. "Mut," she says, and I am getting ready to launch into a spiel and almost don't notice it's the first time she's said it.

"Oh my goodness!!!" I cheer. "Yes, your milk! You're going to drink your milk!"

"Mut," she says and I kiss her.

I notice movement by the door and glance over to see a large group of van Voorheeses enter, but not the Ed branch. I don't know their names but I recognize them from the various funerals the last decade compelled me to participate in—the Elks Lodge, the Golden Spike, the Grange in Revival Junction. This is the old crowd, although there are a couple of young people with them and I wonder where the young people live and what they do. These are the people my mother could have gone up to and been hugged by and talked about ancient sled accidents with, long-ago horse rides, Girl Scout camp, waterskiing down in Gold Lake. She and Uncle Rodney always said they had the greatest childhood. My own legacy in the town is as a gloomy teenager, an eye-rolling waif. But when my grandfather died, then my grandmother, then my mom, I stood with Uncle Rodney and felt the town's warmth as I sampled the enchiladas chilis bean salads potato salads accorded me as a bereaved daughter of Altavista.

It occurs to me that going over and saying hello is an act of filial piety. They haven't met Honey, who is the small but very present, very alive continuation of the Burdock line. I sigh and look at Alice.

"I should go and say hello to those people," I say. "They knew my mom and my grandparents."

"Fine by me," she says.

"You want another glass of wine?" I ask her. "Better not," she says.

"I'll just be a minute," I say, and extricate Honey from her high chair. "We're going to say hello to the people who knew your grandma."

They have been seated on the other side of Spotted Owl and Nancy Pelosi and the latter wave again at Honey as I maneuver around their table. We arrive in front of the van Voorheeses' long table and I address myself to the elderly couple on one end whose names have escaped me. "Excuse me," I say, leaning forward to the woman. "I'm, um, Jeannie Burdock's daughter. Frank and Cora's granddaughter," and they reward my filial piety by saying "Oh oh" and standing up and depositing napkins on the table and giving me a big hug and putting their hands on my shoulder and touching Honey's hand. "And who is this?" they ask and I say "This is my daughter" and like that I just start crying.

"Oh honey," says the woman. "We miss your mom and her mom and dad too." I nod and wipe my eyes.

"I'm sorry," I say. "I just don't really know anyone up here, I thought I'd say hi."

"We were just saying we hardly recognize anyone anymore. We live down in Red Bluff most of the year now. We just came up for the Parade and the Cattlewomen's shindig." Oh god. The Fourth of July parade. The Cattlewomen's Association.

"This is Honey," I say.

"Well hi, little Honey," the lady says. "Bill, just look at her!" That's right, his name is Bill.

"Where do you all live now?" Bill asks.

"Well, we live in San Francisco, but it's a little complicated right now because my husband is Turkish and the government made some mistake with his green card and he's stuck there while we're trying to get it figured out."

"Oh gosh, that's too bad," she says.

"Turkish!" the man says and chucks Honey under the chin. "Imagine that!" and I say, "Yep, she's ah, Honey Mehmetoğlu." "Well hello, Honey," he says and smiles kindly.

"Now didn't you and your mom live somewhere over there," the woman says. "Yeah, we did for a while," I say, and she nods and says "What an interesting experience you all got to have," and I say "Sure did" and the waitress arrives to take orders and I glance at Alice staring off into space and say, "Well, nice to see you all," just as the man is saying "Now, how's Rod doing," and I say, "Oh, real good," and they say good and I say again "Nice to see you all" and they say "Yes, yes," and pat me and I walk back to our table carrying Meltem Mehmetoğlu.

Alice is looking bored by the time I get Honey back into her high chair and cut some more meat for her and start working away on the sinewy pieces.

"How was your visit," she says and I chew and say "Fine" through a mouthful of meat and then I swallow the meat and say "Um, so, would you like us to come with you, to the camp?"

"I suppose that would be all right," she says. Honey starts thrashing in her seat and I smell poop. "Okay," I say. "Good." I want to show Alice that I am not crazy and that I can take care of the necessary arrangements. "So shall I talk to Mark and Yarrow? I mean, I'm happy to get on the phone with them and just tell them I'm a responsible person and I'll, uh, take care of you. Not that you need taking care of."

"Okay," Alice says. "That's probably wise." I pick up Honey. "I have to change her diaper, I think," I tell her. "Would you like to try the ice cream bar? I can bring you something." "No thank you," she says, and I think I might want something from the ice cream bar, but I remember I have the Diamond box at home still and this time I won't throw myself down the stairs.

I sling Honey over my hip and we walk across the room waving at the van Voorheeses and to Kimmy, who points me to the bathroom. "We'll catch up," she says, and I say "Absolutely" and rush Honey to the bathroom because she is starting to cry and squirm and the smell says to me that the diaper has been breached. I feel calm and capable and as we open the door to go into the bathroom I say "We are going to have you fixed up in a jiffy," and then with the mother machine brain I run a quick diagnostic of the situation and recall that I have already put her spare pants on her but then remember that the other pants are just wet with water and so they will work as a switch if the worst has happened. There is a changing table in the handicapped stall and I set Honey down and she cries and squirms and I babble at her "You're fine you're fine you're fine" and think about what we'll need to get done before we take Alice to her last stop. We'll need to clean up the house. We'll need to call Engin send several e-mails to the Institute do laundry and pack everything up. Sure enough there is a smear of poop that reaches up to Honey's back, peeking out of the diaper onto the inside band of her pants but mercifully not her shirt. I regret that poop is getting on the changing pad I've spread over the fold-out changing table but remember also that I have hand sanitizer because I am organized and ready for anything. I wipe Honey's bottom put on cream put on the new diaper put on the damp previous pants and pack everything up and set her down on her feet and glance at my phone which tells me it is nearing bedtime. She grabs my leg and says "Mee-ow mee-ow mee-eow" which I realize with sudden clarity is "Pick me up!" and I say "Ah, yes! Yes I will pick you up! Listen to all this talking you're doing" and I pick her up and kiss her a big dramatic kiss that makes her giggle and I think I don't make her laugh enough and I do it again and again until she's laughing so hard her hiccupy baby laugh it's hard for her to catch her breath. I don't do anything for her enough, I think, not enough talking singing playing teaching.

I knock the door open with my butt and pass by Kimmy who says "Can't wait to get our kids together" and it almost dissipates the all-pervading feeling of desolation I get in Alta-vista, look at this friendly normal person raising her family and having a great life up here even if she is homeschooling them and teaching them god knows what. I file this thought and get back to the table and look around for someone to get us the check and Alice says "I paid," and I consider groping around for cash I don't have and instead just say "Thank you, that's very nice." I set Honey on her feet and get on my knees to clean up the wads of bread and napkin and meat and other shit all over the dense nap of the rug and tuck it into a napkin and when I lift my head I see Honey is running down the room with that forward tumbling run. By the time I've leapt to my feet to go after her she's splayed headlong on the ground and wailing and I pick her up and kiss her grab the bag make sure Alice is out of her seat and walking slowly behind and wave to the van Voorheeses wave to Kimmy and I'm sweating when we get out into the cool night air.

I put Honey down on the crunchy grass that abuts the parking lot and let her run around. It feels so good outside, the air smells so good and feels so good on my skin and it's the first time in weeks I've felt a good physical sensation that wasn't immediately followed by psychic distress. Honey screams just to hear herself and pants, she's so happy to run around.

"Well," I say to Alice, "I guess I ought to take you back and we'll all get ready to go tomorrow."

"Let the little one run around some," Alice says. "You don't let her stretch her legs enough." It's amazing to me that I find a rebuke of my mothering in even the mildest statements from friends coworkers strangers i.e. "Sleepy baby!" or something innocuous but this actual rebuke, this correction, feels so natural I accept it without injury. "Stay on the grass, please, Honey," I say and lower myself onto the low concrete wall that lines the path to the lodge. I'd love to pull the cigarettes out of my bag where I've stashed them just in case but there's Honey and there's Alice and all the promises I've made to myself about not being trash. Not trash. Shouldn't say trash. Alice stays standing. "If I sit on that thing I'll never get up," she says. I wonder at her body, that she's been able to drive out here all alone.

"So how will we work this?" I am feeling efficient ready to bang out some logistics. "So you're going to call Mark and Yarrow and tell them what exactly? That you met a responsible person who is going to drive you out there and then bring you to an airport? I haven't looked at a map yet—do you know what town this place is near?"

"It's in Oregon," she says. "Someplace over the border. I have it all printed out in my folder. It's something like four hours from here."

"That's nothing," I say. "Do you want to do it in one day or break it up?"

"Maybe we can see how everyone does."

"We can stop in Berwin Falls or something if you want

to spend the night. Ooh, if we leave early enough tomorrow we can drive up to Surprise Pass and have a picnic. It has a beautiful view."

"Well, all right."

I have been making a little grocery list for what would make the nicest picnic when I pause to realize that something about our plan makes no sense. Honey runs up to us and throws herself against Alice's legs and I hold a hand out to Alice's arm to steady her and say "gentle, please be gentle" and she takes off whirling unsteadily and falls onto her back in the grass and says "baaak" which is "bonk."

"Sorry, Alice—I just realized—are we going to drive your car? And then we'll all drive back together? You mentioned the airport, I guess I didn't think about what would happen to your car."

"No airport," she says. "If I need to I'll ask Mark to come and drive me home from Altavista. This will just be a day or two, to see the place. We can take your car. It's more comfortable than mine."

"The Buick! Can't beat it," I say. Honey is yanking on my pant legs and she has that shark look like she might bite me. "Shall we . . ." I say, and Alice begins moving toward the car.

We drop Alice off and agree to meet at the motel at 9:30 a.m. after I've stopped at the market to get provisions. She eats everything, she says, except very chewy things. Back home Honey is a damp wriggling critter thrashing in the bath but we get through it then we read the two halves of *The Very Hungry Caterpillar* and she puts her finger in the hole left by the caterpillar and when I put her in the Pack 'n Play she just lies right down with her head on the pillow and her butt in the air and suffers to be covered up with her blanky and the light turned off with no fuss. There is enough vodka left for two little drinks, I reckon, and I carefully pour half into a glass stir in the juice and almost run onto the deck to smoke. Inside Cindy's lit window I see her and Ed toing and froing and when she walks out the door onto her porch I holler at her. "Hi," she says very curtly, and carries a duffel to Ed's truck. "Going somewhere?" I ask, but she doesn't hear or doesn't answer, and I realize I don't care. I have a real friend now, I laugh to myself. Me 'n' Alice, against the world. One more drink, I think, and amble inside to mix it feeling the whole night stretching out before me to relax in my lawn chair on my deck and look at the stars. By the time the relief of being off duty re: Honey has faded and I start to feel horribly lonely I'll be slightly blotto and ready for the king bed to receive me. I sit down with my new drink. I pass my hand over the egg on my eyebrow and light another cigarette and again see how far I can draw it down with one drag.

DAY 8   I have my dream I have all the time where I am in an office trying to talk to a Turkish person, not Engin, someone unknown to me, and I'm saying "Oh of course I speak Turkish," in Turkish, preparing to launch into the explanation of what is wrong, a thing I don't know in the dream, and find I can't speak Turkish at all and can only force a few words out until they smile sympathetically and shake their head and I want to start screaming and I open my mouth wide to do it and nothing really comes out, just a tiny squeaking and I wake up feeling that there's nothing a man can tell me about impotence.

But I wake up feeling surprisingly fresh given the dream and the egg on my forehead, just a gentle throb on my eyebrow. I wake up with the expectation of hearing Honey and realize I don't. The clock reads 6:57. I move very carefully out of the bed and tiptoe around to the closet and peer in and she's sprawled on her back, deep asleep, and I pause long enough to see her chest rise and her fingers move. I scurry away into the shower and take a long hot one listening for her cries. She's still asleep when I emerge and I say the prayer of thanksgiving for how much I am about to get done unencumbered. Now that I am not really doing anything there is nothing I am really unencumbered from but it's still easier to do anything when your baby is asleep. I make coffee. I put laundry in. I pick up the living room. I smoke a cigarette out on the deck knowing I need to call Engin and trying to see if I can pick up Cindy's Wi-Fi which is recalcitrant this morning when I hear Honey beginning to chirp. I go in.

"Hello, sweet pea," I say. "We're going on a trip today!" She doesn't really know what that means I'm assuming but she laughs and claps her hands and waves her arms up and down and I scoop her up do a running jump onto the king bed twisting in midair so that she lands on top of me as I land on top of it and she screams with joy. I put Cheerios banana a little milk into one of my grandmother's glazed white bowls with its spidery gray cracks and she uses her spoon like a big girl and I say the whole time "We're going to go in the car with Auntie Alice, we are going to a new state." I put her on the living room rug with her milk and books and fly around the bedroom and the back porch throwing things into the duffel and the tote keeping up my singsong "Now we put the socks, now we put the comforter, now we pack the Pack 'n Play" until I realize we are packed, completely packed, as though we aren't planning to come back and I'm shocked by how little impression we've made on the place. I notice I have been standing stock-still in the middle of the room chewing on this thought because I feel a silence in the place of Honey's low hum and see her sitting in the corner of the room with her shoulders hunched, listlessly turning over the pages of one of her books. She does this sometimes when I don't play with her or fuss over her for an extended period of time, just goes all mopey and quiet like she's expecting no one to ever talk to her again and it makes me feel like a murderer. So I look at her and say "We could not come back." And then I zoom over to her on my hands and knees and bury my face in her belly and she laughs and revives and gets that awful sad hunch out of her back and climbs all over me shrieking.

I decide to treat this excursion as a possible exit strategy and just put everything in the car and act like when we lock it up it will be the last time. I get the cooler from the garage and look at Mom's boxes. I say "Bye Mom" softly to the boxed-up sleeping things with which she made all our dwellings a home, and then I say "Bye Dad" and before I can hang around and start to feel morose I get the cooler and close the garage behind me. I walk over to the front of the house and straighten Rosemary Urberoaga's For Sale sign and smooth back its folded corner and brush off some caked-on dirt.

Everything is in the car now and we are in the car and we have gotten turkey salami cheese bread banana chips cutlery and two big jugs of water and are making our way to the Arrowhead Motel, which is just past the Golden Spike on the way out of town, when I remember I didn't return the library books and I file this away. They've got a big sign soaring up to the sky like the Frosty, and the customary cattle skulls and old wagon parts with some geraniums and so forth planted around. At the end of the row of rooms and the parking lot is a ludicrous patch of very green grass that they must spend a fortune keeping wet all year around, but right now there are a group of deer on it finding tender morsels and Alice is sitting primly on a bench overlooking the patch and it makes such an oddly nice tableau you kind of see why they do it. I'm turning into the parking lot when I realize that I didn't take a moment to call

Engin before leaving and I'm not sure when I'll be able to and say "Fucker" so loud that Honey startles in the back and drops her cup and says "Uh-oh" and I say "Mommy said a bad word sweet pea" and I think to myself I spoke with him yesterday, I spoke with him yesterday, I spoke with him yesterday, everything's okay and then I drive over to Alice and roll down the window and say "Going our way?" and she says "You'll have to get my bag from the room" and gestures at the open door. I unbuckle dart out and into the damp cave of her room and find a tidy little wheelie suitcase and tote and a big umbrella and see she's left $20 for the maid, which is the ultimate mark of civility as far as I'm concerned. I get her suitcase into the trunk and hover over her while she navigates to the passenger side and onto the soft seat of the Buick. She's holding a folder which she waves my way.

"I got the fellow at the front desk to print out some maps." "Excellent," I say, although it's been years since I read a map that wasn't on my phone. But I see he's printed out the step-by-step directions from Google and I shuffle through these and say, "Okay, I think we're good." He's mapped the route west and then north over the border once we're closer to the coast and this means we can have the hoped-for picnic at Surprise Pass.

I look back at Honey who has her cup but is waving her arms like she wants to throw it and is whining and just generally has an ornery look as she strains against her straps. I say "We're having fun" which my grandpa used to say and then look at Alice who is wincing a little and wriggling in her seat. "Are you sure you're going to be comfortable," I ask, and she says "I'll manage." Honey starts bawling openly so I just say "We're having fun" again, with emphasis this time, and point the car out of the Arrowhead parking lot. Alice points at her car in a far corner spot and says "Goodbye, Rocinante!" and looks at me. "That's the car's name," she says solemnly. I laugh with approval but then I feel my shoulders creep up to my ears as is their wont when Honey cries. Alice twists her narrow body to the extent possible and says "Now what" to Honey, and puts her hands over her eyes and does a creaking peeka-boo, and the little internal combustion engine of joy that runs Honey makes a smile bloom on her wet cheeks.

"There's not a thing wrong with this little baby," says Alice. I notice she is wearing a wedding ring, a yellow gold band around her finger that wasn't there yesterday.

"You're wearing your wedding ring," I venture.

"Sometimes I put it on."

"You never got remarried?" She looks out her window at the scenery, which has given over to sagebrush and will soon climb into scrub pine. A jackrabbit runs across the road before I can even think to slow the car. "I never met anybody I wanted to get remarried with."

"How long were you married before he died?"

"Twenty years." A long time, I think, and then I remember that it's been fifty years since. "How long have you been mar-ried?" She asks as though she doesn't really care to know the answer. She's distracted, staring out the window but I answer her anyway.

"Three years. I met him almost ten years ago and we dated for a month, and then we didn't see each other for five years and then we basically got married right away. My mom got sick in the meantime so I had gone back to be with her and we weren't serious anyway, I mean I barely could talk to him, linguistically speaking." It doesn't matter if she's listening or not, it's nice to be asked about yourself I don't care who you are.

"You can't know them anyway," she says, so I guess she is listening. "I mean you don't know what they are going to do when the rubber meets the road."

"What did your husband do when your kids got sick?"

"Well, he agonized, he loved them, he made up stories for them, he read to them all night long. But he went to work all day long too, and he had very strict politics. He didn't believe it was right to pay someone to look after them, because of the power balance. He was an egalitarian." I almost stop the car. "So what did you do?" "We compromised," she says. "We could accept someone's help if they were getting something in return." "Something other than money?" I asked. "He was a Marxist, I guess you could say." Not a spook then, I think to myself and make a note to pursue further inquiries at a suitable juncture. "So instead of paid help we had fellows come and stay with us after they got out of bad situations, jail and such. I had to negotiate with him about what kind of crimes were acceptable."

I can't help myself, I laugh. "What the fuck," I say and immediately freeze but she actually laughs too. "Anyway, it was very difficult. Even their wheelchairs were huge wooden things I couldn't really get up the stairs. And then after the first of our girls died he up and died too."

"What did you do?" I look back at Honey and she is lulled by the road. "What do you mean what did I do? I despaired. I grieved. I carried on."

I feel there is something accusatory in her tone, as if to say, "I didn't have some little meltdown like you seem to be having over nothing," and I am preemptively mad about this, since I'm driving her ass to god knows where but then she says "But I did finally pay someone to help me out" and I look over and she has a small smile on her face.

She leans her head against the window.

"I think I'll take a little nap, if you don't mind."

"Go right ahead."

My energetic feeling from the early morning is collapsing in its usual midmorning way and I try to muster new feelings. First I think about what a luxury it is to be a Marxist who has an extremely accommodating wife. Then I think about the salami in the cooler and the cigarettes in my bag and the fact that the house is all packed up the bed is made and there's no reason at all to go back. The road is so smooth—kaymak gibi, like cream, you say in Turkish—and the Buick gliding over it. Honey has quieted in the back seat.

After twenty minutes or so Honey is asleep and Alice is emitting light snores next to me. I glance at her and see how very old she looks. We speed along. We begin the slow climb to Surprise Pass and when we reach the turnout I pull the Buick over. To get to the prime grassy spot you have to walk a little way on a trail and it occurs to me that this will be impossible for Alice, something I have failed to take into account. But there is a decrepit picnic table not far from the commemorative stone pillar and plaque and the valley is still a wide sweep before us, with Altavista a few clustered buildings in the distance. The sky is a pallid, milky blue now, save a gray mass to the far north, with the shady apparition of summer rain high in the sky in the far distance. Alice opens her eyes as soon as I turn the car off.

"Hi," I say. She grunts.

"Well, we're here now, if you'd like to have a picnic," I say.

"Sounds nice," she says thinly. She looks absolutely exhausted.

"I'll get everything set up if you want to stay put for a second."

"Okay." Honey is still asleep. I hustle around the back of the Buick and get the cooler and the tote bag with Honey's diaper accoutrements and I lug them to the picnic table and spread out Grandma's plaid tablecloth and take the tomato the cheese the salami etc. out of the cooler and start slicing and putting out mustard and cutlery and I lay out what I think is frankly a very nice little spread. I return to the car and extend my hand to Alice, who looks at it a minute before taking it and allowing me to hoist her up. She shrugs off my hand once she's on her feet and straightens her skirt and walks slowly to the picnic table. "I probably won't be able to swing my legs over that bench," she says, and I say, "We'll face out and look down at the valley then." I begin unbuckling Honey from her seat and she stirs and her face immediately crumples. I coo and make funny faces and peekaboo and she does her cry laugh and I kiss her cheek and her neck and she squirms and snorts. I disentangle her from the seat and carry her over to the picnic table. "We're going to have a picnic," I say to her, and she says "Bibit" and I recognize that she is trying to say picnic and I make a fuss.

"She's starting to try and say a lot more words since we've gotten here," I say to Alice, and she says, "That's good. Smart baby."

"It's only been a week," I say, and she smiles a little wanly and I wonder if this was the reverse of her experience, her babies going backward into themselves and I try to be more subdued about Honey's developments.

"Picnic," I say to Honey. "Bibit," she says. I make her a kind of deconstructed sandwich with cheese shreds salami shreds pieces of bread and Alice says, "She probably doesn't need you to shred it all up like that, she's a big girl. You're a big girl, aren't you?" She looks at Honey and smiles broadly and it looks almost ghoulish compared to her normal expression.

"I guess you're right," I say. "I just don't want her to choke."

I gesture at the valley and say, "This could be apocryphal but I think the reason this was called Surprise Pass is that this was where one of the emigrant trails came through and I guess at some point a group of settlers hunkered down to celebrate their successful passage west, and they were attacked by Indians. I think that was the surprise."

"That's cute," says Alice and it makes me laugh.

"Or maybe the surprise is how underwhelmed they were," I say. "Maybe the surprise is that you make it over a huge mountain pass and see the massive desolate plain you've still got to cross." "Surprise!" Alice says, spreading out her hands.

"Cholera!" I laugh frankly and I feel how long it has been since someone other than Honey made me laugh. But the valley is a balm after the ravages of town, a vast open view of soft-looking green grasses, the yellow sweep of hills moving up into low forested peaks at the basin's far reach. It's not verdant, not gentle, but it looks pretty good.

"When did your people come here?" she asks.

"Eighteen eighties, I think. They had a pretty good run."

"But you never lived up here?"

"My dad was in the foreign service, did I tell you that?" She doesn't say anything. "We always lived in cities. I had a crazy thought maybe we could stay up here for a while but I just can't. The largest group of people I've even seen since I've been here is the damn State of Jeffersoners," I say. "And they're literally separatists. Not to mention my husband could never stand it assuming he ever gets back here." I fold a piece of salami into my mouth. Honey who has been on my lap starts squirming and I set her on the bench next to me.

"You're going to sit like a big girl, oh boy!" I say. I notice Alice isn't eating and gesture at the food. She fumbles for a piece of salami and puts it on bread. Honey has slid off the bench with her plastic spoon and is jamming it into the ground. She bends forward, planting her hands and her forehead on the dirt in a way that can't be comfortable but I can see her upside-down smile between her legs. I stand and grab her ankles and flip her over in a somersault, resting her gently on her back. She screams joyfully and springs up and I brush the dirt off her forehead and she struggles free to do it again.

"What fun!" says Alice. "Such good somersaults!" We repeat this three more times and then I'm winded and I pick her up and dance her over to Alice, who has been watching and clapping cheerfully.

Flies are beginning to descend and buzz. "You're not eating," I note. "Aren't you hungry?" She looks at the beading salami on the paper plate skeptically and says, "I guess not. I only do one big meal a day lately." She must see my concern because she sort of fluffs herself up. "Why don't we stop in the town you showed me on the map tonight and get a big pizza and a pitcher of beer?"

"That sounds like heaven," I say.

"And we can call Mark and Yarrow." I lift Honey to smell her butt, which squishes, and dig in the tote to find her changing things. I lay out the pad on the bench opposite Alice and tug off Honey's socks pants undo her diaper and hush her fake crying. I try to avoid pushing poop into her vagina, try not to get poop on my hand. A wipe tumbles into the dirt and I pick it up gingerly and place it onto the bench behind me.

"Always such a mess," I say to Alice, who is staring into space vaguely in our direction. All I want to ask is How did you do this how did you do this. I want to know how she cared for three sick infants, how it was physically possible, how did she not murder her husband or even the children. I sort out Honey's diaper and Alice has moved everything on the table into a tidy pile. I put salami and cheese slices in Ziploc bags and the bags in the cooler. The last cheese scraps dispatched into Honey's mouth, I look expectantly at Alice.

"Ready?" I say. "Let's go," she says. I put Honey on my hip and help Alice stand. Back into the car, back onto the road, heading toward gray skies.

Alice sleeps and Honey stares blankly. I sing a little Barış Manço to myself, "Dağlar dağlar," mountains mountains, it means. To be honest I don't even really know what most of the words mean—songs give me the most trouble in Turkish. I mean I understand the individual word meanings but not how they fit together. Something about "You plucked my flower and put it in your hands." God forbid I ever be forced to literally translate it for someone. But even if I don't get it it's just the right mournful tone for being around here.

I pass the time trying to think of all the Turkish words I can that still have Arabic and Persian roots because it turns out Atatürk didn't get all of them during his nationalist purges and I wonder, briefly and insanely, if I should go back to school because what am I doing with all this pointless information—it just sits there uselessly until I use it to pass the time on a long drive. I won't even teach it to Honey. But then like that, we are in Berwin Falls on the other side of the border.

When we drive in I get almost a festival feeling. The town is roughly five times the size of Altavista, and has things like a small hospital, a minimall, even a variety of fast-food establishments. We find a motel just by driving along an honest-to-god strip and Alice wakes up and points out one called the Wagon Wheel, with faux-stone pillars and a pleasing old-timey sign and the inevitable wagon wheel out front.

"Let's stay there," she says. I pull in and make to go inside and find out about rooms.

"I'll pay," says Alice and I say "Oh no" and she says "Oh yes" and takes a credit card from an inner pocket of her purse.

"You can't take it with you," she says again. I am wondering whether I should presume to put two rooms on her credit card or whether she might like a roommate and am slightly paralyzed thinking about what is the correct course of action but she says "Get two rooms next to each other, if you can" and I say "Roger" and make my way inside leaving her and Honey in the car.

The interior of the motel is marvelously ugly. There are wagon wheels everywhere—one has even been employed as a chandelier holding faux candles above. I determine that they have two rooms adjacent and I give them Alice's credit card to swipe and return to the car and collect Honey and her diaper bag and Alice's wheelie bag and then scurry around to Alice's side to grip her elbow and try to gently haul her out. I put Honey down next to me and the diaper bag over my shoulder and the wheelie bag handle in my hand. "Two o'clock," I say. "Probably time for a nap," thinking of Alice since Honey has slept most of the day and is probably feeling rambunctious needless to say she needs to eat but we can have a second picnic in our hotel room and maybe maybe she will go back to sleep and I can have a cigarette which I want desperately, it being some five hours since I had one. I think maybe it's just time I smoke in front of the baby but then I imagine her putting her two little fingers together and putting them to her lips and I curse myself for thinking any such thing.

Alice who has been rather aloof about attempts to assist her physically is leaning on my elbow and I am feeling vaguely guilty since she is obviously so frail and we haven't yet spoken to Mark and Yarrow and I'm not sure what kind of exertions this trip is going to portend. Honey trips merrily along next to us onto the maroon shag of the motel, she has a good herd instinct.

The woman at the front desk says "Oh, are we visiting with Granny," and I look at Alice and say "Yes" just as she says "No" and we both laugh and keep walking toward our rooms. When we reach Alice's door I unlock with the mini wagon wheel key and lead her in with Honey at our heels. "Good work, baby girl," I say to her. "Good walking and following," I say. I wheel Alice's bag in and say "Now the woman at the front desk is going to think I kidnapped you and am passing you off as Granny" and Alice laughs.

"We'll hear the police cars any minute," she says. I bark at Honey who has reached up her mitts to try and touch the enormous old TV perched on a rickety stand.

"Should we call up Mark and Yarrow to let them know where you are," I venture. "Okay by me," says Alice, and I pull out my phone and see that, miracle of miracles, I finally have some goddamn cell service. The screen is alive with WhatsApp and e-mail notifications and seeing Hugo's name I immediately experience several physical manifestations of dread, in my stomach and the palms of my hands. I swipe all the notifications away and open up the dial screen.

"Do you have their number?" I ask and Alice begins rummaging around in her ratty leather purse until she pulls out a bundle of tiny squares of paper rubber-banded together.

"My address book," she says and pulls out the top square and hands it to me. "You dial and then let me talk to them." I punch in the numbers and hand her the phone and see with one eye that Honey has wandered into the bathroom where I follow and find her standing with one hand on the toilet flusher and a shit-eating grin on her face. She pulls at it and it clicks and the toilet flushes. I hear Alice's voice in the next room and I do a quick check for death traps and shut the toilet lid and leave Honey to her flusher. I go into the bedroom where Alice is leaning against the wardrobe on the phone.

"Yes, I got someone to drive me the last little while." I hold out my hand as though to offer my assistance and she says "Wait a minute, Yarrow. I'm going to let her talk to you." I take the phone.

"Hello?" I say brightly, and a voice just like mine, a young woman's voice on a woman who probably isn't very young, says "Hello" at the other end. "This is Daphne," I say, and I stand up straight and tuck forearm around my waist and allow the elbow of the hand holding the phone to rest on it. I try to re-inhabit my adult professional self. "It's nice to meet you over the phone!"

LYDIA KIESLING

"I'm Yarrow Passafarro," she says tentatively. Her obvious concern is straining against all our shared instincts to be nice to each other but I have to suppress a strangled hysterical squawk at the rhyme. "Could you tell me how Alice is and how you met her and what's going on?"

"Of course!" I say. "I hope you haven't been too worried! I know it's a little odd to hear that she's thrown in her lot with a stranger. My daughter and I were visiting my hometown and we met Alice at our local coffee shop. She's taking very good care of herself but I know she's very conscious of your concern and she thought it was best not to attempt the last leg of her trip alone." I don't add that she also rescued me and my child and saw me half naked after I drank to excess and fell down the stairs.

"I'm glad she's made a friend," the woman on the other end of the phone says. "We're just really worried—she hasn't traveled far off her property in the fifteen years we've known her and then she wanted to drive ALONE to the other end of the country at her age. It's concerning to say the least."

"I can imagine," I say. I hate it when people say "concerning." This is not the direction the verb goes. In Turkish you could make it go that way, in Turkish you can make a verb be causative by adding a few letters but English does not have this feature built in and "concerning" just seems wrong in that regard.

"Well, what would be helpful now? I'm not actually sure how long she's planning to stay at the camp but she mentioned maybe one of you flying out to meet her and get her car? I'm on a little bit of a hiatus from work so I'd be happy to stick around if that's what makes sense." I look at Alice and she has the sourest expression on her face and no wonder when she's sitting there while two mere children decide how to transport her like she's a piece of valuable furniture.

"I'm not even sure where you are. We had talked about her just going out to Colorado so this is already a big change. Could you let me know some of the nearest towns so I can talk about it with my husband? And what your number is?" I rattle off Bend Medford even Reno and my number. "To be honest you're looking at a big drive no matter where you fly. Maybe I could drive her down to San Francisco and you could fly in there." This would be a good way to solve my problems, I think—just let Alice bring us back home like a rising tide. I decide to lobby for this course. "Yes, actually—that really makes sense. You'll have a lot of flight options that way and you won't have to drive."

"But what about her car," says Yarrow. "How would we get the car back?"

"You're right," I say. "I don't know if Alice is up to the long drive" and Alice cuts me off and says "Just tell her to do that. I can make the drive."

"Alice is saying that the drive will be okay. And we can caravan and stop every so often on the way down."

"I mean getting the car back here," she says and I've got nothing.

"Tell her we'll call her back tomorrow," says Alice.

"Yarrow, Alice is wondering whether we can all confer and then talk again tomorrow."

"Okay," she says, obviously not okay. "But look, I don't know how much she's told you about herself."

"Not too much," I say, looking sidelong at Alice and angling my body away from her.

"She's had a really hard time," says Yarrow.

"I have heard some of this, I think" I say, feeling very awkward with Alice watching me from against the bureau. I go toward the bathroom and poke my head in and see Honey sitting on the floor with an expression like she is trying to poop.

"She lost her husband and three children and we're all she's got," she says. "I mean there's been some really really awful stuff in her life."

"Well, yeah, she told me just a little of it." There's a pause. "I don't really know what else to say," I say, which is true. I don't know why the hard life should equal being trapped in your home for the rest of your days. I feel a little flare of indignation on Alice's behalf. Why shouldn't she go where she pleases, meet who she likes, be where she wants, power of attorney be damned. She's not even driving the car. She's her own woman.

"Okay, well Alice and I will talk about the car situation and maybe you can confer with your husband and then we'll call you back tomorrow," I say, trying to sound adult and soothing and responsible.

"Okay," she says. "I guess that's all we can do. Please take care of her. I mean you sound like a normal person but I don't know you at all—no offense," she says.

"I totally, totally understand. This must seem super weird. But I promise I just want her to get where she's going safely." Alice is now in the bathroom door glaring at me and making a hang up gesture.

"Okay, well, talk tomorrow, Yarrow. Nice to meet you." I tap the phone to hang up.

"Did you hang it up," says Alice.

"Yes, you just press the screen," I say.

"Make sure it's hung up."

"It's hung up!" Honey is hugging my leg and making tentative nips to my pants. "NO BITING," I say, and she bursts into theatrical crying that I first assume is fake but I see a tear squeeze out and I have to pick her up and kiss her and say "I didn't mean to scare you, Honey-pie" and nuzzle nuzzle. "But you know we don't bite."

"I don't know how reassured she felt," I say to Alice. "She's awfully protective of you, it sounds like."

"I want to lie down," she says abruptly. "Okay," I say.

"When you wake up we can have the pizza and beer," I say mostly because I really want this and hope she still does too and she smiles weakly. "That's right." I scoop up Honey who reaches her arms out to hug Alice and Alice smiles and reaches her arms back and we do an odd group hug with Honey squirming between our bodies and I feel her bony hands on my arms, the first person besides Honey who has touched me in a long time. Alice turns on her heel and walks out of the bathroom.

I start to carry Honey to our room and then realize I don't have the Pack 'n Play which I will need to put her to bed. I poke my head back into the room. "Actually, sorry, do you mind watching her," I say. "I need to run and get her crib and so forth from the car."

"I don't mind," Alice says, and smiles at Honey who runs toward her skirt and buries her face in it and laughs. I walk briskly out of the room and down the corridor not insensible to the fact that this means I can smoke a cigarette. I get the Pack 'n Play and the various other things and I find my cigarettes and sit on the bench outside the front door of the motel looking out at the wagon wheel and the highway. Beyond is a row of mountains two of which have the slightest little bit of snow on them. I feel like seven minutes is a reasonable amount of time to leave them and while I recognize the addict's brain serving forth this logic I don't care and light the cigarette and as usual the first drag is both less and more satisfying than anticipated. Now that I am sitting still I realize I should call Engin and then I remember all of those notifications waiting on my phone to upset me.

I decide to get the worst over with and look at the Institute e-mail and whatever is going on with Hugo and Meredith. It is calming to first delete all the things that do not matter so I select everything that falls under this category, all the cheery euphemistic updates from the University's head cheese, all the e-mails about various sexual assaults that have taken place on campus, all my mass mailings from the Council on American-Islamic Relations. This leaves behind several e-mails from Purchasing which portends that my reimbursements are probably not forthcoming because I need to submit a different form than the form that was initially provided to me by Purchasing. There are twenty-two e-mails from Hugo one of which reads EMERGENCY, and twelve from Meredith. There is one from Karen that says "Are you okay" in the subject line so I know that she must be back from vacation and that things must not be going very well. I smoke more of my cigarette and then I open EMERGENCY and it says "This is not acceptable, Daphne—we have lost the key box and need to be able to give keys to our visiting scholars. I understand you have your family situation but you need to get in touch." Six months ago I would have composed a florid apology outlining all the ways

I was going to solve this problem and ensure that no other person ever have to face anything like this ever again but now I don't care. The last e-mail from Meredith says "Hugo is on the warpath, you probably need to check in soon" which is pretty decent from Meredith all things considered but then I see the e-mail preceding it which is her asking for me to get her an exception for a travel expense since Karen is swamped and I decide that was the real emergency. I consider writing them now but I remember Honey is with Alice and Alice is frail and Honey is a wiggleworm a grenade a timebomb and I pull down the last of the cigarette and stand up feeling lightheaded and hurry back into the motel with the bag and Pack 'n Play and various other things.

Inside Alice's room Honey is sitting in the hard little chair that goes with the desk and Honey is painstakingly trying to pull Alice's shoelaces out of her sensible shoes. "Hi hi," I say, "Mommy is back. Sorry it took me so long," and I realize I didn't do gum or wash hands or anything and now Alice will know I smoke but what's it to her and I drove her across state lines and am now probably under investigation by a concerned and concern-causing but not concerning hippie named Yarrow Passafarro.

"Do you need me to help you with anything," I ask Alice, looking around at her suitcase and the bed and wondering whether she will need to be lifted into it or anything like that.

"No," she says irritably. "I'm fine, thank you."

"What about your shoelace," I point out, and she rolls her eyes and nods and I bend down and return the sturdy lace to its eyes and tie it in a firm knot. Then I pick up Honey and carry her to our room and realize she hasn't had a lot of fun or edification today and I decide to do the bed-jumping thing and clutch her tight and run and fly onto the bed which groans alarmingly and she laughs and pats my face so hard it hurts. I pull back the nasty comforter pull *Goodnight Moon* out of the bag and give it to her to look at while I set up the Pack 'n Play. While I shake the sides of the thing until they finally become rigid I realize that I am thinking about the damn e-mails and that I will have no peace until I can resolve them. Once the cattle gate of distressing reminders is open the thought that I have not spoken to Engin today barges in. It is three o'clock now so it is 1:00 a.m. there but I think Okay must prioritize let's call him and I find the Wi-Fi info on a ratty postcard in a rattier motel binder and open the phone and gather Honey unto me and show her her own face on the screen as Skype does its customary ringing song which I once found comically monotonous, it's fake music, it's anti-music, and which I now hear as ominous. Honey scrabbles to touch her face on the screen and I hold her with one arm and stretch the other arm out so that she can't hang up the call. The British woman's voice comes on and says "The person you are trying to reach . . ." and I decide to gratify Honey on this one single thing and hold the phone close and guide her tiny finger to the red circle. "Bye-bye," I say, and she says "Bye-bye" and while she knows how to wave I don't think she's ever said that before.

"Baban seni çok özledi," I say which means Your dad misses you very much. In fact it means Your dad missed you very much which is one of the mysteries of Turkish I will never figure out, why some verbs never take the present continuous even though they are describing an act that is ongoing, that cannot be put away in the past, like Missing or Liking, but not

Loving, which Turks recognize as a present continuous situation, although Falling in Love is something that is always behind you in the simple past. Honey just looks at me and I think about how I am denying her her father tongue and then I think Will you take a nap and then I think probably not and then I think *I* need to take a nap. I realize there is a television with cable which is a novelty and I turn it on and click away until I find Dora the Explorer and sit Honey on the bed and I put a pillow behind her back and one between her and the edge of the bed and I lean over her curly brown head and run my hands over her back which is warm and small and slightly hunched like mine and I stretch out next to her and curl my arm around her butt and she stares rapt at the television and I doze.

A knock on the door and I am up only after I register that the knocking has been going on for quite a while. Engin is not like this, he has insane cat reflexes and when the smoke alarm erroneously goes off which it does periodically because we need to get a new one he flies out of the bed before I even open my eyes which leads me to believe that maybe he has more anxieties than he lets on about home invasion things, disaster things, and I feel sad thinking that he might be thinking anxious thoughts on the other side of the world. Honey is slumped against the pillow behind her with her eyes half-open and an advertisement is blaring on the screen and my next thought is that my plan actually worked and I got a nap and Honey stayed in one place although at the expense of rotting her brain. "Just a second," I say and I look at the clock and see that it's almost five o'clock which is incredible, that she would sit still for so long. I sit up and see my wan face in the mirror my purple eyebrow my hair nest and I pick Honey up and say "Hi little buddy" and walk over to the door and open it and Alice is standing there and she looks at me and says "I'm hungry." "Me too," I say, which is always true, and I say "Let me put on my shoes and change her diaper" and I hurry back into the room leaving her standing in the doorway.

"Come in," I say.

"I asked the girl up front where to get pizza and beer and she told me about a place called Berwin Pies."

"Excellent," I say. I deal with Honey's diaper and get her diaper bag and reach for my phone to see where this place is and then remember all the e-mails Engin etc. and think Fuck fuck fuck but find the map type in the place and say "Ten minutes away" and she says "I guess that thing can tell you everything" and I say "When it has service."

Berwin Pies is on the other side of town and we drive there past more boxy warehouses, Altavista on a grander scale, but with more check-cashing and more big parking lots. We drive past the beautiful lake we missed on our entrance to the town and Alice keeps her own counsel while I attempt to parallel park and then give up and pull into one of the big empty lots kitty-corner from the pizza joint. It is what you might expect, neon sign pleather booths the light a little too bright, just needs a bulb three notches warmer and it would be homey instead of bald and flea-bitten but I see they have several beers on tap and I smell pizza and we find a booth and a friendly rotund lumberjack type brings us a high chair for Honey. Alice who has been mostly silent the whole drive looks at him almost flirtatiously and says "We want beer and lots of it" and he laughs and says "Well I think we can take care of that for you" and asks what kind of beer we want and Alice says "Whatever you got" and I intervene and ask for some Oregon thing and we order a large supreme pizza and sit back and wait for all this bounty to flow in.

I expect a town of this size to feel less depopulated than Altavista but there are only three sat tables in the restaurant. I reflect that almost everyone I've seen since we came north besides Kimmy has been a teen or the aged or aging.

The beer comes and I cheers Alice and she says cheers but then sits there silently and I am not sure whether or how to make a conversation go. Honey is shredding napkins and banging her spoon gently and she is occupied and before I know it the pizza arrives and I serve all of us and cut up Honey's piece.

Alice tries to pick up her piece and then sets it down again.

She drinks some of her beer. I've almost finished mine and realize I need to pace myself if I'm going to drive us home.

"I wanted to be a playwright, you know," she says out of nowhere. I don't really know what to say so I say "I thought you were a teacher" and she says "Yes but in my spare time I wrote plays." She goes again. "Do you want to be a teacher?" She looks at me. "Since you work at the University?"

"No," I say. "I don't know what I want to be exactly. I was going to get a Ph.D. but I never really had a plan for after. I just like to know things and feel useful."

"You should be sure you have a way to support yourself," she says.

"My mom always said the same thing," I say. "When my father died it was like we lost the thing about our family that said what our family was and then she had to make herself over."

"When I had all those babies they kind of railroaded the rest of my life." She takes another long sip of her beer. "This just tastes so good," she says, as though she had not just issued an utterly devastating statement in Berwin Pies. Honey is playing and spilling milk and I try to shovel some more pieces of pizza into her.

"Why are you AWOL from your job now," she asks.

"One of our work-study students and her classmate got a grant from my Institute to go interview refugees in Turkey, and I helped them plan their trip and when they were there they got into a car accident and one of them was killed." The mustard gas doesn't accumulate behind my eyes like it normally does. She doesn't say anything. "I don't love the way my institution does things normally but, like, this girl *died*. I can't cope with listening to everyone fall all over themselves to abdicate responsibility. Even though it was an accident and it technically isn't anyone's responsibility. We're supposed to be in loco parentis."

"You're never safe from bad things happening," she says. This thought is so profoundly depressing I hope the earth opens and gently swallows everyone on it, right now.

She seems to feel how despondent that makes me and she looks at me with some fond light in her eyes and she says "I want to apologize if I've been bad company for you," and I say "Alice no, no" and she cuts me off and says "I don't make friends easily. I say the wrong thing" and I say "Alice I don't know what we would have done if we hadn't met you" which is true because at the very least she got us out of the damn house.

"I told you about our farm," she says and I nod and she says "It was going to be a place for the girls to run around and catch fireflies" and I can just picture it something verdant and humid and the lightning bugs flashing. "There was a long time after they died where I was so angry I didn't try to make the house nice, when I didn't always behave nicely with people. I was in the . . . abode of pain." I don't exactly see what this has to do with being good company to us but I just say "I find you delightful to be with," which is basically true.

"Ever since I got in the car to come west I feel some of it falling away," she says and I just say "I'm glad."

The air feels fresh when we get outside, I mean really really fresh. It must be the proximity of the lake because we are as high as Altavista here but something feels a little cooler, a little more moist, than the plain where Altavista sits. Honey struggles to get out of my arms and I say "Do you want to ride on my shoulders" and carefully put her up there and hold on tight to her ankles. My blood feels loose and I wonder momentarily whether I should drive but I think why not it was only one and a half beers and still holding tight to her ankles I touch my nose with one finger then the other and walk in a straight line and it all seems in order. I get her into the car get Alice into the car and drive very slowly back to the motel seeing maybe three cars on the way. Honey is asleep before we get to the motel—I remember she had no big afternoon nap and instead stared at television while I snoozed beside her. She stirs when I get her out of the car seat and then puts her head back on my shoulder and goes back to sleep, a rare event.

"We can get an early start," I say to Alice before we head into our rooms.

"Seven o'clock," she says.

I keep the lights off and the door to the room open and

find my way with the illumination from the motel hallway. I strip off Honey's shoes and her socks and her pants and I leave her in the onesie underneath, none the worse for wear. I lay her gently on the pillow and cover her with the blanket and stare at her for a minute. I go over to the dense drape at the window and realize our room looks out at the bench which in turn looks out over the parking lot. I calculate that if I open the window it will take me about thirty seconds of negligent parent time to get from the room through the lobby and to the bench, from where I can smoke and look at all the e-mails and hear Honey if she cries out. So I open the window, collect the essentials, make sure I have the key, close the door gently behind me, and sprint down the hallway and out through the front door of the Wagon Wheel and confirm, from the window, that I can see my sleeping child through the gauzy second curtain. I move six feet to the right and light a cigarette and take the phone from the pocket. It's still light out. I open Skype and press to call Engin. It rings and rings until the British woman is there. "The person you are trying to reach . . ."

I finish my cigarette and look at the e-mails. I hear a reedy sound through the window adjacent. "That's poison, you know." It is the voice of Alice, presumably talking about my cigarette.

"I know," I say. "I'm quitting when we get back." Her window slides shut.

I write to Hugo awkwardly with thumbs, the cigarette perched on the bench beside me. "Dear Hugo," I say. "Once again, I am sorry for the delay. The key box is in the bottom drawer of the reception desk—Meredith at one point knew this; perhaps she's forgotten. My grandmother has passed away; I am settling some things at her home and I will be back in the office next week." I cc Meredith and Karen and send the message and hope that it will be good enough. I write to Meredith. "Dear Meredith, I have written to Hugo and cc'd you. I am so sorry for the trouble I have caused. For your exception you will need to have Karen write a letter from you to the Acting Vice Provost explaining why the extraordinary expenditure was necessary, and then he will need to sign off." I feel like I've dispatched these two items well, but I can't ignore the electronic evidence of all the things I'm really supposed to do. There is an e-mail from our friendly local Gülenist organization with which we have agreed to plan an interfaith Iftar dinner and from which Hugo is always encouraging me to "raise money" although their office is absolutely threadbare and the manager applies for every job the University posts which indicates it may not be a likely avenue for fundraising. There are the reminder e-mails from the federal entity that grants part of our funding reminding that it is one month until our quarterly compliance report is due, a task that takes approximately one month of agony to dispatch correctly. I try to remind myself that I have successfully dispatched them in the past many times and that nothing will stop me from doing so again. I smoke another cigarette and try to think calmly about my calendars and spreadsheets and efficiency tools back in the office but for some reason they fail to calm me and then I go back inside the motel and illuminate our room with the screen of the phone to set the alarm.

I pet Honey's head—she is stretched out abandoned to sleep with her head squished up against the netting of the Pack 'n Play. I see for just one instant how long she is compared to the last time I was able to look at her with that rare flash of objectivity. Before she died my mother told me when she looked at me she saw me at every age I had ever been which makes me cry every time I think of it. When I tried to tell Engin I choked so hard I had to go in another room until I could come back and get out the sentence. I thought that this all-ages panoramic vision was something everyone got with motherhood, some new way of seeing. But whenever I look at Honey she is the age she is at this moment and I strain and strain to see her perfect tiny baby head the first time she crawled the first step she took and the only thing I can see are the photos we took, photos which unbeknownst to us at the time of taking them would obliterate all other records. I wonder whether I have stunted my memories of my child with the very tool I used to capture her various epochs, or if women who didn't have cameras were left with nothing but the child they had at that moment, whatever age she happened to be. If in the absence of a camera the only way to recall the memory of holding your sweet baby was to have another, grasping at something by its nature out of reach and aging and exhausting yourself in the process by suddenly having a whole herd of them to look after, any number of which could still then die or find some other way to break your heart. I think about having another baby and feel the thrill of longing and dread, although more longing since it is the idlest of fancies, since there is no one here to impregnate me. I lie in the motel bed and concentrate very hard on Honey as a baby. I remember sitting on the bed, I am holding the small baby, I try to enter the memory and look down and see her in my arms, to be with my baby again.

DAY 9   The next thing that happens is the sound of the alarm and the squawk of Honey who is exactly the age she is and no younger. I sit up and see her standing looking gleefully over the railing of the Pack 'n Play her curls twisted up in a peak above her high forehead. "Good morning, Miss Critter," I say to her, and she beams at me. I crawl to the foot of the bed and reach into the Pack 'n Play and drag her up on the bed with me and lie back and she lies on me and puts her head under my chin and I am thinking Keep this moment, let's keep this one and while I am trying to fossilize the moment or X-ray it or photocopy it or do something that will make it stay with me forever she is squirming thrashing rolling and she is off the bed, she is on the move and suddenly I have what I think may be my most important epiphany about motherhood which is that your child is not your property and motherhood is not a house you live in but a warren of beautiful rooms, something like Topkapı, something like the Alhambra on a winter morning, some well-trod but magnificent place you're only allowed to sit in for a minute and snap a photo before you are ushered out and you'll never remember every individual jewel of a room but if you're lucky you go through another and another and another and another until they finally turn out the lights. I pack up our things and consider this while Honey uses the cord to pull the telephone off the nightstand onto her toes.

Alice is standing outside the door when I open it and she says "I was wondering when you'd wake up" and it is only 7:05 and I start feeling annoyed right off the bat but say "Good morning, Alice, I hope you slept well." I leave Honey in her care to get her bag and ours and haul them down the corridor to the lobby where I confer with the attendant who is a young man with flaming red hair about breakfast. The Wagon Wheel does not offer a breakfast. I leave our bags and things and trundle back down the hall and say "There's no breakfast, we can snack with our leftover picnic things or the manager says we can go to the Black Bear diner or we can go to the Safeway," and she says, "You just feed her—I want to get on the road" and I say "Ten-four" and dig out a banana and peel it and give a piece of it to Honey along with a verbal contract for a string cheese when she's finished. I ask Alice to wait with her and haul everything to the car but when I walk away Honey cries and toddles after me and I say "Wait with Alice" and she cries louder and I say okay and heft her up and take what bags I can with the remaining arm and we make for the car. The attendant trots out from behind the desk and grabs the Pack 'n Play and I feel so indebted so grateful so helpless so guilty and I hate this feeling but I just say thank you.

We hit the road. It's two hours to the camp and I try to suss out the plan on the way there, because I realize we still have no plan.

"Is there a museum or visitor center or something we can go to?" I ask and Alice says "No" and she sounds irritable and I say "Sounds good" and think about what I am going to do, then, because now that we are away from Altavista I know with great certainty that we can't go back, we can't go back to the mobile home, we can't go back to the High Winds Market. We have to go Elsewhere. Alice doesn't make a peep and Honey doesn't make a peep and I'm thinking why did I sign on to chauffer this person around who I don't even know, etc. But I'm bored and I've had so little conversation in the last week, the last eight months, that I decide to make some.

"Can you tell me about this camp thing? I don't know about it." She turns from gazing out the window and faces ahead. "During World War Two they let conscientious objectors do public works instead of putting them in jail or making them take office jobs in the army. But they gave 'em awful jobs, working in mental institutions and doing heavy labor, like where we're going. He liked it, though, the harder the better."

"Was this the thing where they sent Depression guys to plant trees?" and she raises her eyebrows at me. "No, that was before, but they used the same camps. The 'Depression guys.' Huh. What do they teach young people? It was three million people," she says. "It's why you have all these nice parks and the country didn't just blow away with the dust storms." She frowns. "It was segregated, though. So my husband disapproved. But the CO camps weren't."

"You said you came out here to see him?" and out of the corner of my eye I see her nod. "When I got out of the service," she says. "We had been writing letters. I met him in school. Quaker college. I joined up halfway through school, after he left, but I was only in for a year. I came and visited him and then I went back to school. We waited for each other."

I don't know whether she means sex or just generally waiting. "How long were you apart." "A couple years, all told," she says. "And now fifty years." I look over at her.

We are taking the shorter route rather than the truly scenic one that would have wound around the big mountain and covered more California ground than Oregon. We pass farmland, pine forests, little tiny towns: population 54, 240, 300, 76. It's good to have that feeling again of the endless west rather than the circumscribed plain of Altavista and the unrelieved sagebrush and juniper scrub. We are beginning to leave the monotony of the high desert and there are green hills like dells I think they are called, and the trees are different and when I press the switch to roll down the window I can feel the influence of the sea in the air just the slightest bit. This feels like Humboldt land, Del Norte land, the trees are taller, the air is wetter. Honey blats in the back and I crane my neck and catch her eye in the rearview and say "Hullo baby" and she kicks and grins at me and pants and doesn't look the slightest bit ruffled. The sky, which has been foreboding since our picnic yesterday, is dark and ponderous to the west.

"Looks a little unpleasant toward the camp, weather-wise," I say.

"I brought my umbrella," Alice says looking ahead.

We haven't been driving for very long when she starts speaking extempore.

"I keep thinking about that trip to Turkey, the one you made me remember." I glance over at her and make a sound for her to go on.

"We took a train all the way to the east part of the country, Diyarbakır it was called." Diyarbakır where Ellery died, my mnemonic device until the end of time. "It was such a boring train ride—very long unbroken expanses of countryside." She laughs. "I remember that's what he said to me, 'My goodness, this is a rather unbroken expanse of countryside,' and then he flashed me a little look and suggested we pass the time by kissing and I said all right so we set about kissing, and it made a tremendous scandal. There was a lot of tsking from the ladies around us." She laughs and her voice is rusty in her throat. "I was always such a prim young woman, I can't believe now that I did it." I'm honestly stunned by this story. "I'm amazed someone didn't attack you. In 1960!" It's hard to picture this woman behaving like a drunk Brit on a beach package tour, rolling around in the sand while the aunties and uncles cluck their tongues with scorn.

She looks out the window again. "I remember when I first met him I thought he was nice looking. Someone introduced us at a potluck and I remember the feeling of waiting to be introduced, as though we were in a play. I liked the shape of his hands." She smiles again.

And now she is quiet and I wait to see if she will start again but she doesn't. Her eyes are open. "The girl who died," I say. "She was in Diyarbakır. I've never been there. I keep trying to picture what it was like."

"You should be thankful that you don't have that in your mind's eye."

"It seems like the least I can do, to sort of witness, I guess."

"You suffering won't ease anyone else's suffering," she says drily and then she doesn't say anything else and I don't either.

The drive is much longer than I thought and after a very long stretch of silence during which Honey is mostly sitting glassy-eyed we finally pass the sign for the camp, a regular state highway sign as you'd see for a town, and I make the turn. We travel a nicely maintained dirt road for ten minutes and then we turn onto a very bad dirt road and I have a pang like what if I can't get the car back up what if we slide off the road and then we come to a small clearing in the trees with a ramshackle cabin and a very faded interpretive sign. "I think . . . this must be it."

I pull the car over near the sign and cut the engine and Honey is immediately squirming squelchily and cooing to be let free of her seat. There are no other cars to be seen. I can't tell what kind of land we're on. It doesn't seem to be parkland but there were no Private or No Trespassing signs, but it also lacks the assiduously nicely kept signage of a national forest or state park or county forest or state point of interest or whatever they call the lesser administrative entities. I unbuckle and get out of the car and stretch and peer into the back seat where Honey is trying very hard to wake up and has a look on her face like it's the worst thing she's ever done. I leave my door open and walk over to the cabin, which is flaked and cobwebbed with a padlock on the door. I walk to the interpretive panel which is peeling up at the corner and faded all to hell, a mottled beige surface crisscrossed with scratches. I can make out "many original structures are no longer extant," and I trot to the car to report back. She says, "I expected as much." Unease is gathering in the trees and the gray clouds above. Honey cries in the back seat. "Hi buddy," I poke my head in and say. "You just sit tight." "This isn't the camp," Alice says. "It was down a hill," and motions at the dirt road ahead and I marvel at her memory. She smooths her hair behind her ear and I'm stuck for a moment admiring the elegance of the gesture. "Okay," I say. "Here we go."

I start the Buick and edge its nose down the road, which declines down past the cabin and is furrowed and rutted but dry. The shocks of the car absorb the bumps beautifully but I'm perturbed by how much the hood rises and falls with the changes in terrain. "Bumpy," I say. I look at Honey in the rear-view mirror. "Bumpy," I say in a singsong for her benefit. It takes us a long time to wind our way down this dirt road, guessing on some unmarked forks, always choosing down, down, down. We inch our way down for probably twenty minutes, trees crowding us on either side, and then we are in a large clearing—a small valley, with tree-covered hills gallumphing up on all sides. Some collapsed wooden structures dot the clearing. I drive out into the middle of the field. "Wow," I say. "Looks like this is it."

"Yes," says Alice. She looks at me. "This is it." She looks sad. "Now I'd like to get out and have some time by myself."

"Sure thing," I say. "We'll just hang back by the car and have a snack."

"No," she shakes her head vigorously, hands in her lap. "I want to be alone. I don't want anyone hovering around." Shit.

"Alice, I'm sorry, there could be all kinds of holes and uneven ground and I just don't think you should be walking around here by yourself." She looks at me and puts her hand on my hand, which is still on the steering wheel.

"Please," she says. "Go find us a motel and check in and then come back for me. I want to be alone. I won't be foolhardy. I promise. Give me two hours." She gives my hand a little squeeze. I agonize for a second. "Okay," I say, hearing Yarrow's worried voice on the phone. "But first I'm going to get out and do a lap and make sure there aren't any big holes or snakes or anything. You're going to let me do that." I try to sound commanding. She nods. "And you're going to let me pull some food together for you to keep in a dry spot. And you're going to let me drive you over to the buildings." "Sure," she says. I go around to the trunk and get Honey a cheese out of the cooler and I collect the other leftover picnic materials crackers and cold cuts and put them into a couple of gallon Ziplocs. I put these on top of the car and give Honey her string cheese and think about getting her out of the car but then consider what it will then be like to get her back into the car seat. She is whimpering and straining but the cheese pacifies her for the time being. "Tseeeeeeeee," she says. "Tseeeee." I start a slow jog toward the buildings and am encouraged that the ground beneath the ankle-high grasses is dry and reasonably flat. I feel my lungs scratching and protesting and my ancient sports bra riding up over the underside of my breasts and I slow to a brisk walk. One of the long, low bunkhouse-looking buildings is a ruin, not burned, just collapsed in at one corner, splintered planks raised in mute supplication. Some of the buildings are in better shape, but all appear to be padlocked. I try to shake off my overwhelming recent feelings of helplessness and try to be the person I am at my job during my most successful efficient and results-getting. I have written a multimillion-dollar federal grant, I think to myself. "What are the things I need to assess this situation," I say aloud, but I don't know, I just don't know what exactly is the right thing to do. Some kind of bird of prey caws hoarsely above and I think For god's sake. I go to the edge of the clearing, a hundred yards or so from the nearest structure, and there are some huge worn stumps right before the forest starts in earnest and I find the flattest one, about the height of my thigh, tucked under an enormous pine, and I say, "Okay," and I run back to the car and point out the stump to Alice. "This is where I'm going to put the food and everything," I say. "Do you feel like you can walk that far from the buildings? I'm going to drive you right up to them." She nods. "Sit tight a little longer" I tell her and she is sitting there as is Honey who is crying now and she laboriously twists her back to try and wave a crooked finger at her and get her to smile. I get the food, and one of Honey's blankets, and the trunk flashlight for good measure and scurry back to the stump and lay them out. Back at the car Alice raises an eyebrow. "It looks like you're getting ready for me to live under that tree."

"I'm anxious about leaving you here with the sky gray like that. You know I am. Do you want a sweater or something?" and she shakes her head.

"They're all packed up. Don't need you messing in my suitcase." I go back to the trunk and rummage in my duffel and pull out the "I Climbed the Great Wall" sweatshirt and I run it back over to the stump. Back at the Buick I'm out of breath.

"I put my sweatshirt there, just in case." Honey is crying in the back seat and my shoulders start climbing up to my ears like they have done since I first heard her first tiny infant cries. I take my phone out of my back pocket and look at its barless screen. I hop in and start the car and drive slowly over to the most official-looking structure.

"I'm pretty sure they are all locked up, and some of them are in real bad shape," I report. "Please don't try to walk up into one and find yourself falling through a rotting floorboard."

"I won't," she says. I fish her maps out of the center console and figure if I go back east on a different state road I'll eventually come to the interstate and all the motels that cluster around it. I look at the clock on the dash. "It's ten forty-eight right now," I say. "I think it will take me around an hour to get to a motel at the outside. If it gets to be noon and I haven't found one I'm just going to turn back around. So either way I'm going to be back here at one-thirty. That seems like an awfully long time for you to be by yourself here."

"I've been 'by myself' for longer than you've been alive," she snaps.

"Yes, I understand that, but you weren't living outside for twenty years." I am feeling and sounding shirty. Honey is shrieking. I point up at the amassing gray. "And it looks like rain."

"One-thirty," she says. "That's fine."

"You have your purse?"

"Yes."

"Did you take your pills?"

"Yes."

"Is your cell phone in your purse?"

"Yes." She digs for a long while and pulls it out. "I don't get any reception, though."

"You can still dial 911, I read somewhere. So if something happens, you get out the phone and dial even if it says you don't have service." I get out of the car and circle around and get her umbrella out of the trunk and open her door and offer a hand, which she takes imperiously. She stands and I give her the umbrella which is the right height for her to lean on and she taps on the glass of the back seat. "Bye-bye, little Honey," she croons at the screaming Honey. Alice reaches out a hand and I open the door for her and they briefly link fingers. "Take care of your mama."

I take Alice's shoulders in my hands. "Please, please be careful. Walk slow."

"That's the only way I can walk," she says, and pats my hand on her shoulder. "I'll be fine. We'll be just fine."

I get back in the car and drive slowly back to the road, praying that the weather holds, the center holds. I reach a hand back and touch Honey's foot. "Hi sweet baby," I say, and she kicks at me with her little shoe and yells "NYO" and I say "Why don't you take your shoes off" because that could be a fun project for her and I wonder again why I never have any legitimate activities for her in the car but then again I think entertaining yourself is important. As is always the case on the way back the road feels shorter and slightly less treacherous than the way there when we didn't know what was coming and soon we are back up at the shack and the washed-out sign. I stop the car and crane my neck to look out the passenger side window to see if I can get a glimpse of the clearing below but it's all trees, trees, trees. I sigh and consult Alice's printout maps to reassure myself on the direction of the interstate. We turn onto the county road from whence we came and head east. Once the car has picked up real speed Honey settles and I settle and we zip along and I think Alice is fine, she made it all the way out to California by herself which is an incredible feat given the state of her.

The road is windy and the sky is gray but holding steady, no drops, and around the time I think we ought to be nearing the interstate we start seeing signs for something called Wildlife Safari Experience and I think Jesus Christ, but then I think that actually might be a fun thing for Honey to do other than sit in the damn car for hours and hours and the mobile home for days and days with her neurotic mother. What's more it appears to be enough of an attraction that there are motels clustered in proximity to it so we roll into one that proudly advertises a $49.99/night room. I am yearning for a cigarette when I pull in and Honey is asleep and I am conscious of the fact that I could maybe sneak one in standing by the car and this is exactly what I do, bending my knees so I can look at her through the window and throwing the butt down when her body eventually senses the cessation of motion and she twitches herself awake. I feel high and I think I can't wait to have Alice back safe so I can relax and then I have the small rogue thought that it will be good to get her off my hands wherever we work it out with Yarrow and then I banish that and imagine the tumbleweeds rolling down the road in Altavista and know that more than anything else we've got to be rid of the town.

I get Honey out of the car seat and now she is cheerful enough but her diaper is a big sodden mass and before I do anything I think we ought to change that and I make some space to lay her down in the trunk and instead of lying calmly she rolls and twists while I'm trying to get the new one on her, undoubtedly due to being so cooped up for two days, and I have to hold her tighter than I want and I think Oh god I'm the woman smoking in the parking lot being forceful with her child and I finally get the damn diaper fastened and I lift her up and cuddle her but she wants to be down down down and all I can do is direct her forward and I say "This way, Honey, this way!" and run alongside her toward the door like a sheepdog.

I get us two rooms with my credit card which makes me pause to think about the damn pending reimbursements and

I take a moment to confer with the attendant about whether there is a more direct route back to the camp and he says yes we could take the interstate for a stretch if I go left out of the parking lot instead of right and straight and it is 11:51 which is perfect according to the timeline we have established with Alice. I take ten minutes to feed Honey the remaining cold cuts and a piece of bread and a banana and then three minutes to get her thrashing and yelling into the car and then one minute to put my forehead against the wheel and it's 12:06 when we are pulling out of the parking lot.

We've been driving about five minutes when the sky opens up and I say "FUCK" and Honey says "UCK" and then I say "SHIT" and she says "IIII" and I say "Sorry Honey, we don't say words like that, we say SHOOT" and she says "Ool" and I press the gas and we are flying faster but then I think about hydroplaning and take my foot off the gas and my heart is pounding thinking about Alice in the soaking rain trying to make her way to shelter and I have to say "She has the um-brella, we are almost there, we are all going to be fine" and it's only going to take us thirty minutes now by the safari motel attendant's reckoning and then I think about the dirt road turn-ing to mud and the Buick sliding down it and I feel my heart start to speed up again and I just keep saying "We'll be there soon, we'll be there soon," and I see Honey looking quizzical in the rearview and I try to breathe in through my nose and out through my mouth to still my pounding heart.

I've just slowed the car to round a bend in the road and when we clear it and are on to a long straightaway I have the rapid impression of something bad in the nearish distance— an accident, lights flashing big cars a group of people and I slam on the brakes and feel us juddering forward on the pavement, the wheels no longer turning like they should. I make a yipping sound into the car and I hear Honey make an echo of concern in the back and my heart is bursting in my chest but then we are slowing slowing slowing and I feel the brakes working and something floods my body leaving me exhausted and damp and cold and I say "It's okay it's okay" and I see now through the rain that it's four pickup trucks and a giant green banner strung across their beds and a bunch of people in camouflage slickers and are they holding yes they are holding rifles and I think it's a hunting thing a rural thing some kind of jamboree or something until I see the yellow on the green banner and it's a flag and it's the State of Jefferson flag with its two X's and I say "Jesus fucking Christ." The Buick is at a stop now and there are three cars on the road between us and the blockade, each one with a camouflaged figure leaning into the driver's side window. I look in the rearview and there are no cars behind me and I'm not sure what to do so I start up the car and roll slowly toward the red SUV that's last in line and when I'm about ten yards from the blockade I see it's about ten or fifteen people and a few of them reach their hands in front of them to gesture slow and stop and one of them starts striding toward me with his gun. I pause for a moment to think Should I be afraid and though I don't have that feeling, my body in flight as it felt in the Buick hurtling down the road, I know this feeling of surreality is a kind of fear as I watch this man approach the window with a rifle over his shoulder and a sheaf of papers in one hand and I roll the window down unthinkingly and the rain is sluicing into the car and now he's at the window I give him a smile and hope for the best which I know is my dubious birthright as a representative of youngish reasonably attractive white American motherhood. It's a tall, stringy white guy with a weathered face a mustache and a high forehead visible under the hood of his slicker.

"Is everything okay?" I say and then I say "I'm just here with my baby" and he looks toward the back of the car where Honey is very quiet, sensing unprecedented currents in the air and he hands me a piece of paper and says "Ma'am, we've occupied this land for the State of Jefferson, the fifty-first state of the United States of America to be governed by the Constitution drawn up by the founders of the Republic" and I look slack-jawed down at the paper and read "PROCLAMATION OF INDEPENDENCE" and say, "Oh. Okay, well I'm just trying to get back to Camp Cooville, we're meeting a friend there" and he says "Well ma'am I'm afraid right now we're in Phase One which is securing our borders, so I'm going to have to ask you to turn back until that Phase is completed" and I say "Well how long is that going to be because our friend is ninety-two years old and she's alone and it's pouring rain" and I can tell he hasn't prepared for this particular very specific contingency and he looks somewhat apologetic and the first car in the line ahead of me is turning around and driving slowly past and I see a resigned-looking elderly man at the wheel and then the next car after him drives off the road and turns around to line itself up with the fucking blockade and the man leaning into the window of the car in front of ours appears to be having a lengthy conversation and I'm looking around through the rain to see are there any police officers here any firemen what is the fucking deal and I look at the group huddled behind him and I see, can it be, yes, it is Cindy fucking Cooper and I crane my neck out the window and stare. "Excuse me sir." I look back at him. "I actually see my neighbor Cindy there" feeling like maybe I can get on top of this situation and he looks behind him in surprise and I say "Cindy Cooper. From Altavista. Do you think I could talk to her?" and while he's still looking behind I yell "Cindy. Cindy Cooper" and she peers out from under her hood and makes her way over to the car. "I know her, Jeff," she says. Behind her I see what looks like Ed van Voorhees detach himself from the group and follow.

"Cindy, what is going on?" And she says "He told you, didn't he" and gestures at the paper. "Phase One." She has a determined look and an honest-to-god smile on her face. I know it's a kind of worldwide luxury to find this situation maddening and ludicrous rather than truly terrifying but see-ing Cindy's familiar face I can't fully believe that it is real. "But what about the vote you were so happy about, um, two days ago? I thought now the Board submits the petition or whatever, to the state" and she says "Some of us decided we're sick of waiting, we're sick of hearing what we owe the BLM to graze on our lands" and I hear the phrase "our lands" come out of Cindy from San Bernardino's mouth and I start to feel afraid. I say, "Well okay, but I have to get through. That old lady? The one from Altavista?" and then I realize Cindy's never seen her, has no idea who I'm talking about and I start over and say "There's a very old woman I dropped off at the Coo-ville Camp this morning and I'm supposed to pick her up at one-thirty at the latest, and it's pouring rain and there's no shelter there or anything for her" and Cindy pauses the wheels turning in her brain and I say "Please, please just let me through so I can get her" and then she looks behind her at the men and shrugs and says "Like he said, got to secure the borders before we can do anything else" and I feel my heart racing again and I say "Are you saying I couldn't get in to go back to Altavista to my own property?" and she says "Well we're letting residents in but you'd have to go east and enter down closer to the state line. I mean the California one. We don't want a lot of unnecessary people inside the borders right now unless you're ready to join up with us." I think this is so stupid and I am suddenly beside myself and I yell "CINDY SHE'S NINETY-TWO YEARS OLD SHE COULD DIE OUT THERE" and I have never yelled at anyone in my adult life other than Honey sort of and Honey starts crying in the back and I say "I don't know what to do" and Cindy says "I don't know what to tell you" and I think I have to try harder.

"Are you telling me that you've sealed every road between here and Sierra County? There aren't even that many people in your whole goddamn movement!" and she looks a little beleaguered and says "We're targeting key roads around the border counties" and I think okay so I can probably get there another route and the fact that they are doing this for what amounts to a pointless symbolic gesture makes me so furious I wish I knew how to punch someone because I would reach out of this window and clock Cindy except her friends would probably shoot me. I feel something rise in my throat something I know is bad and I say "I don't know where the fuck you came from but my family has lived up here for five generations and a bunch of fucking rednecks aren't going to break up the goddamn state of California" and god help me it feels just like the feeling of squeezing a tantruming baby's arms too hard, something horrible horrible but almost delicious and she says

"Bitch you don't live here and you need to go back where you came from" and moves toward the car and my violent urge deflates and I think I've made a mistake and I put the car in reverse zip backward do an ugly humiliating three-point turn and think Please don't shoot us through this car window and I speed away in the rain with my shoulders up to my ears but there is no bullet no sound of Honey screaming and then I think what if Engin was here and thank god thank god thank god he isn't here and then I think Alice Alice Alice oh my god and once I've raced around the turn and find a shoulder pull over and I look at my signalless phone and try to call 911 just like I've read you should and nothing happens so I turn the wheel to get back on the road crying and hyperventilating along with Honey. I have a deep horror of being unpunctual under the best circumstances but this is real, this is so much worse, and I feel pinpricks all over my skin thinking about what is happening to Alice in this downpour but I also know that if I drive in this state in this rain I am going to get in a car accident and Honey is facing frontward and so will be more likely to be killed or maimed and I have to calm down and I try to take deep breaths, try to say soothing things to Honey "It's okay sweet pea, everything is okay, everything is going to be fine. It's okay, it's okay" and breathe in through my nose and out through my mouth which is a tactic I have developed from my hours on the phone with the National Visa Center and I turn around to face Honey who is sniffling and I hold her moist small hand in mine and give her a big smile and she looks at me so reproachfully and says "Wah" and I put my hand on her cheek and wipe tears and then I make my hand into a little pincer with two ears and dart it toward her like a puppet and first I think she is going to cry more but then she laughs and I think Okay. I look at the soggy paper in my lap and read aloud to her and after "PROCLAMATION OF INDEPENDENCE" it says "The citizens of the State of Jefferson hereby state their intention to secure the borders of the 51st State of Jefferson which will be governed according to the United States Constitution" and farther down there are a list of things and one of them is "You are driving parallel to one of the greatest areas for copper and other mineral mining in the western United States which the citizens of Jefferson have been systematically denied access to through unwarranted federal and state regulations" and Honey is looking at me curiously and I say "This is nonsense" and I thrust the paper onto the passenger seat and feel my breathing slow to normal and give Honey a squeeze and pull back onto the road driving the Buick as fast as I can and feel like the brakes will still work and trying to think positive thoughts about Alice.

Finally we skid into the motel parking lot and I leave the heat on and the blinkers and debate whether or not to get Honey out of the car and say a prayer and risk it since I'm just running in the front door, which I do, leaving her in a car for the only time in her life and contravening every horror article I've ever read and I feel sick as I tell the attendant who is white and scrawny and freckled and named Ivan what's going on over on the interstate and I crane my neck to check the car is still there outside the door and he raises an eyebrow and as he starts to lift the phone from its cradle I put a hand on his arm and say "And the older lady I was with—she's in Camp Cooville right now, I'm supposed to get her at one-thirty and I'm gonna try the other road but I'm already going to be half an hour late and she's ninety-two and out there with no shelter" and he says "Uh, do you want me to tell the police that too" and I hesitate and first I say no then I do the math and think if I get there at 2:00 and I can't find her or she's hurt it's another forty-five minutes before I'm back here so I say "Yes, please tell them, she's ninety-two, we might need an ambulance, I'm going to go now."

I am a little worried about how he is planning to present all this information to the cops and wonder idly what will happen to Cindy but I write down Camp Cooville and my name and my phone number even though my phone is useless and then I run outside jump back in the car where Honey is screaming bloody murder and I kneel by her in the back seat and wipe her face and give her kisses and find her sippy cup which has a few fingers of warm milk in it and give that to her and say "I'm sorry I'm sorry I'm sorry Mama's so so so sorry."

We go back the original way, the way I'm hoping will not be blocked by Cindy if as I imagine they have had to spread their sparse-ass movement across hundreds of state and county roads across hundreds of miles of territory. The rain has barely let up and I am driving slowly slowly and I creep around every corner in case of blockades and mercifully there are none which just makes me feel more furious that I lost all this time to have a fucking procedural argument with Cindy when it was a moot fucking point anyway since I could go five miles over and achieve my desired outcome and I almost want to turn around and tell her what a fucking moron she is but then I remember and I start a running prayer Please let Alice be okay Please let Alice be okay. Honey is doing a low moan in the back seat and I think about how long she has been in the car and how generally unenriched unstimulated and then I think Well she won't remember any of this anyway, but that makes me oddly sad too.

When we pull onto the dirt road to Camp Cooville it's 2:07 which isn't that bad but I'm terrified of getting the Buick down that road which must be a mud river in this downpour but I tell myself it's American-built, thousands of pounds, made for hard North State winters and we inch slowly down the road and when the road finally levels I race forward to Alice's stump and she's not there, just the cooler bag and the blanket and the sweatshirt slumped in a pool of water on the surface of the stump. I see the umbrella leaning neatly against the stump and I wonder what this can mean. I put my head on the steering wheel and yelp and then I get out of the car pulling my jacket over my head and peering through the rain for some sign and I can't leave Honey in the car but I can't take her out in this so I get back in and start driving bumpily slowly around the buildings praying not to hurdle us into a sinkhole or a stump. My eyes strain so hard to make out the navy skirt the white turtleneck and the gunmetal hair that I keep seeing apparitions through the trees, but none of them are her.

I drive around slowly with the window down calling Alice's name with rain coming in sideways onto the door panel and dash. But then I imagine the horror of running over her prone in the tall grass and I stop and start honking the horn and screaming her name intermittently. Finally I think I have to get out so I look at Honey and I try to really get through to her and say "Mommy is getting out of the car, but she's not leaving, okay. I'm going to be *right back*. Mommy's coming *right back*." I don't know if she understands this but her face crumples once I unclick the seat belt and by the time I've gotten myself out of the car she is sobbing and I think five minutes, we can have five minutes. I sprint around the clearing holding my breasts with one arm and putting my hand over my eyes with the other. "ALLLLIIIIIIIIIICE" I scream and I stop panting under the eaves of one of the buildings to catch my breath. The rain is relentless and I think an insane thought what if she has just been rained away pounded into the earth by the deluge. I recover my breath and run a series of jagged loops around and between the buildings and then I run back to the car and Honey is crimson in the back seat and looks at me in furious reproach and I kiss her and I am crying too and I reach in the diaper bag for the halves of *The Very Hungry Caterpillar* and I say "I'm sorry I'm sorry I'm sorry" and "We're gonna leave real soon" and then I am back out into the rain. I run to the stump and look helplessly at the evidence which tells me that she touched nothing but leaned her umbrella against the stump and I think maybe she went into the woods to get out of the rain which would make sense and I think I'm going to have to go in there and I walk a few feet in and look all around me but then I think This is madness I can't leave the car I can't leave Honey in the car you always read about how getting lost in the woods is the easiest thing you can do and the very thought of not being able to get back to Honey makes me panic and spring back to the stump which is where I think it should be and then I consider bringing Honey into the woods with me but the problem of being lost remains, it's just that we would be lost together. I start to bawl. I don't understand how all of this went south so quickly but I guess that is what I've told myself I was waiting for, things to go quickly south.

I think I will just have to get Honey and we will have to look together so I take the umbrella from the stump and run to the car squishing into the mud and open the door and Honey knows that things are weird and I say "Hi" brightly and "We're just going to get out for a minute to look for Auntie Alice" and I unbuckle her and wrestle her out of the seat and pick up the umbrella and hold her in one arm to my hip, hitching her up to make sure of my grip and put the umbrella over both of us and enter the woods at the stump. I turn back to look at the car to try and orient myself and think hysterically that I need some kind of marker so that I can indicate our location because I'm irrationally terrified that we are going to be swallowed into the forest and never get out. I think we will just walk directly forward in a straight line and then after two minutes turn around and walk directly back and then we should I think get back to the stump or thereabouts, as long as we can get to the tree line at the edge of the clearing. The rain isn't coming through too badly so I put Honey down on her feet and she clings to my shins and I close the umbrella and pick her back up and hold her tight with the umbrella sticking out perpendicular under my armpit and we walk forward and I look left and right and within a few yards we've climbed up a partially buried boulder which I think Good a landmark and then at the top I see on the other side Alice, Alice lying on the ground curled on her side with her head on her hand looking like a sleeping child. I cry out and say "Alice Alice Alice" and she doesn't stir and I spring around the side of the rock and put Honey down as gently and quickly as I can and I put my hand on Alice's neck like someone on a television show and I just feel cool soft papery skin and I put my head on her chest and try desperately to hear something beyond my own panting and I don't but have no idea whether or not I would and I try to gently shake her shoulder and think she stirs but I'm not sure and I smooth her hair down with one hand the hair I've always wanted to touch and then I hear faintly a wailing through the rain and the wind in the trees and I pick up Honey and run back toward the clearing, straight back from the boulder where yes there is an ambulance barreling down the road and it appears Ivan from the safari motel has come through. It crosses the field and stops short just by the Buick and I run to it yelling "She's back there" like a madwoman and it's a man and a woman who emerge and they say "Calm down ma'am" and they go into the ambulance cab and say something into a walkie-talkie and then retrieve a stretcher and I point toward the woods and pant along beside them into the trees holding Honey who is absolutely silent and wide-eyed. Once they see Alice they drop to their knees and start their ministrations and I'm darting around saying "What's happening is she okay is she okay" and the man says "Ma'am why don't you take the baby and go on back to the car" and I turn tail with Honey and run back to the Buick and set her on the passenger seat next to me and I say "Fuck it" and "I'm sorry" and get out a cigarette and open the window all the way down but water comes in so I raise it up halfway and light the cigarette and she stares at me in quiet wonderment and starts to fiddle with the buttons on the passenger side seat and once I chuck the butt out the window I see the paramedics coming through the trees with something on their stretcher and the man looks at me and nods his head, one swift, grim motion.

I haul Honey onto my lap and get out of the car holding her and run to the paramedics who are putting Alice into the ambulance. "Honey, we've got to get her to the hospital, she's real frail," the woman says kindly and Honey the baby turns her head from my cheek to look at her. "Where are you taking her?" I say and they tell me the name of a hospital which is Bernville Emergency Clinic and the man barks some directions at me that I try to hold on to and then they have loaded her up and closed the door and I think I should have said goodbye and then I wearily get Honey back in the car and follow to the best of my ability the ambulance and once it has made its way up the dirt road and peeled out into the horizon I try to keep the directions in my head, mercifully the hospital is not back in Berwin Falls but just thirty miles from here. I think I did it once so I might as well count this day as a wash and light another cigarette and smoke out the window while driving which I don't think I have done in ten years.

I say a prayer for Alice but while I am doing it my mind wanders and I callously think of all the administrative bullshit that is about to come my way. I will have to explain no doubt to the hospital and maybe the police who I am and why I am the one who had the old lady in my care and failed her and they probably won't tell me anything about Alice because I'm not a relative and Mark and Yarrow will probably try to send me to prison not to mention that I am a witness, maybe among the first, to the attempted secession taking place up the road and I just pull hard on my cigarette and think It's all out of my hands.

We reach the outskirts of the town where the clinic is and it's so small we find the place right away and I park and get Honey out who is almost almost almost asleep, probably stupefied from the carbon monoxide of the cigarette, and I open the front door to the low-lying clinic which reads Emergency along its top and I ask the gal at the front desk for the older lady who just came in and she says "Oh okay, yeah they have a couple questions" and gestures toward a towheaded policeman sitting legs spread against the wall of the clinic and he stands while she calls behind her "Dooooooc." "I'm Officer Bentley," he says and I say "I'm Daphne Nilsen," isn't it strange, I'm a Nilsen not a Burdock not a Mehmetoğlu and extend a hand while holding Honey and he says "Can you tell me what your relationship was to the woman who got brung in?" and I say "I actually hardly know her," feeling a small stab of disloyalty. "I met her in Altavista where I've been staying at my grandparents' house. She was passing through and she asked for some help getting to Camp Cooville. Her husband used to be stationed out here and she wanted to visit. So, uh, I drove her out and when we got there today she asked me to give her some time alone and this was before it was raining" and I can feel myself speaking too fast and try to slow it down and I'm also starting to cry and I say "I'm sorry" and compose myself and Honey whines and I say "While I was trying to get back to her I ran into this State of Jefferson blockade thing—I have the piece of paper in my car—they were giving out some kind of Declaration of Independence" and I pray he will know what I'm talking about and not think I'm insane and his face, previously impassive, almost imperceptibly nods and I say "Yeah, so I had to turn around and was late getting back to her but only by about forty-five minutes, I also stopped at the hotel to tell them to call you all, that's the Safari Motor Inn, and when I got there I found her on the ground in the trees." While I'm talking a good-looking thirty-something brown-skinned man in blue scrubs comes out and is standing at a little remove, clearly listening to my account, and I turn to face him and he gives a very very subdued smile and says "I'm Dr. Bakhtiyar" and extends a hand and my insane brain thinks Bakhtiyar, from Persian: *lucky*, *fortunate* and I say "What happened to Alice?" and he says "Are you a relative?" "No," I say. "I was giving her a ride. I have their phone number though." I take my phone out of my pocket and pull up the call from yesterday and hand it to him. "What's going on?" I say helplessly and he says "Just a moment" and writes down the number and says "I'll be back shortly" and disappears into the back of the clinic with his slip of paper. I hug Honey and kiss the top of her head and exchange a small smile with the receptionist and re- alize I must look like hell, my clothes plastered to me, my knees and shoes covered in mud. Honey is in much better shape but I feel her shivering in my arms and I say "I'm going to get her some clothes from the car" and run out to find her spare pants which I had thank god packed in the diaper bag. When I get back in the clinic with her dry things Dr. Bakhtiyar is back in the waiting room holding a phone and says "They'd like to speak with you" and I take the phone and say "Hello" and Yarrow is on the line crying and manages to get out "Well, she's gone," and while this is half what I'd expected I still can't really believe it's true, and I just say "I'm really sorry" and she cries and then a man's voice which I presume is Mark is now on the phone and says "Can you please tell us what happened"

and I don't actually believe that it has happened, and I try to
think of how to explain it all, Cindy and the blockade and the
Proclamation of Independence, and I just say "She asked to be
left alone at the camp and when I came back for her she was
gone" and again I say "I'm so sorry, I didn't want to leave her
alone but she really insisted" and Honey strains to get down
and I put her on the floor and she falls down and cries and
Mark says "We're trying to figure out how one of us can get
out there if you can manage to stay put until we arrive" and his
tone is bitter and I have to just accept that, of course he's going
to be furious and I say "Of course" and he says "Yarrow and I
will talk and call you back at the number you called on yesterday" and I say "Okay" and give Dr. Bakhtiyar back the phone
and then I gather Honey and sit down on one of the plastic
clinic chairs and bawl my eyes out while Officer Benson or
Bentley or whatever it was stands awkwardly next to me, his
police bells and whistles creaking.

After making my statement to Officer Benson and Dr. Bakhtiyar both of whom seemed bewildered but not really angry, not
really judgmental I finally get Honey back into the car and
then back to the motel and I explain what happened to Ivan
who kindly opens Alice's room and gets her things out and
puts them in our room and even bless his heart gives us a box
of granola bars and two packets of ramen and I feed Honey
and me and give us a hot bath and get us into the bed and despite the scratchy white sheets the physical comfort of being so
cozy with the rain coming down outside feels obscene. Honey
is leaning quietly but alertly against me contravening all of her

usual ways and I have the TV on and on the local news there is the blockade and there are Cindy and her friends looking grimly into the camera and there are police cars parked before them and the police appear to be standing around in a clump and the camera cuts to several other blockades, maybe three others around the two states and it's only a matter of time before it's national news but I can't bear to put on CNN Fox News or any of the others can't bear the thought of their scrutiny on this parcel of the earth.

The phone rings and I answer and Mark informs me curtly that he will be landing in Medford, Oregon, tomorrow at 4:00 and I say "I will pick you up and drive you wherever you need to go, and back to the airport. Whatever you need" and he says "I'd appreciate that. And I just really want to get to the bottom of what happened" and I say "Of course, I can't imagine what you must be thinking and feeling" and I get choked up and he hems and haws and says "Well, we'll get everything sorted tomorrow."

I pull Honey to me and kiss her head over and over again and prop her against the pillow and get up and get Alice's hardbacked suitcase and hoist it onto the foot of the bed. I click open the two snaps and on top of neatly folded clothes there is a folded paper reading "In case of emergency" and I think Jesus Christ and I unfold it and it is a piece of stationery from the Wagon Wheel motel and on it are written two phone numbers and below that in a crabbed cursive it just says "I'm not coming home" and her little day-by-day pill box with today's pills untaken and yesterday's too and I lie down next to Honey and cry like my heart is breaking.

DAY 10   One of the State of Jefferson guys was shot by the police early this morning when they moved to retake the interstate here at the northernmost point of the fifty-first State of Jefferson. He fired and then they fired and now he is in "stable" condition in the hospital, probably the same one as Alice, probably having his life saved by Dr. Bakhtiyar who, if I had to guess, is probably the only doctor for a hundred miles and who if I also had to guess is probably not the person the wounded man pictured sharing his new state citizenship with not to mention having his life saved by. The blockading groups were apprehended pretty quickly after that and the roads are clear but one group of five has moved into the national forest along the border and is claiming to be hunkering down for a long siege. I wonder if Cindy is in the forest or in jail. I wonder whether she made common cause with the Cunt after all. I hope I never see Cindy again.

Honey is sitting on the floor leafing rather deftly through a Gideon Bible that she found in the drawer which she herself opened. I have already smoked a cigarette out of the motel window this morning while she slept so my parenting is not off to a good start in any case.

Last night while I was trying to fall asleep I thought about kinds of death. I shooed my father my mother Ellery out of my mind and I tried to empty everything but Alice out in the wood. I pictured her walking across the clearing and turning toward the trees on some mission of communion. I saw her moving with certainty across the uneven forest floor while I was laboring in futility with Cindy and her coconspirators. Under the forest canopy the rain would have taken on a new sound, not the pounding of water against the defenseless grass but something gentler and hushed, a sound like an expectant audience whispering in an amphitheater at dusk. And maybe her foot slipped on a root and then she was on her back in a divot of earth looking up at the trees. I pictured her lying in the divot just the right shape to cradle her with her face up to the sheltering canopy. Maybe she felt the pine needles under her hands and made a tentative move to try and stand and she couldn't get anything to cooperate and she was dry and more or less comfortable and she closed her eyes. I closed my own eyes and clasped my hands under my body. *Please God*, I say to myself. *Let her be out of the Abode of Pain. Let her be with her husband and her babies.*

I will pick Mark up at the airport in Medford this afternoon at 4:00, and then I will take him to the coroner and then I guess and hope he'll take over from there. I take a photo of Alice's note in case they've decided to sue me or arrest me which I guess is not outside the realm of possibility. I hate the lizard part of my brain that made me avoid saying anything like "I feel responsible" to Mark, but I somehow also feel that Alice knew a sucker when she saw one and that sucker was me and when I think back there's not really one particular thing I would have done differently and whether I *should* have done something differently has not yet revealed itself.

I watch a commentator on CNN interviewing a man in

camo and there is a graphic of a map of the State of Jefferson, and there within it, unmarked, is Paiute County, Altavista, Deakins Park. I open the laptop and I look at my Institute inbox and think about all the things I have to do and I open my Tasks spreadsheet and start to make a list and then I look at Honey who is tearing pages out of that Bible like a heathen and I think about Engin and the culture of my family and the brevity of life and how you could spend fifty years missing someone who is gone and never coming back and I close the spreadsheet and open Skype and it rings and rings and rings and there is no Engin and I will have to trust that he is not dead not with another woman and I don't want to lose this feeling while I wait for him to call so I open WhatsApp on my phone and write "Aşkım sana geliyoruz" which is "My love we are coming to you" which is pop-song corny but just what comes to mind and like that it's decided, at least assuming they let me out of here. And then I close the computer and get off the bed and look down at Honey and she looks at me with her father's eyes and my eyebrows and her very own look of self-reliance and determination and I say "Well, Miss Honey. Shall we go have a look at this Wildlife Safari?" and she scrambles to her feet and reaches up her arms to her mama.

ACKNOWLEDGMENTS

Endless thanks to Claudia Ballard for giving me the courage to try this, and to Emily Bell, Maya Binyam, Jackson Howard, Sarita Varma, and everyone at MCD/FSG for making it a book. Special thanks to Oya Topçuoğlu, who read portions of the text and provided valuable insight, and to Alex and Petter, who provided inspiration.

C. Max Magee and *The Millions* gave me the space to become a writer and I'll never forget it. I'm thankful also for the many writers who have provided encouragement and community over the years, in person or in the ether, especially Adam Boretz, Kirstin Butler, Nicole Chung, Ingrid Rojas Contreras, Katie Coyle, Vinson Cunningham, Michelle Dean, Jen Gann, Emily Gould, Rahawa Haile, Garth Risk Hallberg, Jane Hu, Vanessa Hua, Brian Hurley, Crystal Hana Kim, Reese Kwon, Edan Lepucki, Kara Levy, Lillian Li, Lili Loofbourow, Yael Goldstein Love, Michael David Lukas, Manjula Martin, Laura Miller, Kate Milliken, Caille Millner, Nick Moran, Ismail Muhammad, Mark O'Connell, Meaghan O'Connell, Katie Raissian, Lisa Srisuro, Lucy Tan, and Laura Turner.

I am eternally grateful to the people who helped me learn Turkish over the years—professors, fellow students, and friends—among them: Gökay Abeş, Begüm Adalet, Toygun Altıntaş, Helga Anetshofer, Hakan Karateke, Kağan Arık, Özge Atamtürk, Fatih Ateş, Rezeda Azangulova, Osman Balkan, Özgür Baykal, Valantin and Murat Bilir, Andrea Brown, Christopher Markiewicz, Yaşar Tolga Cora, İpek Hüner-Cora, Öcal Çetin, Coşkun Çokbilir, Madeleine Elfenbein, Molly Laas, Murat Gökdemir, Emma Harper, Glyn Harris, Özgür Hekimoğlu, Bengi Hürriyetoğlu, Ekin Enacar-Kömürlü, Fatih Kurşun, Zuhal Kurtcebe, Stephanie Ruggles, Merve Sarı, Ahmet Tunç Şen, Sümeyye Yar, Zübeyde and Mitul Sheth, Oya Topçuoğlu, and the Izmir CLS Yaşlılar. There is no way to sufficiently thank Linda and

Gary Caldwell, my second parents, or Müge Bal, Gaye Gülenay, Esra Girgin Gümüştekin, Sema Gökmen Ölmez, and Dilara Nergis Şabciyan, with whom I passed so many afternoons in the teachers' room. I'll never forget your kindness.

Thanks to the *Hodgsoniyya*, particularly Terry Burke, Prairie Sundance and Lindsey Kroll, Nelda and Reuben Smith, Gretchen and Tom Spicer, Fanou and Bryan Walton, and John Woods. This project also benefited indirectly from the Title VI program of the Department of Education and the Critical Language Scholarship of the Department of State. Many thanks to Hossam Kaddoura for providing a place to work, and to Xiao Yan Li for providing wonderful childcare.

Thanks and love to all the friends who always told me I should do this, especially the Rats and the Boehners, Hope McGrath, Emily Behl, and Erin Hall. I started being a writer while working for John Crichton at the Brick Row Book Shop. David Beckman, Georgia Prosalentis, and Fatima Makhzoumy all took care of me in different ways.

I would be nowhere without the love and support of my mother, Phyllis, and my father, Brady, who gave me a wonderful childhood. Thanks also to my extended family: the Grahams, Kieslings, Mohrs, Quayles. I wrote this thinking of my beloved grandparents June and Doug, who are now where the grass grows green and lush and stirrup-high.

And finally, to Tim: without you, none of this. Thank you for our girls, this life.

A Note About the Author

Lydia Kiesling is the editor of *The Millions*. Her essays and criticism have appeared in *The New York Times Magazine*, *The Guardian*, *Slate*, and *The New Yorker* online, and have been recognized in *The Best American Essays 2016*. She lives in San Francisco with her family.